THE LONG SHADOW OF
PANJSHIR

THE LONG SHADOW OF PANJSHIR

W.T DELANEY

Author's Introduction

This book is written as a tribute to the men and women of our Military, Special Forces and Security and Intelligence Services.

I would like to thank my very good friend DM, whom I had the good fortune to serve with in the military and afterwards in Iraq, for the long hours he has spent being my sub-editor, sounding board and on-the-spot advisor throughout the writing of the book.

I would also like to thank my wife, Marion, for putting up with my time in semi-seclusion in my office, tapping out the chapters.

The novel is purely fictional, though it has been shaped by my own background and both current and historical events. I spent over five years working alongside the USMC and the British Army in Helmand, Afghanistan. During that time, I watched both the USA and the UK drain away blood and treasure for, ultimately, nothing in return. To quote from this book:

Afghanistan really was 'The Graveyard of Empires'. The NATO mission had arrived with a fanfare and left with a whimper, and all the hype of milestones, progress reports and security force assistance had since been hurriedly buried in the same boneyard.

I met and befriended courageous Afghans who did their best for their own people under a corrupt regime. Many of them have now been abandoned, left in dire circumstances and justifiably feeling betrayed.

I was also part of the NATO effort in the country until 2016, and I was privileged to deliver lectures to NATO officers on the intricacies of operating as a military mentor in Afghanistan. If you had told me then how things would eventually work out, I would have said that, like this novel, "that's purely fictional!"

Finally, my thoughts today are with the new Afghan insurgents of the National Resistance Front of Afghanistan, who are still fighting for their country in the Panjshir Valley. May their valiant struggle be one day rewarded with success.

FOREWORD

WT Delaney, a former Royal Marine and a good friend of mine, has asked me to provide a foreword to his fourth book, *The Long Shadow of Panjshir*. This gripping novel is an espionage-based military adventure that explores the murky and dangerous worlds of political contract killing, covert intelligence collection, armed insurgency and deadly treachery.

The story starts in the Valley of the Five Lions, in Panjshir Province, Afghanistan, where a malignant past has shaped the violent present to produce an uncertain future. It moves to London in early 2022, several months after the fall of Kabul to the resurgent Taliban, and when Vladimir Putin is ominously massing his forces on the border of Ukraine. A beautiful but battle-hardened Russian spy, codenamed Babushka, arrives openly in town on a mission that baffles Britain's MI5 and MI6. At the same time, a pathological serial killer is on the loose, wreaking bloody havoc with a Spetsnaz combat knife among expatriate Afghan agents on the books of the British Security Service. Are the two mysteries in any way connected?

The action moves back to Afghanistan and uncovers a spider's web of murder, deceit and power struggles linked to the heart of the Kremlin, with alarming echoes of Cold War nuclear weapons deployment. As the story unfolds, spy chief Collette Brown and former soldier Christian 'Mac' McCann, of MI6, race to discover the truth that connects a savage betrayal during the Soviet occupation of that unhappy country to the current insurgency against the brutal regime of the Taliban. There, against the hauntingly rugged beauty of the Panjshir Valley, MI6 uncovers secrets about Babushka, the sinister knife assassin and the imminent Russian invasion of Ukraine that could save thousands of lives.

Once again, WT Delaney has drawn on his extensive experience to conjure up a feast of thrills and spills with a plot rich in imagination, yet one that reflects so much of the reality of covert and complex security intelligence operations, in both the UK and one of the most dangerous places on earth. *The Long Shadow of Panjshir* will certainly not disappoint readers of his earlier enthralling stories and is warmly recommended.

DM

The Panjshir Valley
Afghanistan
1976

Prologue

In Panjshir, a folk tale is entrusted from one generation to the next on a tribal timeline and, like the valley itself, sculpted and eroded into shape over time. The girl would never forget her first story. It was during the deepest winter. She was huddled with the other children, wide-eyed and expectant, in a snow-topped house clinging to the side of a mountain in the Valley of the Five Lions. She felt the ambient warmth of the family's livestock at her back and the heat of the fire on her face. She remembered the excitement, the laughter, and the orders from the adults to ensure a respectful silence.

They called the man who sat behind the fire the storyteller or Niqali. He smiled benignly at the audience, resplendent in bright clothes with a long white beard that reached down to the scarlet wrapped tightly around his portly frame. The flames flickered, highlighting his ever-changing facial expressions, and made a hundred shadows dance across the whitewashed walls. His stories were told the old way, with the flame's heat matching his fiery rhetoric. He conjured up raw emotion using smoke, mirrors, and just a pinch of opium dust to deepen the mood. By palming the contents of an ancient rifle bullet onto the fire at the right time, the sound effects were created for both ancient cannon fire and God's mighty thunder. The heroes and heroines were always Tajik, always Afghan, and only the enemies changed.

First, the invading Macedonians under Alexander the Great, then the wicked Mongols, followed by the devilish British and the heathen Soviets. The best Afghan folk tales are about war, courage, love, honour, heartbreak, and that inevitable Afghan tribal ingredient, revenge!

A classic Afghan story has a life of its own, but, like a whisp of smoke curling off a flame, it often inverts itself and changes in the telling. Like life, it sometimes twists, contorts, and changes over time and does not always end up when or where you want it to. This story starts with a girl wondering if anybody would ever tell her story.

And if so, when would it be told?

Chapter 1

The Panjshir Valley, September 1988

The pilot felt the helicopter shudder in the cold sky over the Hindu Kush. The two turboprop engines momentarily struggled to gain traction as he banked the aircraft into the thin air above. At 15,000 feet, the pilot could see the thin opal ribbon of the Panjshir River glimmer in the bright sunlight. The valley that the river had carved out of the rock through untold millennia looked inviting, but for a Russian, it wasn't. But at least, at this height, they were safe from the American Stinger missiles supplied to the fanatics below.

The outline of the helicopter became more apparent as it corkscrewed down from altitude. Its silhouette, an ominous black shadow momentarily framed like a dangerous dragonfly against the rugged backdrop of the mountain, was instantly recognisable as a Soviet MI 24 gunship. Its unmistakable shape, with an assortment of shiny bumps and guns, seemed to add to its power. It was a deadly war machine, designed for death and uniquely suited to flying over the Panjshir Valley.

The pilot had made this trip many times. He brought the machine down to reduce height quickly until he was skimming along at under three hundred feet. The aircraft that the 'Dooshman' (Mujahedeen) called 'Shaitan Arba' (The Devil's Chariot) powered up the valley. It was only safe against the Stingers when it was contouring against the rugged mountainside, and the speed meant that it presented only a fleeting target for the minimum amount of time. The pilot glanced down from his cockpit to where the sun glittered off the gunner's glass cupola. He could see the man's head scanning and tracking the Yak-B 12.7mm Gatling gun housed under the aircraft's nose turret.

Nobody wanted to be there! Not now, as the first rumours of withdrawal solidified into fact.

They were all nearly on their way home, and this was not the time or place to fly over the Panjshir in a Russian war machine. Before he left, he had been given by his future wife and comrade soldier a cassette tape that was being listened to everywhere. He made the next flight calculation as the song was still in his mind.

It was called 'We are Leaving'.

The gunship was on its final mission, and nobody wanted to be the last Russian soldier killed in a lost war far from home. But he was flying the Spetsnaz, and they were always the last to leave! He had six Soviet special forces soldiers, a senior Russian general, and a silent Afghan tribal leader, all squeezed together in the cramped troop compartment. He was flying at full capacity, but he didn't know why they were there. All he knew was that their combined weight and the secret cargo made the helicopter much more sluggish in the high mountain air.

He hadn't been told the whole mission; he didn't know because he wasn't important enough to know! He only knew he was going to drop off his passengers in the valley below.

Kabul, 31 December 1988
We are leaving, we are leaving, we are leaving.

She liked this song; its melancholy tune summed up her feelings - their feelings! She scratched the inside of the frost-beaded glass to look out. As she opened the window, the sweet, woody smell of a Kabul winter drifted in with some snowflakes. The walls were sparsely decorated, with only the slightly tilted picture of a smiling Afghan President Najibullah on one whitewashed wall, facing her own giant poster of Che Guevara on the other. The girl was living in a room of the large Soviet safe house in Wazir Akbar Khan. It was high-ceilinged and spacious. A locally-woven carpet covered the floor. There was a single bedside cabinet, an army-issue straight-backed chair, and a grey metal desk. The only flash of bright colour was on her bed, an Afghan blanket bought on Chicken Street, Kabul's main market. A mournful sound again drifted from the cassette recorder. It was the latest Soviet Army war song called 'We are Leaving'.

Farewell, mountains! You witnessed
What we had and what we gave.
What enemy we haven't finished off.
What friends we lost there.
Goodbye Afghanistan, this ghostly world.
We are leaving, we are leaving, we are leaving.

She picked up the small portrait photo from the bedside cabinet. A handsome face shone back from under the brown leather frame. A black ribbon was tied around it. Her fiancé, a pilot in the Soviet Air Force, had died before he had been given a chance to leave Afghanistan. She mourned him both as a comrade and as a lover. He was the man she had thought she would spend the rest of her life with, but his life had been lost in the cold mountains of the Hindu Kush.

She looked again at the photograph, kissed it gently, and whispered his name, Mikhail, as she laid it inside her army-issue suitcase. He had not returned from a Level One security mission. Nobody had. She made a silent pledge.

I will find you one day, my love, and bring you home!

For the last time, she hung her uniform in the room's only other piece of furniture, a Soviet-issue wardrobe. She laid it into its resting place with a sense of reverence. The uniform was part of her and, like her, made in Afghanistan but unmistakably Russian. She glanced at the badges and insignia on the jacket with a profound sense of loss. These were, after all, a collection of her achievements. The gold Soviet paratrooper badge, the infantry combat badge, and the medal ribbons. Her eyes lingered longest on the lightning bolt and dagger flash of the elite Alpha Group of the Soviet Spetsnaz (Special Forces). She was the only woman in her unit to wear them.

This was the uniform of a Moscow-educated orphan who had so far achieved much but who had so much more to give. She glanced at her reflection in the small rectangular mirror affixed to the wardrobe door. A beautiful girl stared back. She had light blonde hair that fell forward in the latest Western style, and her father's pale Russian skin fused beautifully with her mother's Tajik, greenish-blue, opal eyes.

The eyes in the mirror seemed older than the face; they reflected the sadness caused by an overdose of combat operations. The slightly scratched steel mirror framed the face of an 'Afghansy' soldier in a war that was coming to an end. She had only just turned twenty but had already spent her entire lifetime of luck. She had watched friends die and killed those who had tried to kill them. She had mastered her self-discipline in a hundred cold ambushes in the Afghan mountains and had learned to control her fear.

She opened the brown leather issue holster that lay on the bedside cabinet and removed her sidearm, a 9.27 mm Makarov pistol. She felt the reassuring weight in her right hand and racked the weapon with her left to feed a round into the chamber. She moved the working parts back to check for the dull glint of brass. It was loaded correctly. She now placed the pistol in her covert holster under her coat. Two of her soldiers would soon arrive to take her to the airport. She was ready to go to Moscow.

She glanced at her uniform again; it was now part of an Afghan story that was over. As a Soviet GRU (Military Intelligence) officer, she knew that, as in the song, and after ten years of wasted Soviet blood and treasure, they were leaving. She looked again in the mirror; the lyrics of the song had reached the chorus.

We are leaving, we are leaving, we are leaving.

And so was she! She was transferring from the GRU to the Soviet KGB (the Committee for State Security). Her training would take place at the 'Red Banner' spy school, hidden deep in the woods only fifty miles from Moscow. There, she would perfect her tradecraft, train as an agent handler, and change from fighting the Mujahedeen to working against the capitalist governments that had financed them. She had volunteered for the 'First Directorate', the department of Soviet Intelligence that operated against the security services of the West. A new part of the story had begun.

But how would it end?

Chapter 2

January 28th, 2022
London

Yousef walked towards his home. He had once been a big man but had shrivelled with age, although his mind and instincts were still 'operator sharp.' He walked quickly along his road, not entirely understanding why he felt so uneasy. He knew things had changed. The Taliban had ruled Afghanistan for over six months now. All the talk of reform and reconciliation was over, and the Sharia noose was tightening around Kabul. The news was beginning to filter through of a bloody mass killing in the small village of Qala-e Malik where he had been brought into the world kicking, screaming, and covered in blood over sixty years before. He had also just received a strange call that he instantly regretted answering. He now had that nagging feeling that he was being watched. It was a type of sixth sense, a feeling a veteran intelligence officer develops over time. But that's what kept you safe.

Yousef Aziz was an intelligence officer by trade, trained by the Russians and intimately familiar with what agent runners call 'The Circle of Knowledge. It was a straightforward concept: the more people knew a secret, the less secret it was! His circle was tight but not tight enough, and it was the others that shared the secret with him that worried him. He needed to tell his handler to get the level of protection he needed. Maybe it was only his imagination, but he could almost feel danger closing in on him. He rationalized: he had always been a careful man, *and if you could survive in Afghanistan, you could survive anywhere.*

He had arrived in Britain hidden in a lorry thirty years before and had claimed asylum as soon as his feet hit the ground. But, unlike the other Afghans sealed with him in that fetid and airless place he had a life-threatening secret sealed within him. He now knew that as the last malignant ripples of the fall of Kabul reached London that grim secret could end his life. He loved living in the quiet London suburb of Kingsbury. It was a long way from the Panjshir. He looked down his quiet tree-lined street, glittering in wintry sunlight after a burst of rain.

The cold breeze at his back moved the branches as some lost but intertwined Coronavirus masks skipped and danced towards his front gate. He felt the pavement slippery underfoot as he glanced quickly up and down the street. Everything was as expected, and nothing had changed. He pulled his keys from his coat pocket as he passed the usual collection of parked cars and plastic waste bins. The handle squeaked as he opened his garden gate, and the tomcat from next door eyed him with his usual suspicion.

He felt safer inside his own refuge, protected by high hedges, as he selected the key to open the steel-lined security door. He carefully scanned the outside of the door; everything was the same. He checked the tiny sliver of Sellotape that he had affixed across the door and the frame. It was intact. He looked around again and moved the key towards the lock that would simultaneously open the three deadbolts inside the reinforced concrete frame.

The tall blond man pressed his back firmly against the red brick wall at the side of the house. He controlled his breathing, calmed himself for action, and listened for the first curse of frustration.

He held a knife by his side, his right hand wrapped comfortably around the rubber-reinforced polymer hilt. It was a Spetsnaz issue

6.5-inch Bopoh-3 fighting knife of deadly black tungsten steel, and it felt good in his grip.

He was only twenty feet from his victim, and as soon as he heard the first Afghan curse, he moved.

"Harami" (bastard).

The killer moved soundlessly around the corner of the house.

By the time Yousef had grunted his second Afghan swear word, "Kus modar" (motherfucker), the blond man was behind him.

The old Afghan realized that somebody had blocked the lock as he tried his key for the third time. He swore again in English.

"Fuck this!"

Then he felt a strong hand on his face and a searing pain in his throat. His final thought was in English.

"What the f...!"

The blond man had cupped the old man's mouth with his right hand while he pinched his nose between his thumb and forefinger to stop the scream. He pulled back his head with force, smoothly pushed the razor-sharp Kizlyar blade halfway through his neck, three inches behind his victim's thyroid cartilage, and sliced it forward. The big man's last vision was of his blood haemorrhaging against his own front door. Yousef couldn't scream as he left life the same way he had entered it - kicking and covered in blood.

Chapter 3

At Thames House, MI5's London headquarters, Lou, the murdered man's agent handler, had been the first to get the news. At the last meet, he had thought that 3036, codenamed Flame, was getting increasingly worried about something. He had run the agent for over a year, and he knew about the asset's complicated past and his increasingly perilous future. He also knew that the old Afghan intelligence officer had been almost paranoid about his own personal security. The news of his death had come as a flash message on his secure mobile just as he had finished his latest MISR (Military Intelligence Source Report).

The message was simple and told him everything he needed to know. It just said:

3036 dead! Phone soonest.

It had been a busy week for the Joint Task Force, the MI5/MI6 agency set up to oversee Human Intelligence (HUMINT) operations in the UK. When Kabul had fallen so suddenly the year before, the Taliban had inherited all the biometric records of the Afghan Army, Police and NDS (Afghanistan's US-funded security service). The same data that had been painstakingly compiled over ten years was used to both validate friendly forces and locate enemy ones.

The biometric information had been collected by a piece of portable American wizardry that gathered a whole spectrum of personal data from every soldier, policeman, and Afghan government official. The handheld device, developed at huge expense by the US military, looked like an oversized pair of binoculars and was able to simultaneously gather facial recognition, iris scans, and fingerprints. It was designed to differentiate between the good guys and the bad, so its capture had gifted the new Taliban government an intelligence gold mine. The implications of the data loss were still echoing around the walls of Britain's security services, including the large building perched by the Thames at the Albert Embankment, which was the not-so-secret home of Britain's SIS or Secret Intelligence Service.

To Mac, the MI6 building at Vauxhall Cross looked like either a giant Mayan temple or an antique cash register waiting to slip into the river. He glanced up quickly as he checked his watch. He didn't particularly like the look of the place; it was a strange mixture of angular cream concrete and glittering green glass.

It had taken him only fifteen minutes to briskly walk across Lambeth Bridge from Thames House, a building whose 1930s post-imperial look he much preferred. His scheduled monthly meeting with the Joint Task Force had been cancelled. The JTF had lost an agent and he had been asked to 'VX' (Vauxhall Cross) for a crisis meeting in Collette's office.

Christian McCann, known to his MI6 colleagues as Mac, felt a hint of sadness. The death of a source is sometimes like the death of a friend. Mac had recruited Lou's source 3036, or Flame, and quite liked him. They both came from a time and place that he knew, and they had often discussed the old times in Panjshir.

As a young Parachute Regiment officer, who had passed selection and was then serving with 22 SAS, he had been deployed at the request of MI6 as one of Ahmad Shah Massoud's military advisors in the dangerous but unbelievably beautiful Panjshir Valley. Flame had been working with the Soviet GRU on the other side. As he walked towards VX history was repeating itself and another defeated army had left Afghanistan - though the Soviet withdrawal had been conducted with far more dignity than NATO'S hectic scramble last year. He glanced again at his watch.

Unlike those who had died after they had co-operated with the West in Afghanistan, he still had plenty of time!

Lou had been rushing to get to conference room Z3 at the MI6 building, and he was the last to make it. He hurried along the corridor, an incongruous figure amongst the conventional suits and ties. He wore his favourite Bob Marley tee shirt, and his long Rastafarian locks swung most unconventionally. But the suits in VX were used to the odd surprise. Agent handlers are the least conventional of people, and Lou was just that! He was half Irish, half Afro-Caribbean, and also an ex-Marine Commando who had served with both the Joint Support Group in Iraq and the Defence HUMINT Unit in Afghanistan. He had then been recruited by MI5 and later headhunted for the JTF by Mac.

As Lou finally entered the meeting room and the steel door wheezed shut behind him, Collette Brown, his boss at the JTF, was already in full flow. She paused momentarily and gestured with her eyes towards where Mac and Ahmad Talabani, his fellow source handler, sat. With her immaculately manicured right hand she flicked back some of Nicky Clarke of Mayfair's finest work from her brow and pressed the remote to activate the monitor. Lou joined Ahmad behind the conference table as the MI6-issue Swedish-style chair groaned under the weight of his 16-stone frame. There were four buff brown files in a neat row on the shiny white wood, along with four sets of board markers. There was a moment of silence and reflection as the killer's gory handiwork flashed up on the screen.

"The files in front of you are the latest police and forensic reports. It looks like a professional hit." Collette leafed through her brown folder.

"The locks on the door had been superglued to keep the victim busy. The CCTV cameras covering the street and the garden had been covered with black tape at some opportune time before the attack. That, I think, means that the killer carried out a CTR (Close Target Recce) of the house before the murder. Not that it would have made any difference, as the cameras hadn't been working for some time." She clicked the remote and another photo appeared.

"So, this is what he left behind." It was a graphic image

There are three types of scenes-of-crime photographs: the overall, the midrange and the close-up, and it was the close-up that they were looking at now. Yousef, asset 3036, was lying on his stomach in a pool of blood outside his front door, with his head contorted to the left. His left eye was still open and staring blankly at his own blood that totally covered his door. The gaping hole that had once been the front of his neck could be clearly seen. The blood had congealed and was dark and crusted around the wound.

"Ok, guys, for the sake of time and clarity I will give you a quick sitrep." She was clipped and concise with her presentation.

"For those of you who hadn't met him, this is, or more precisely was source 3036 or Flame, and he's been run as an asset for the last ten years."

Collette clicked the next slide. A picture of a healthier-looking Yousef flashed onto the monitor.

"This is from his source file, which is quite a thick one. 3036 was especially useful concerning the growing crime links between the Taliban and the London drug gangs."

The senior MI6 member of the JTF then clicked the button again.

"The scene of the crime," Collette's voice was emotionless as an exterior shot of the house was displayed on the screen.

The picture had been taken from outside the front gate. It showed the garden path of an ordinary red brick semi-detached house leading up to a shiny black front door with an ornate-looking brass knocker in the shape of a lion's head. The murdered man's body was slumped against it, outlined in a blackened pool of blood.

"Here's the house at 4 Ranford Gardens, Kingsbury, NW9." A Google Maps photo of the quiet street flashed onto the screen.

"It's an unremarkable area with a low crime rate, with the average semi selling at about £750,000. The nearest CCTV that we have accessed is outside St Andrew's Church at the bottom of the opposite street, although this was only a low-quality camera installed after some vandalism last year. The police are now examining the footage in case an organized surveillance of the victim's house emerges." Collette looked back from the monitor to the audience.

"We have asked for a cell site analysis to try and pick up anything by local Wi-Fi routers for MAC addresses (Media Access Control), just in case the killer's mobile was on Google Maps, but it's a long shot if it's a professional hit. They would be aware that any house that had a Wi-Fi signal could be tracked back in any subsequent enquiry. And that's all we've got!"

Collette pulled a whiteboard towards the conference table. The board had the detritus of a previous workplace meeting scrawled over it. It stated, 'Mental Health in the Workplace. She scowled as she attacked it with the board wiper. She always seemed to be cleaning up after the Health and Safety Nazis at VX. "Let's work through the folder together and see what we can come up with, OK? I suggest we break for coffee and reconvene in an hour. When we get back, we mind-map it." She glanced towards Lou.

"We need to chat; stay here," she said, as the others left the room.

Only seven miles from Vauxhall Cross, the winter sun filtered through some old-style Venetian blinds and illuminated the killer's face in bright vertical slats of light. They flickered upon a man perfectly at peace with himself. He smiled as he worked the knife easily across the leather sharpening strop. He paused every now and then to appreciate the keenness of the blade. The repetition of the movement had a calming influence on the tall man. It wiped his mind after every kill and helped him rationalize his actions; after all, it was a job that he had acquired rather than applied for. Like everything else in his life, his suitability for his post-military career had been determined by chance.

The doctor had said it had been a billion to one chance that the small fragment of the Mujahedeen RPG missile had hit the part of his brain's limbic system that the doctors called the amygdala and had lodged there. It was the area of the brain that controlled both fear and emotion, so, in that uniquely strange Afghan way, it had ensured that killing was a job he enjoyed. The Soviet Army had provided the training and the Mujahedeen had supplied the shell fragment, and that combination made it easy for him.

He was a man of simple needs. His modest flat just off Kilburn High Road was sparse, bright white, and immaculately clean. It had been his refuge against the wider world since he had arrived in London. His only luxury was the low hum of classical music, never loud enough to annoy the neighbours. His job meant that he had to keep a low profile. He checked the blade again as his computer tinged. *Another mission?*

All his instructions came through TOR on the dark web now. His MacBook Pro laptop acted as his middleman and ensured his employer's anonymity. He insisted upon strict computer hygiene, the VPN ensured that he could change his virtual location at will, and he only used ever used *ProtonMail* for email messages.

He clicked and downloaded the folder. He now had his next victim.

Ting! The blond man smiled: a Bitcoin transfer. He had just been paid in full for the last job!

Chapter 4

"So, what do you think?" Collette said.

"I don't know what to think. Flame was a competent agent who knew his subject matter. It's the loss of a decent asset," Lou replied.

"A bigger loss for Flame, I should think!"

"Yeah, poor bastard. I don't think he expected to get stiffed, but I knew he was worried about something." Lou furrowed his brow.

"Any idea what?"

"No, but he'd asked for an emergency meet."

"Like any other of our Afghan sources in London, then?"

"Pretty much. The security implications of the data loss in Kabul are now emerging." Lou looked thoughtful.

Collette knew that agent runners sometimes got to like the people they worked with.

"He had no family left in Afghanistan," Lou continued. "He was worried about something else."

"Did he mention anything specific?"

"No. He once said that his biggest secrets would always be locked inside and in the past. Maybe he wanted to get them off his chest, but they died with him," Lou said mournfully.

"OK." Collette was business-like. "Work with the collators. We need to go back through every file we have on him. Every meet, every source report, every handler's comment, and any thread we have actioned based on his information. We must determine if this murder has anything to do with his work for us."

"Understood," Lou said.

Collette picked up the brown folder with the last photographs taken of 3036. She glanced inside and frowned.

"Let's hope this is a one-off and linked to something else."

Two floors below, in his office, Mac opened the buff brown folder positioned centrally on his desk. He prepared his MI6-issue moleskin notebook and cheap MI6-issue Chinese biro and started to make notes. This was how ideas were gathered, and problems were solved at the JTF. The handlers and their senior managers had an initial meeting to discuss the situation. They then went their separate ways, developed possible solutions, and then returned to discuss them and mind-map the options. It was a sound system, though hardly foolproof. Agent handling was a complex landscape to navigate, and the correct direction was not always found.

He stopped writing and flipped a large silver coin from his desk into his right hand. He started moving it on the outside of his fist from one finger to another, and as he considered the problem, the coin moved faster. It was a Maria Theresa silver thaler that Ahmad Shah Massoud, the famous Afghan resistance leader, had given him in the Panjshir Valley over thirty years before.

These coins had been a universal currency in the Arab and broader Muslim world for two centuries before the advent of the evil Yankee dollar. He liked the weight of it. It was his lucky talisman and manipulating it was his way of concentrating on a problem. As his thoughts clarified, the shiny coin gained speed over his fingers until he had a conclusion.

Could he have been working as a double agent?

Sources are complicated human beings sometimes with a hidden agenda. And it was not unknown for even a well-paid informer to jump track and become a double agent. He remembered his instructor's voice from his agent handling course:

The coin that buys the absolute truth has never yet been minted!

Mac flipped the coin; it spun, glistened in the light, and landed in the palm of his hand. He slammed it onto the desk and turned again to look at the last mortal remains of Yousef, or agent number 3036.

True secrets are sometimes protected only by death, and now you will keep yours!

When he had recruited Yousef almost two decades earlier had been a *Walk-In*, an intelligence agency term for somebody that volunteers his services. The source had established himself within the thriving Afghan community and been able to report on some of the extremist Islamist groups that had started to thrive in what Mac's CIA colleagues called the Islamic Republic of Londonistan.

London's Afghans had arrived in three consecutive waves. The first refugees came after the Communist takeover of the country and the fall of King Ahmad Shah in the '70s. The murdered man had arrived in the second exodus when the Taliban took power in the 1990s. A third government-assisted wave had settled in Britain after the Taliban's 'victory' over the West. The mass migration was like a brain drain every twenty years: as one Afghan regime dissolved and another took power, the most educated and wealthy always left their country for a new life in the West. Mac knew Afghanistan and thought:

A civil war in Afghanistan is always waiting in the background. No doubt, just like a London bus, another one will be along soon.

Mac was MI6's current expert on all matters Afghan, but, like all things in that complex country, he knew his knowledge had a limited shelf life. If he had been asked in September 2021 about how long the very corrupt Afghani government of Ashraf Ghani would last without US support. He would have confidently said, "at least a year". The only precedence was the government that the Soviets had left in place in 1989 under Najibullah, which lasted over three years, even with people like Mac, MI6, and the CIA actively supporting the insurgency against it.

But the MI6 man and SME (Subject Matter Expert) on that country had got it as badly wrong as everybody else. He glanced at a framed photograph that had pride of place on his desk. It featured a younger Mac with an equally youthful-looking Ahmad Shah Massoud, perched on a rugged mountainside in Panjshir sometime in the late 1980s. He remembered both the good times and the bad, the intense comradeship and the senseless

killing. As the current SME, he was supposed to fully understand that strange and complex place, but he didn't think anybody could.

He thought the quote about intelligence during the Cold War era, by the renowned CIA man James Jesus Angleton, summed up working as a spy in Afghanistan. It was a place:

Where truth and falsehood endlessly reflect and refract one another, and nothing is quite what it seems!

The MI6 man glanced across at his Massoud photo again. It was a snapshot taken at a time when life was simpler. It was in another place, at another time when things seemed clear cut. When Islamist insurgents were the freedom fighters, and MI6 supported their efforts. He still remembered how he felt on the day the French journalist had taken the picture. The warm sun was on his face, and he could feel it seeping through a light covering of dust. He was tired and thirsty; adrenaline had coursed through his body, making him feel elated but dog-tired.

They had just ambushed a Russian convoy. He had trained the Mujahedeen to use the new British Army Blowpipe missiles that MI6 had supplied, and they had 'brewed up' three Russian armoured personnel carriers and a new T72 tank. The Soviet soldiers hadn't stood a chance. Everything had seemed so clear then - *Soviets bad, Mujahedeen good* - but twenty years at the sharp end of counterterrorism had taught him to examine things from a different perspective.

The USA had wanted payback for Vietnam, and the Western world revelled in the discomfort of the USSR. It was a tonic for the West during the height of the Cold War that, over time, had become a very bitter poisoned pill. But he didn't really blame his younger self. He had been in his twenties, patriotic, single, unafraid, and on a military adventure of *Boy's Own* proportions.

The numerous lectures that he had attended before his deployment had added to his only other knowledge of Afghanistan. He had read a book called *The Great Game* by Peter Hopkins, and he had a boyhood love of the adventures of the *Wolf of Kabul*, a British Army Intelligence Corps officer and heroic character in the Hotspur comic of the 1970s. His mission had been a simple one. He was to train insurgents to kill as many Soviet soldiers as possible, all young men just as patriotic as himself. He could have had no idea then that, twenty years later, he would be eventually fighting the same enemy as the Russians faced. The historical irony encapsulated the riddle that had always been Afghanistan; it really was 'The Graveyard of Empires'.

The NATO mission had arrived with a fanfare and left with a whimper, and all the hype of milestones, progress reports, and security force assistance had since been hurriedly buried in the same boneyard. The blood and treasure spent propping up a corrupt political elite were gone, leaving the bent politicians lording it in their private villas in Dubai and the demoralized ANA (Afghan National Army) giving up as soon as the Yanks left. And that was just the way it was when you relied on Western logic in that peculiar country. The only thing that really hurt the ex-Para was how NATO had abandoned the very people that he had been with in the mountains. The West had given up on the people of Panjshir, who had helped take the country from the Taliban after 9/11.

He was beginning to have doubts about his future. The ultra-politically correct woke and gender pronoun-obsessed MI6 of 2022 was no longer the organisation he had joined. Conventional spy craft was being increasingly replaced with online recruitment and computer algorithms, with cyber becoming increasingly more important than cyphers. He was sick of the constant hectoring to attend some opinion-moulding lecture or symposium rather than getting on with his job. *He was what he was,* an aging ex-paratrooper with anger issues who felt increasingly out of touch with the new generation of Six who preferred to conjure 'truth' from conjecture using a computer keyboard rather than find it in the field. *Every dog has its day,* and Mac was beginning to realize that his was over. He now thought more about retirement than attainment.

He looked again at the body of his ex-source. He had inhabited the same world. He had been a good agent, but, like Mac, he'd also had his time. He had once supplied valuable and insightful access to the unholy union of religion and politics, which had fused to create radical Islam in London. Flame had been useful, and he had liked him! Mac closed the file and checked his watch.

I've time to squeeze in an hour at the gym.

Chapter 5

Dublin

Dr. Linda O'Sullivan had joined the medical profession to help the sick but had ended up 'helping' the dead. The long journey from Trinity College Dublin had meandered somewhat after her first five years, and she was now a state pathologist. It had seemed a noble ideal, subliminally moulded by those episodes of CSI and other murder mysteries on RTE television. Sometimes it was rewarding, working with the dead, but occasionally upsetting as well. It was also a daily reminder of the fragility of life and your own mortality. You needed a sound mind and a strong stomach for the job, but either one could fail you at any time.

You eventually got used to some aspects of it. The strange metallic smell of blood tinged with antiseptic. The chilled, sometimes almost ghostly atmosphere of the pathology suite and all those awful sights you had to leave enclosed behind the teak door on Griffith Avenue to live a half-normal life. In thirty years, she had seen just about every way of exiting this world for the next, but the evil of torture had affected her most.

They didn't come along often; her last one had been a body picked up on the Irish side of the border during 'The Troubles'. It reminded her of man's constant and recurring inhumanity to man. She looked at the battered and burnt corpse on her mortuary table and felt an involuntary tear dissolve into her surgical mask.

As a forensic pathologist, she was there to determine the cause of death for legal purposes. But these injuries were so numerous and so severe that, if it weren't for the semi-severed head that rested at an awkward angle against the shiny steel of the table, she would just be guessing.

The corpse was that of an overweight Asian man who was identified as Abdulaziz Karimov. He had been about 60, with eye colour brown and hair colour white, with the only other identifying features being a series of fully healed scars from what appeared to be war wounds and a very faded tattoo of what looked like a sword. *A military man*, the doctor, guessed.

The chalky white cadaver was like a study of prolonged suffering. When this body had been a terrified human being, it had been beaten, stabbed, slashed, and seared with what could only have been a blowtorch. It also had other tell-tale signs: equally spaced circular scorch marks, something she had seen on her border torture victim. A *picana*, or modified cattle prod, had been applied all over his torso and genitals. A swab revealed that a saline solution had been applied to the skin to maximise conductivity.

Had the dead body now lying on her shiny steel table once been a man with a secret? Was it that secret that eventually stole his life?

★★★★

Vauxhall

On the fifth floor of the SIS building in London, Lou knocked on Collette's office door and waited for the electronic lock to click as he spoke into the intercom.

"You asked to see me, Boss?" Lou was now attired more conventionally but not as comfortably. His Rasta locks were tied back into a man bun, and his dark grey work suit was now stretched tight under pressure and looked ready to explode. Some people looked good in a suit with a man bun, but the burly black ex-Marine did not. Lou suppressed a smile. The suit was three years old, but he still claimed for it on every annual clothing allowance.

As he entered the office, Collette was sitting at her mahogany desk with her back to him. The office screamed senior management to all that visited it. Large and airy, it had an almost panoramic vista of the other bank of the Thames through the large, green-tinted window. His Boss was as immaculately turned out as ever.

She's probably spent more on that hairdo than I did on this suit.

Collette turned her head and smiled. She had a soft spot for her agent handlers in general and Lou in particular.

"Come in, Lou." She pointed at a file on the shiny mahogany desk.

"This has just been pushed over from JTAC."

The Joint Terrorism Analysis Centre had been doing what it was designed to do. An office deep inside MI5's Thames House, it brought together counterterrorism expertise from the police, government departments, and other agencies so that, as officially stated, the information could be analysed, processed, and shared.

Collette pointed towards her opened laptop.

"I have just shared a report with you from Dublin's SDU (Special Detective Unit). An associate of 3036 has turned up dead and not looking his best."

"Do we have a name?" Lou reached for his own secure laptop from his bag and placed it on the desk.

"Yeah." Collette leaned across to the desk and then clicked the laptop to display the autopsy photograph of a man on a shiny steel slab.

"Abdulaziz Karimov," she said as she scrolled down. "Again, as I said, not looking his best!" The photo showed his injuries. The face on the battered semi-severed head seemed to be asking, 'Why me?'

"He was an Afghan, an ethnic Uzbek Abdulaziz is a common name there. It means Servant of the Almighty, although it turns out he was a servant of the KGB during the Afghan/Soviet war."

"He was one of Flame's sub-sources," Lou stated.

"Yes and supplying information on the Afghan/London drug scene concerning domestic terrorism. They both worked together in Afghanistan."

Collette peered into her laptop as if it were the crystal ball that the public thinks all spymasters should have.

"So," she continued, "we have two bodies within a week: approximately the same age, same nationality, and linked by Russian tradecraft. The plot deepens. Any initial thoughts? You were his handler. Over to you."

"Could it be someone cleaning house, maybe tying up loose ends?" Lou was now seated behind his laptop.

"It's something linked from the past, but the two murders are unalike: one clinical and professional and quick ..." Lou scrolled down.

"And the other, very professional in a different way, a painfully slow way." He again looked at the injuries sustained by the Dublin victim. "This second murder was carried out to extract information and committed by someone trained to do it." He looked again.

Nobody deserves that!

"Poor bastard!" Lou mouthed the words under his breath.

Collette noticed that there was a slight rip on his grey work suit, which had given up the struggle with his rear deltoid.

"What do you think - the usual suspects?" Collette was still looking at the rip.

"The Russians? Not sure; we need to ask Mac. They've maybe old scores to settle. He knows more about the geopolitical dynamics of that era, but to me, this looks like revenge!"

"OK," Collette nodded. "Work on this, and I'll chat to Mac. We need to try and find out what's happening and if any of our other assets are under threat. Run this by our other Afghan friends and sub-sources. After all, they have a vested interest in finding out. They could be next."

"Yes, Boss." Lou closed his laptop and prepared to place it into its bag.

"And you have a rip in your suit under your arm. Try to buy a larger size next time you are in M&S."

"That's a big Roger, Boss." Lou only reverted to mil-speak inside the portals of VX or Thames House. "I take it that the purchase will be OK'd on my white sheet or my clothing allowance, then?"

Collette smiled sweetly. "No, absolutely not!" She looked away and dialled Mac's number.

Oh fuck. Mac grimaced as he felt his secure line vibrate in his pocket. He had wanted some time away from the confusing world of HUMINT, to go to his gym and punch a heavy bag or, even better, a fellow Krav Maga enthusiast.

He was now a senior member of the Secret Intelligence Service, but he still had to feed the Para beast that lurked inside him, and, strangely enough, the controlled violence seemed to help him problem-solve when he got back to the office. The modern MI6 was markedly lenient about most things but still a bit worried about how you spent your free time. It was perfectly acceptable to spend lunchtime in *'one's club'* but still considered strange to batter a heavy punch bag or a person.

He lifted the phone. "Hi, Collette," he said, masking his disappointment.

"Hi Mac. I bet you were sneaking off to the gym."

"Yeah, you caught me."

"No problems; at least you never pollute the office with gin fumes after lunch."

"Hey, want me to pop back?" Mac said, hoping for a negative.

"Yes please. You'll need to explain this Afghan puzzle to me."

"Where?"

"Your office?" Collette suggested.

"OK, I'm on my way up." Mac turned towards the shiny steel lifts and abandoned the idea of training that day.

The sound of his office door opening broke his thoughts. Mac was immediately aware of a waft of perfume and smiled. He liked her. She was one of the older members of the Firm that still represented the MI6 he had joined. She also served as his firewall against the new 'woke' breed in Five and Six that made up the younger members of those organisations. She was carrying her laptop and a brown folder, similar to the one Mac had on his desk, along with her own pink moleskin notebook and a gold pen the previous Chief had presented to her. Collette now used the Montblanc for everything she wrote. Her constant carping about the standard of the biros supplied to MI6 had made the pen an easy choice. She had got it as a presentation gift after her tenth year with the Firm. Mac also knew that when Collette was carrying her laptop and her precious 'pink brain', as she called it, she needed answers and was in receive mode.

"Sorry about that, Mac."

"Not a problem; work first, PT later."

"I just needed a steer on a theory," Collette said

"Happy to help." Mac stood and prepared the office guest chair for her.

Collette opened her laptop and quickly gave the Afghan expert the same download that she had just given Lou.

"That looks nasty." Mac grimaced as he glanced at the autopsy photographs. He had seen a tortured dead body before; it was an expression of human nature at its worst, and the sight made him sadder as he got older.

"I have my own theory about why these murders are happening at this particular time. Can I run it by you?"

"Fire away."

"I don't know for sure," she said, but maybe it's after the Salisbury thing."

"What, you mean the Russians did it?" Mac joked.

"Well, that seems a distinct possibility. Look at this."

She turned her laptop's screen in his direction. It showed a clear recent photograph of a woman that he quickly recognised. She was descending the aircraft stairs of what looked like a Learjet 75.

"You worked the Russian desk; did you ever work against a senior SVR (the Russian Foreign Intelligence Service) woman codenamed Babushka?"

"Colonel Katherina Sokolov- that's a blast from the past. Yes, she's hard-core and old-school Moscow Centre; the SVR calls her Matryoshka. We called her Babushka, just like that Kate Bush song from the '80s. We codenamed her that for the same reason as them because operationally, she's just like one of those Russian dolls."

"Like the ones you can get at Camden Market?" Collette smiled, but Mac didn't.

"Yeah, the same." He looked serious. "Sokolov was called that because of her exceptional operational abilities."

"I think I know what you seem to be saying but explain the logic." Collette was now tapping her gold pen gently on the desk. She did it when she was particularly interested in a subject. Mac explained.

"A Matryoshka doll is an old piece of Russian folk art. The outer shell of the doll has another five inside it, all slightly smaller, all fitting snugly inside each other, and that aptly describes Colonel Sokolov. One cover story was always carefully hidden within another that perfectly fitted inside the next. With Babushka, you never really knew who you were working against or who was running whom."

"Sounds like a formidable adversary."

"She is! So, we would know she was here if she wanted us to know."

Mac looked again at the screen, "Do you think she's behind the murders?"

"Maybe or maybe not, but it does seem like a bit of a coincidence. A top Russian operator arrives in town, and our assets get stiffed."

"Do we know where she is?" Mac said.

"Yes, she's not trying to hide. She's over here in plain sight and staying at the Lanesborough."

"If she was covert, we'd never pick her up. Who's on it?" Mac enquired.

"Bob Simpson's team from A4." Collette referred to MI5's surveillance specialists. A4 was one of the departments of 'Box' that was universally respected in the security services, and Bob Simpson was an ex-Royal Marine and SBS operator. He was the senior A4 controller and was only used against the most challenging targets.

"Yeah, but even Bob's team will have to be on its toes. She was a Tier One objective for our Russian desk and ran rings around us."

Collette pointed towards the laptop again. "So, you think that this is definitely Babushka?"

Mac looked again. "One hundred percent, or at least somebody who looks identical to her."

"What, like a doppelgänger or body double?" Collette seemed sceptical.

"Anything is possible with her." He was still looking at the photograph. It was at least ten years since he had last worked against her.

"OK, I have another pic I need your help with." She snapped shut the Mac Book Pro and handed across a colour photo. "Because this could be part of the murder mystery puzzle."

It was a close-up of the tattoo taken by the Dublin coroner. Mac looked and smiled.

"Hey, yet another blast from the past."

"You've seen one before?"

Mac studied the photo again. The tattoo was old and distorted, reminding him of how long it had been since he had worked in Massoud's backyard. It showed a long sword on an Afghan shield. The ink at the outside of the design still retained a purplish colour, although the badge in the centre had been burnt off by the attentions of the torturer. It seemed almost deliberate.

"Yeah, the last time I looked at one of these was after an ambush in Panjshir. It's faded, but it looks like the badge of the KHAD."

"KHAD?"

"Yes, sorry, Collette: the *Khadamat-e Aetia,at-e Dawlati,*" Mac said in Dari. "Literally meaning the State Intelligence Agency."

"A bit strange, don't you think, a tattoo on a covert intelligence operator?" She looked puzzled.

"Yeah, should be, but Afghanistan is a place where our rules don't apply. Afghan men don't wear vests or tee shirts unless they are under a shirt, and modesty is a big thing in the Islamic world. KHAD handlers had this tattoo partly through unit pride but mainly to identify themselves to their fellow operators. It was usually tattooed high on the upper right arm, where this one is, so it wouldn't show during *wadhu,* when they washed and prepared for prayers."

"They were religious Communists?" Collette again looked puzzled.

"Well, they were supposed to be Communists, but their tradecraft was good."

"They worked for the Soviets, though?" Collette's voice rose slightly.

"Yeah, or more precisely, they worked for the Afghan government, but a lot of the KHAD were actually trained in the USSR."

"A successful unit?"

"Very successful and hated by the Mooj since they were very good at what they did. By the mid-80s, they were running sources within all the so-called Peshawar Seven, or, more officially, *The Islamic Union for the Liberation of Afghanistan*. That was the organisation we supplied with the funding and weapons during Operation Cyclone."

Collette had heard of what MI6 and the CIA had called Operation Cyclone.

"Yeah, if only we had known then how it would turn out," Mac said, almost ruefully.

"What do you mean?" She had always thought Cyclone was a success and the key that finally unlocked the Iron Curtain. It was still heralded in intelligence circles as the classic example of how to support an insurgency.

Because," said Mac, "all the US, Qatari, UAE, and Saudi funding was channelled to the insurgents by Pakistan's ISI, or Inter-Services Intelligence. They made sure the cash went to only the most extreme Islamist groups. But only after they had taken their cut, of course. Most ISI officers ended the war very wealthy men."

"And the Firm?" Collette thought she already knew the answer; it was one of those hazy pieces of MI6 history she had learned of during training.

Mac continued. "We and the French DGSE (General Directorate for External Security) backed *Jamiat-i Islami*, also one of the Peshawar Seven but a bit more liberally minded and pro-Western under the leadership of Ahmad Shah Massoud, known by the press as *The Lion of Panjshir*. And that's why I ended up over there as one of his military advisors and trainers."

Collette pondered on it. "So, what do you think about these murders? Are the Russians over here cleaning house? Is Colonel Sokolov mopping up spilled secrets?"

"It's possible, but there is also something else to be aware of."

There was a moment of silence.

"What's that?"

"The Afghansy."

"Please explain."

"They are Russian veterans of the Soviet/Afghan war, and like our Afghan vets, they stick together like glue. They, especially the ex-Spetsnaz elements, are also a powerful political force inside Russia and are naturally allied with SF veterans of the Chechen war. They have influence that reaches right into the heart of the Kremlin."

"A type of unofficial political power base?" Collette said.

"Yes, and remember that Sokolov was Afghansy, and she will not be above wanting some payback for what we did to them in the past." Mac looked thoughtful.

★★★★

It was Colonel Katherina Sokolov's first full day at the Lanesborough Hotel on London's Hyde Park Corner. As she peered into the mirror on top of the expensive dressing table, she could still recognize the young GRU girl that trained at the

KGB spy school all those years ago. The last three decades as an intelligence officer had managed to etch some fine lines around the eyes. They had a green-blue opal colouring of stunning clarity that reflected sadness and inner turmoil in equal measure. Those same eyes had, in service to her motherland, both attracted some men and witnessed the last gasps of others. Moscow had expected much, and she had delivered!

She smiled when she thought of where she had trained all those years ago. A gated facility about fifty miles from Moscow and tucked deep inside the forest, the Red Banner Institute specialized in training KGB officers to work against the West.

The training was partly conducted in a Soviet-constructed 'village' meant to replicate everyday British life. There was a village post office, a pub, and even a town hall, and red post boxes and telephone kiosks were everywhere. Every conversation with her instructors was conducted in English, and every exercise was conducted as if on operations.

But it turned out to be the KGB's chocolate-box idea of British life and totally different from the grim reality of the towns and cities where she had eventually plied her trade. They had also taught her fluent 'Oxbridge' English. But her operational life had shown her that all languages have different accents, and she could now converse in several regional dialects in various European languages.

She had been in London for two days in what the old KGB handbook called commercial cover, also known in intelligence circles as hiding in plain sight. She was not hiding; she had been playing the game long enough to know that the alarm bells would now be ringing at both Vauxhall Cross and Thames House, and she wanted them to ring. As a former KGB officer, she had no doubt that she would have been on the UK Border Force's warnings index list and spotted as a passenger on a Moscow billionaire's private jet before it had landed at Heathrow.

She would now be under some form of surveillance. In fact, she would be disappointed if she were not. Since the botched GRU assassination attempt in Salisbury in 2018, an SVR intelligence officer was not that welcome. And especially not in London, where so many Russian dissidents had gathered, but that was part of the plan. The British used to call spying against the Russians *The Great Game*, and the Russian spy liked the term.

The Great Game is on, and I will play it to my advantage.

She deliberately had the minimum amount of cover in place. She had travelled under her own name, with the usual legend used in Europe. She was officially a senior executive of a Moscow-based company called 'The Moran Security Corporation', the maritime arm of a private military company also known as The Wagner Group. It had been a busy schedule that included meetings in Paris, Dublin, and now London. The hook was baited, and she hoped they would bite!

Kilburn, North London

At the same time, a tall blond man was relaxing on his sofa and listening to Vivaldi at the other end of Edgware Road. His small overnight bag was still packed after his last business trip. Torture was tiring, so he just closed his eyes and let the music flow through him. Before his brain injury, he had never been interested in any type of music, but now he loved it.

On one side of his living room was a ceiling-high bookshelf neatly lined with books and a vinyl collection of classical records. As he closed his eyes and half drifted off, he thought back to his time as an intelligence officer during the Soviet occupation of

Afghanistan. The things that had haunted him before that fragment of shrapnel altered his perceptions did not worry him anymore. He used to feel guilty about his service, but now he realised that he was just doing his job at a challenging time.

He had been an intelligence officer in the 10th Directorate (Afghan Foreign Intelligence Branch) attached to an elite KGB special forces *Kaskad* unit that was operating in the north of Afghanistan. He had been trained in Moscow and Kabul and had liked working with the Russians in the north. He even looked a bit like them. His Nuristani heritage had gifted him his height, straw-blond hair, and light blue eyes. And, as it was never good to stand out too much in an intelligence job, he blended in quite easily with his Soviet friends. He remembered the first time he killed and the first time he had to get someone to talk. Pain-enhanced interrogation used to bother him then. He smiled. *It didn't now*.

Chapter 6

Knightsbridge, London

They were good. They were very good, but Colonel Sokolov had worked against the best, and they weren't quite good enough. Spotting surveillance is an acquired art, and success only comes with years of experience; training only scratches the surface of it. The four-person team following her hadn't made any glaring mistakes. The MI5's A4 watchers were very professional, but eventually, she was able to identify them. It helped that she had worked in London before and was particularly familiar with this part of it. It was an affluent area, a little oasis of calm in a worried city. She had dressed the part. Her black Burberry hooded trench coat was high-end but not overly ostentatious. Her low heels were by Jimmy Choo, and a Chanel shoulder bag contained some quick-change anti-surveillance clothes.

She was having fun.

She had already taken them for a reverse taxi ride. Five stops on the number 22 bus route and an underground experience on their subway system. And was now going to subject them to what all London-based watcher teams secretly fear: the 'Harrods Experience.' As Babushka passed the green-liveried doorman, she could almost imagine the internalized groans of her watchers, especially the one who had been wheeling the dust cart outside. They had been following her now for about eight hours.

There are three types of foot surveillance for a four-person team. They are loose, close, and a combination of both. She would make sure that the MI5 team got to work them all!

She thought she detected a small amount of panic in the eyes of a smartly dressed older woman, her closest shadow, as she changed direction and lost herself amongst a group of Japanese tourists. She reached the escalator unsighted and took it to the fifth floor. She quickly looked at the offerings in what Harrods calls its 'Shoe Heaven' - *she really loved shoes* - and then quickly descended to the first floor, to Women's Wear. She glanced at her watch.

Bang on time.

She spotted the other A4 watcher just as she stepped off the Egyptian escalator and could almost see him wince as she made her way into the luxury lingerie section. He was a tweed-jacketed middle-aged man, and in that part of the store, he wouldn't blend at all well. *He will switch close cover with the woman.*

Codename Babushka made straight for the 'La Perla' section for her prearranged meeting before the two A4 people could switch.

There she is!

An Arab woman with a full-face niqab, elbow-length gloves, and a long flowing robe of expensive black silk was pretending to examine a black lace corset. She switched her bag from her right to her left shoulder in a visual signal. It meant *I have recognised you and I'm ready for the switch.*

The Arab woman walked towards the ladies' toilet, and the Russian followed. The switch was quick and efficient, and two minutes later a striking-looking woman, similar in height and appearance to Babushka and dressed in the same Burberry trench coat, opened the door of the ladies loo and continued to shop.

Babushka waited and peered through the partially opened door until she saw the A4 woman tag the decoy and whisper into her chest mike. The Russian agent then glided out of the restroom, dressed from head to foot in black. It would only be minutes until the team knew there had been a switch, but minutes were all she needed. The now black-garbed Babushka spotted the other watcher as she moved towards the escalator. She moved in behind and bumped into him.

"Sare" (sorry), she said in Arabic, and then, louder in English, as she turned away, "Check your pocket. It's an old-school brush contact."

The A4 man was momentarily dumbstruck as the black shape faded into the crowd. He tentatively reached inside his right trouser pocket and pulled out a note. In neat block capitals, the message was clear.

'I need to meet soonest. Ring me on this number, followed by a mobile number, and then: 'This training has been brought to you by the Russian SVR.' It was signed Babushka.

In Collette's office, the winter rain was hammering hard against the window and supplying the soundtrack to her thoughts. Her notebook was opened on her desk and adorned with precise lines of writing. It was always in the same neat italic script, applied with the Montblanc pen. She read through her notes one more time.

It doesn't seem to make sense! Why?

Her thoughts were interrupted by a knock on the door.

"Come in, Mac." She had asked to see him for an update.

"You know this woman. What do you think?"

Collette handed the note to Mac, who carefully examined it, turning it over in his hand, and searching for some hidden meaning. But there didn't appear to be one.

"Have the techs looked at this?"

The message was written on a half sheet of A4 copy paper. It appeared to have been neatly cut in half with some scissors.

"Yes, they've dusted, sampled, and even checked it for secret ink."

"And?"

"And it is what it is, Mac. It's a cut piece of A4 paper with a message, without fingerprints, and neatly printed in block capitals in black biro. She's a class operator."

She had a hint of a smile on her face.

"I chatted to the A4 man who received it. He was quite embarrassed by the whole thing. He had no idea that his team had been blown."

"Yeah." Mac placed the note on the desk with a respectful nod. "She's one of their best."

"And she seems to have a wicked sense of humour."

He looked again at the note. "But why go to all that trouble to just meet us?"

Collette considered the situation as she looked at her notebook.

"She wants it unofficial. She's made her presence here blatantly obvious and in plain sight. So, she must have known that we would put a team on her. She has something to discuss that can't go through normal channels. Maybe she wants to come across?"

"Defect?" Mac's voice mirrored his doubt.

"No, listen." Collette looked up and smiled. "What do we look for when we start a recruitment plan?"

Mac listed the priorities as a mantra. "Capability, Access, Motivation, and Point of Contact. Are you suggesting that we should pitch her?"

He used the standard slang used in the security and intelligence services for an offer of employment as a source. The M16 veteran had named the textbook requirements that were essential for any successful recruitment of an informant. But the list meant far more than that. It was the very essence of agent handling.

A source had to be capable of operating as a spy and adjusting to his or her new existence as an MI6 agent. The newly recruited source also needed to have sufficient access, current or potential, to the secrets the Firm needed. To make the risk and effort worthwhile they also had to remain undetected while they passed back those secrets from the penetrated organisation. They further required the motivation or reason for agreeing to work for the Firm. That was one of the most important factors. And finally, you needed a POC or point of contact to make the recruitment pitch in the first place.

What could motivate a Kremlin hardliner like Babushka to turn? None of the usual reasons!

Collette still smiled sweetly. "Well, she has the first two - and has the thought occurred to you that she may be planning a Walk-In?"

"What do you think?" Mac said.

"I think this woman has an angle that we haven't thought of yet, and I think she is looking for a chance to recruit one of ours."

'Who?" Mac said, already understanding the drift.

"You!"

"No way." Mac's voice had an offended tone.

"Why not?" Collette expanded the thought. "You have all the attributes the SVR is looking for, and maybe she intends to supply some other motivation. After all, you are single, and she's an attractive woman."

She winked, and Mac realised Collette was teasing him as she continued with the theme.

"Or perhaps this whole thing is just smoke and mirrors to disguise her true intentions. It seems strange that a senior SVR officer has just arrived in London while the Russian Federation is building up troops on the Ukrainian border and when two of our sources have been murdered."

Collette picked up her pen, replaced the cap, and asked a question.

"And what do you think she wants?"

"Knowing what any woman actually wants is well out of my comfort zone, but I do know there are much simpler ways to defect." Mac sounded mournful or even bitter. Collette remembered that he was just recovering from a painful divorce.

"Well, call it women's intuition if you like" - Collette fluttered her eyelashes - "but I think she might want to come in from the cold. And, since we are part of this great organisation, whose purpose is to recruit and run agents to protect HMG's interests abroad, I think you should at least try to pitch her before she pitches you."

"I think she wants to talk about something that she doesn't want the Russian Embassy to know, but I don't think that recruiting me is her plan," Mac responded. "Have you thought of running her name past Spellcraft?"

Collette seemed to visually recoil at the suggestion. "Too early for that, but it's an option that we could use after your initial assessment."

Spellcraft was the codename used within MI6 for the closed cell of handlers that ran a very special double agent within Russia's FSB. The FSB was the Russian Federation's equivalent to MI5, and SCORPION was the most secret of agents, so the sealed unit had been formed to protect the source and his impressively accurate information. There was also a personal angle Mac had not considered, which Collette would never mention. The man who controlled the product that the agent produced, Damian Brown, was not only of the same rank as her and vying for the same promotion but also her ex-husband. The ex-husband bit didn't matter too much as they got on surprisingly well, but the promotion race did. The product had delivered some stunning successes over the last two years, and her former husband was now riding high on the results.

Collette moved the conversation forward.

"So, what's your plan?" she said, as she flashed a smile.

"I have her number; I'll give her a call."

"As simple as that?" Collette's voice had a sceptical tinge. "You'll need close cover; I'll organize a team."

"No, no need; she would spot them anyway. I will be safe enough; I'll go for a public space. Maybe dinner."

Mac scooped Babushka's note up from the desk and glanced at it again. "After all, a note between intelligence agencies passed at a brush contact is almost like the spy's version of Tinder."

★★★★

At the same time, the blond man, whom his fellow operators called *Belaya Smert* (White Death) was stalking his prey on Oxford Street. He was following his target at the proper distance for a rainy day in London. He was close because you could afford to get closer on a wet day. English rain brought its advantages: people seemed to walk in a controlled rush everywhere and were much less aware of their surroundings. Additionally, the black umbrella he carried shaded him from the numerous CCTV cameras on London's main shopping street. The pitter-patter of rain also had a calming influence on him. He was enjoying the hunt.

The killer caught his reflection in the plate glass of M&S as he checked the rear for surveillance. He was dressed in a black raincoat that, draped around his long body, gave him a sinister outline that reminded him of something. He smiled as he checked the knife that nestled comfortably inside the leather sheath strapped onto his left forearm. A thought flashed into his damaged brain.

The Grim Reaper? Yes, most definitely. After all, that's my job!

He was still smiling. He knew the man he was following and had worked with him once. He was a good comrade from the war and a nice man, but he would soon be a dead one!

★★★★

Two miles away at Thames House, Lou, Ahmad, and Mac were in what the unit called 'the Binner' or Room 3. It was a cyber-sanitized, soundproofed, and steel-lined room on the third floor of Britain's domestic security agency. Nobody really knew why Room 3 was called the Binner; it was one of those archaic nicknames passed down from the FRU (Force Research Unit) days in Ulster, and it was where the agent-runners processed their reports into a centralized and cyber-sealed server.

Ahmad had just returned from a meet with one of his sources in Whitechapel and was in a brown, tailored shalwar kameez and waistcoat. He was one of the JTF's most experienced handlers. A medium-height, dark-complexioned ex-British Army Afghan veteran of Kurdish extraction. He blended easily into an increasingly multicultural London, even in its more monocultural areas. He was sitting by Lou, still compressed inside his uncomfortable work suit, opposite Mac, dressed at the other end of the sartorial spectrum in some of the best tailoring that Savile Row could supply.

I bet that's not covered by the Firm's clothing allowance, thought Lou.

They had called the meeting to discuss whether there had been any apparent link between the unit's operations and the subsequent demise of 3036, and Chris, the tech guy, had the floor.

"So, explain it to me again." Mac was talking to the man they called 'Computer Chris'.

MI5's premier IT expert stared through his latest blue-framed acquisitions from Specsavers. He wore a pained expression, like a very patient primary school teacher dealing with one of his thicker students.

"It's called a forensic financial profile, and I have processed it through Panatile."

"Panatile?" Ahmad asked.

"Yeah; sorry mate," Mac interjected to explain. "It's a network analysis program and an advanced computer software developed by the Israelis and the Cousins (CIA)." Mac glanced across at Chris. "Not that I know much about it, but we used it on the last job. It apparently gathers computer algorithms, swirls them around, takes what we need, and then gives us an answer. Is that right, Chris?"

"Yes, that's one way of looking at it, but it's still only a powerful tool. Its job is to process data on your subject matter area (Chris still had the same pained expression), but it's like any type of processing software: it entirely depends on what you put into it. In other words, if you put rubbish in, you get rubbish out."

"So, what have we looked at?" Lou still seemed a bit baffled.

Chris took a deep breath as if in thought. "At the moment, we have dumped two major chunks of data into its server. First, any common commercial and banking links between the two victims and, second, any telephone and email traffic that links them to anybody else. That is overlaid with any online material, including personal social media."

"And the result?" Mac said.

"This is what we have so far." Chris switched on the large wall-mounted monitor with the remote.

He pointed to what in intelligence circles is a LAD or Link Analysis Diagram. It was a pictorial representation of the people and organizations involved in any investigation.

It looked like a spider's web of different coloured lines and boxes that crisscrossed, interlinked, and identified their relationships. It looked like something you would see at the Tate Modern to a casual observer.

"Here's the LAD from our two victims' phone data. As you can see, they were in constant contact over the last year. Hits from both of their mobiles' MAC addresses linked to local towers put them together on several occasions, although never in London. They had three meetings last month: two in Newcastle and another in Dublin."

Chris gestured towards the diagram displayed on the large TV monitor. He used a laser pointer, as he explained.

"And here are the financial links overlaid onto the mobile data." He tapped his laptop; another profile fitted neatly over the first and intermeshed with it.

"As you can see, there were also substantial financial exchanges when these two met, or sometimes just after a peak in phone traffic between them. Always with large withdrawals of cash. That indicates that they could have used the Hawala system to move money quickly."

"Can we trace that?" Lou asked.

"No. As you know, Hawala is almost untraceable, as the system is based mainly on tribal trust, family, and a coded reference in a phone call. You pay in at one end, minus a handling fee and the money is paid out at the other, and it's virtually untraceable. That's why it's used in the drug trade. The cash is given in at one end, through approved Islamic bankers called Hawaladars, and is retrieved at the other with a prearranged codeword."

"What sort of money are we looking at?" Mac was studying the analysis diagram on the monitor, trying to work out the color-coded links.

"Large - big numbers and on numerous occasions." Chris clicked the screen again. "We are also discovering just how individually wealthy our ex-source 3036 was. It seems he had significant funds offshore, and he didn't get that rich on the money we paid him."

Mac looked impressed. "Something illegal?"

"Yes. Look at this." Chris used a laser pointer to highlight five different money movements.

"Jimlit flashed these up." Chris sometimes used terms that only he knew. He responded to the team's almost universal blank looks.

"Sorry," he smiled. "The JMLIT is the Joint Money Laundering Intelligence Team. They look at this sort of thing because of the way dirty money is moved around."

"And?" Lou asked the question.

"They have recorded numerous SARs and CTRs. A SAR is a suspicious activity report, and a CTR is a currency transaction report." Chris pre-empted the questions this time.

"Where did the money originate?" Mac was studying the screen.

"It's difficult even for us to work out because of how complex these transactions can get. It's being unravelled by the NTFIU (National Terrorist Financial Investigation Unit) now, but it looks like they got lucky. The results of the investigation into offshore tax haven that the press is calling 'The Pandora Papers' have just come online. It's the most comprehensive exposé of how international elites hide their money. It highlights the accounts of 35 world leaders, billionaires, celebrities, and business leaders."

"Was Flame directly linked?" Mac asked.

"We think so, but it takes time to unpick the connections. We think the payments could have originated somewhere in Russia and been routed through Panama before transiting the Hawala system and ending up with our ex-agent."

"Do any of the mobiles indicate traffic with Russia?" Mac continued to study the link diagram.

"No. Not so far but we know that five different mobile phones are linked, and those are the ones outlined in red." Chris used the laser pointer again and hovered the red dot over one of the phone links.

"As you can see, our dead source Flame was using this number, and that one belonged to the Dublin torture victim." He then indicated the other three links with the red dot.

"We have applied for a warrant to trace the WAP addresses of the other three."

Ahmad raised his hand. "Yes, mate?" Chris said

"Would I be right in thinking that the associates who possess the other three mobile numbers are in danger, then?

"Yeah, it's a strong possibility," Chris concurred.

Lou gave his opinion, "Or one of them could be the murderer. What do you think?"

There was a quiet hush over the room as the JTF team considered Lou's conjecture.

In her office at the SIS building, Collette opened the coroner's report that had landed on her desk. The MI6 liaison officer at SO15, or what used to be called Special Branch, had spotted the link straight away. Unfortunately, a stabbing wasn't unusual in London, but this one was different. The victim was confirmed as an older Afghan man, dispatched with a single stab wound with military precision. The knife had entered his back in between his ribs and hit his heart.

There was bruising around the man's nose and mouth, indicating that he had been dragged backward before the stab wound ended his life.

Collette clicked the link for the full report on her laptop and scanned through the very depressing photographs. It had initially been reported as a gangland stabbing - there had been three the day before - but this one was different. It was apparently military, it was professional, and it was almost clinical.

And I bet the murder victim also worked for the Russians, she thought as she opened her pink notebook.

Mac was in a thoughtful mood, two floors down, as he pulled his desk drawer open and selected one of the burner phones. He then inserted a cheap supermarket sim card and flashed it up. He was strangely nervous as he waited until the Nokia was good to go. It reminded him of one of those phone calls he had made.

Will she, or won't she?

It wouldn't be the first time that a girl had volunteered her number but then had doubts. It was almost like the dreaded Aldershot first-date syndrome when he had been a young 'Tom' in 2 Para in the early 1980s. A chance meeting with a nice girl slumming it in a hard-core Para pub like the Globetrotter would always end up as a no-show as soon as she mentioned the dreaded word 'Para' to her parents. He smiled as he thought about those early days, a young soldier cutting about without a care in the world. Life had been simpler then. He had his own plans and not reacting to somebody else's. That had always made him feel a bit uneasy or even vulnerable. Especially when the woman he was calling was old-school Moscow Centre and a serving colonel in Russia's SVR.

He composed himself, took a deep breath, and tapped in the number. He let the phone ring four times, hung up, and then rang again. He was guessing that the Russian phone procedure was similar to the Firm's, and so it proved to be.

"Hello, I thought you'd never ring," a dulcet-sounding voice said.

"Colonel Sokolov, I presume?" Mac said, immediately regretting the hackneyed phrase.

"Yes, you presume right, but why do MI6 officers always want to sound like Victorian explorers or Sherlock Holmes?"

"When and where?" Mac cut the small talk. "Elementary, my dear Watson. Your city, your choice. Your name isn't Watson, is it?" There was a gentle laugh. "Or am I talking to Mr Christian, but you can call me Mac, McCann OBE QGM, the current expert on all things Islamic Terrorism at VX?"

"Yeah, but you can call me Mac."

Babushka laughed again.

"A good deduction," Mac said, staying with the Holmes theme. "I guess you have the same files on us as we have on you?"

"Yes, Mac, pretty much. When and where do you want to meet? I suggest a public place on neutral ground."

"Nobu."

"Sounds good, and on whose expense account?" There was another soft laugh.

"Ours, of course," Mac said. "I don't want to get you into trouble with the bean counters at Directorate R."

There was a moment of silence on the other end of the phone. Mac had name-dropped the actual department that Colonel Sokolov usually ran. Directorate R was the Operational Planning and Analysis department evaluating SVR operations abroad.

"Perfect, Mac." She quickly recovered her composure. "Just text me a time when you have set it up."

"Thanks, Colonel Sokolov. I will arrange it."

"Hey, if this is dinner on you, you can call me Katya."

"I will be in touch, Katya."

"Yeah, well, don't stand a girl up!" she said as the phone went dead.

Mac returned to his desk and considered the task and the question that needed to be answered.

Why was she here? Was it a classic Walk-In?

Even with so many possible motivations, it was a historical fact that the best and most successful agents were almost always volunteers.

But if she was walking in, what was her motivation?

The lexicon of the spy world was littered with acronyms, and the one that applied to motivation was simply called MICE. It listed the four main motivating factors for successful recruitment. They were firstly Money, then Ideology, followed by Compromise or Coercion, and finally, the self-motivation of Ego.

Money was probably the most popular and the easiest to supply, and Mac knew from bitter experience that most people had a price. But he thought financial remuneration was perhaps an unlikely motivation for his dinner date. A quick look at her bio showed that she was more patriotically inclined and, therefore, unlikely to be motivated by a bag load of cash or a Cayman Islands account. He thought it especially unlikely in Babushka's case since she had arrived from Dublin in a private jet owned by a billionaire Russian who seemed to own the other half of London not owned by the Arabs.

Ideology was a more complicated motive but sometimes supplied the best agents. Maybe she'd had second thoughts about the Russian Federation's foreign policy. An ideologically driven double agent is the crown jewel of spying, and if she was in London to walk in and offer her services as just such a double agent, he needed to plan for it.

Compromise or coercion was the dangerous motivation in the agent recruiter's arsenal and was prone to blowback. Blackmail is a blunt instrument, and unresolved resentment can cause severe problems for a handler further down the line.

The final factor, Ego, is a self-generated motivation and easy for a skilled HUMINT handler to exploit. Looking at Babushka's file, he considered it and then discounted it.

Mac closed his eyes and tried to concentrate as he thought about his best angle for a pitch.

CHAPTER 7

Nobu, Park Lane, London

Secret agents sometimes meet in the shadows and sometimes don't. On some occasions, it is more secure to meet in plain sight. The Russian knew the restaurant well and had dined there before. Nobu was an upmarket place to eat. She liked the food, a unique blend of Japanese and Peruvian cuisine, and the decor, with lots of mirrors, backlighting, white wood, and natural stone. It was a global brand with restaurants in thirty-two different countries. *A bit like McDonald's for rich people.* It had the advantage of being the sort of place where the tables were spaced for privacy. This was intended more for romance than espionage, but it served the same purpose.

Katya was seated in one of the restaurant's mirrored booths with her back to the entrance. She looked at the reflection opposite her and checked her watch. The Russian adjusted her hair with her fingertips and confirmed that her lipstick was applied correctly. She then pressed the small button on her left sleeve to check that her covert earpiece was working. Three clicks immediately got two bursts of static from the tiny pea-sized receiver inside her ear, telling her that minders were monitoring the downstairs entrance. She had dressed for the occasion, business-like, formal but upmarket. She had chosen an Alexander McQueen tailored blazer and trousers in a turquoise blue that complemented her eyes. First impressions were always important, so the outfit was accessorized with a leather Bottega Veneta crossbody bag in the same colour that contained her perfume, lipstick, and her pistol, a 7.62 mil MSS Vul.

Not that she felt that the man she was meeting posed any threat. *Brits were far too civilized for that*, especially in their own capital city. But the SVR officer had always operated on the old Moscow Centre premise: *It's better to have a gun and not need it than to need a gun and not have it.*

The Vul, or PSS, a small magazine-fed pistol that the KGB had developed at the height of the Cold War, operated on a closed-cartridge system and was almost totally silent. *Silent was the way to go if you were going to shoot anyone at night in London.*

Outside, on Park Lane, Ahmad signalled and maneuvered the big Mercedes and spoke to Mac.

"This OK?"

"Yeah, looks good," said Mac, as he unclipped his seat belt and reached for the door handle. "I will walk the last bit. Give her guys a chance to warn her that I'm on my way up."

Lou was doing the close cover. He had already spotted the two men in the parked car on the opposite side of the street. He concluded they were protecting the meet because two stocky men in a car aren't the best way you carry out surveillance in town.

They must be her minders. Lou knew professional watchers would be a lot harder to spot.

They're probably just a trigger for the meet and maybe close protection; nothing more sinister than that.

As Mac opened the door and stepped onto the pavement, he tested his comms.

"Hi, all stations. This is Mac." He heard Ahmad's voice first.

"Lima Charlie," and then Lou's "Lima Charlie."

Mac hit the Send button in his pocket twice to confirm he was now in non-speaking mode. Two bursts of static from the handlers in sequence confirmed they understood.

Mac looked towards the car where the two Russians were eyes down on the restaurant's front door.

They didn't look that much out of place, he mused. *There were a lot more bodyguards in this part of London than spies! This is a strange, artificial part of town. It's like a little oasis of calm away from the madness of Paddington and the in-your-face energy and sleaze of Soho.*

London's rich people and their support network of advisors, political connections, security, and servants were corralled and protected in one of the most over-policed areas of the city. The safe zone consisting of Mayfair and Knightsbridge ran up to the lush green of Hyde Park on London's famous Park Lane. This was where the super-rich lived, played, and partied, and it was owned by Qatari and Saudi oil money or Russian oligarchs. This was where Londonistan crashed into Londonograd, and money flowed on impact.

He looked towards where two more Russian heavies were waiting for his arrival and strolled towards Nobu. He liked the look of the place. It was an impressive building. The façade was a modernist stone block with a thin glass-roof portico that projected over the entrance.

Upstairs, Katya heard three bursts of static in her earpiece. *He's arrived.*

Mac was still thinking about clever one-liners as he ascended the wide stairs to the dining area. At the front desk, an immaculately attired hostess looked the new arrival up and down and made her instant assessment, the way only senior front-of-house staff can do. It was the usual scan from the feet up.

Shoes, Church's - check. Suit - looks Savile Row – check. Watch – Breitling – check.

The only thing to confuse her was his maroon Parachute Regiment tie. She hadn't seen one before. *It looked a bit like the Aston Martin logo.*

"I'm here to meet Katya," Mac said. The concierge indicated towards the right of the restaurant.

"Yes, a table for two. Madam is expecting you, sir. Enjoy your private dining in mirror pod three."

The woman Six called Babushka was still mentally rehearsing how she should act. She would have her back to him as he entered the restaurant. She would be friendly but cool. The colonel felt strange: *it was almost like a first date.* She smiled at the thought, and then Mac appeared reflected in the mirror, and her heart missed a beat.

Sometimes the subconscious past suddenly propels itself into the conscious present!

She was amazed because the man approaching her table was strikingly familiar. The hair colour was the same, along with the similar build and height, and even the same confident walk. It was like looking at an older version of Mikhail, her forever love, who hadn't returned from Panjshir thirty years before.

Mac had almost walked past the booth before he caught Katya's reflection in the uplit mirror. She sat straight backed, with a strange expression on her face.

Not shocked but perplexed, Mac thought.

He used her name as a question. "Katya?"

The colonel quickly recovered her composure.

"Yes," she smiled up at her dinner guest. "I thought you would just walk on past there, Mr. McCann."

"No, there was no way I was going to walk past, not after all the trouble I went through to get this place cleared."

"Wow! Did your people think it was too dangerous?" There was a slight mocking lilt to her voice.

Mac sat down opposite her and smiled.

"No, it was more like the heated discussion I had with our bean counters. Nobu's a bit rich for their taste. Is it the same in Moscow?"

"Yes, precisely." The Russian agent returned the smile. "We've two Nobu restaurants in Moscow, and I've had our accountants querying the prices in both." She sighed.

Katya shifted uneasily as she looked once again at her dinner guest.

Is that nervousness or attraction?

Mac glanced across at her as he took in his immediate surroundings. He was usually happier in a gym or hanging off a mountain than in a high-end eatery, but a place like Nobu had obvious advantages for a covert meeting. The venue suited their needs because the wealthy clients that used the place were not always with their actual husbands, wives, or partners, so the staff were discreet and well used to illicit meetings, especially ones with the odd whispered conversation.

He looked towards his dinner guest as he watched her make her initial assessment. The most important part of any agent meet was always the first five minutes. This is the time set aside for the handler to develop empathy while covering all the basics for a first meeting. When Mac had been at 'the Fort', the trainers had called it the *Five Fingers*. It was the way that they were taught to cover all the bases when they met a new source.

The first finger was Initial Greetings. It was generally better to start well and put the agent at ease; such an approach is designed to build a bond of empathy over time. And then the more business-like question known as the second finger: *Anything important for me?* You ask this question early so you do not spend too much time empathy-building when you should be collecting time-sensitive information.

The third finger is a practical question: *How much time have you got?* A handler needs to fit his debrief into the agent's schedule, as the source is usually the one under time pressure. The fourth finger is another question: *When can we meet again?* It is used to arrange the next meeting and how it will be achieved.

And the fifth: *What will you say if anybody asks what you were doing here with me?* That final important question ensures the agent has a plausible but uncheckable cover story.

I wonder if she's had the same lecture. The thought made Mac smile, and she smiled back.

She was a beautiful woman. He didn't think he had ever met anybody with such striking features; they were a delicate fusion of east and west, and she looked younger than it said in her file. Her age was hard to guess, like so many other things about this mysterious woman.

The MI6 man shifted in his seat as she inspected him, still with the hint of a smile around her lips. She tried to assess Mac's age. *She thought the late forties or mid-fifties* with fine lines that splintered from his eyes and made him look distinguished rather than old. His shoulders were set square, and he was slim and athletic but on the well-muscled side. He looked like a soldier, and his face, weather-beaten, tanned by the sun and hardened by exercise, glowed healthily. She noticed his eyes for the first time, the same cobalt blue as the boy she had lost in the mountains.

Mac had known she was an experienced spy as soon he felt her opal green eyes almost boring through him as if they were scanning his soul. He broke the brief silence.

"Welcome to London, Katya. How long have you been here?"

"I think you know that. Your people have been following me since I arrived."

Having been repulsed by the empathy-building part, Mac went to the second default question on the Five Fingers.

"OK, what have you got for me?"

"Hey, I'm glad the old-school ways are still being taught at the Fort," Katya smiled.

"The Five Fingers were also taught at the Institute in the old days. Not so much now, though - it's all cyber, online recruitment, and fake websites and algorithms. Is it the same at Six?"

"Yeah, pretty much so." Mac's gaze met hers. "So, why go to so much trouble to arrange this meeting?"

Katya's fingers brushed back her hair near her left ear, and she removed her earpiece and placed it on the table.

"I suggest comms dark," she said. "I have things that I want only you to hear."

Mac removed his earpiece and placed it alongside hers.

She then reached inside her blazer, switched off her encrypted radio, and looked at Mac, who mirrored her actions and switched off his.

"I have no other recording equipment," he formally stated.

"I know; my guys scanned you when you arrived." She again smiled sweetly and added, "Do you want to eat while we talk?"

"Yeah, seems logical," Mac said as he picked up the menu. "Do you want us to order?"

"Absolutely." Katya picked up her menu.

Mac smiled and asked a direct question.

"So, why are you here?" The Russian spy avoided eye contact and continued to studiously examine the fare.

"Why do you think?"

"The obvious," Mac stated.

"Explain." Mac could pick up only the slightest Russian accent; it was just enough to make Katya seem even more interesting.

"Let me give you a scenario and see if it fits. You OK with that?"

"I'm intrigued." The Russian put down the menu and sipped her wine.

"I'm glad." Mac toyed with his table napkin as he went into his rehearsed pitch.

"You were in Afghanistan at the same time as me, and you know what the place does to you." He paused in thought. "It changes you," he added. "It changed me, and not for the better. And I think it changed you and made you think differently. Am I right?"

"Yes, we call our Afghan veterans *Afghansy*," Katya agreed. "The politicians think soldiers are emotionless and should never question their political masters, but we know differently, don't we, Mac?" As she spoke, Katya's soft face seemed to harden. "Hate drives war." Her voice also became more pronounced. "Especially in Afghanistan, where no quarter is either asked or given. And that hate leads to permanent anger in your soul. Do you know the feeling? Maybe not, but I think your latest Afghan veterans do."

"And is that why you are here? Even though the relationship between our two countries is somewhat strained at the moment, no?"

"Yes, but let's order and discuss my reasons later. Your surveillance branch – it's A4, isn't it? - have given me exercise and an appetite, and I need to explain something before you can appreciate my situation."

Mac nodded and tried to read the menu in the restaurant's tasteful low light but had trouble doing so; his optician had recommended spectacles, but he was sure it was just the poor light to blame. He eventually gave up trying to decode the squiggles (*which might as well be written in Russian*) and just opted for the main course he'd enjoyed on a previous visit.

"Can I recommend the shrimp and lobster with spicy lemon dressing and the Montes Sauvignon Blanc? It's a great combination."

Katya smiled as she looked at the menu. "I'm not a seafood person. I'm having beef tataki with ponzu sauce. I suggest we share. It's a lot for one person and, like a secret agent's dinner date, it's for two people. What do you think?"

"And the wine?" Mac smiled back.

"It could only be the Pinot Noir Russian River Valley 2017."

"Russian River. Very apt."

"Yeah, I thought so, but it's actually a Californian wine and a great match."

"I will follow your lead." Mac was trying to place her accent: soft, almost gentle, classic Oxbridge English with the slightest Moscow twang.

"Great. I hope it's going to be the same with the rest of the evening?"

"I can't promise that!" he said. Mac knew that whatever his Russian counterpart had to talk about would be far from straightforward.

"Anyway, that's why we are meeting like this: we are both dinosaurs from the Afghan wars that want to make sure that such dangerous things do not happen again," said Katya.

"According to your file, you are dangerous as well. A veritable T-Rex of the intelligence world," Mac whispered in reply.

Katya smiled, bared her white teeth, and growled.

CHAPTER 8

Collette looked at the latest report on her desk and tried to solve a murder mystery. The secret folders hadn't changed much since she had arrived at SIS, or just the Firm, as insiders called it. The thin, blood-red folder had *Secret UK Eyes Only* emblazoned at the top, with a series of columns on the right-hand side with the dated signature or initials of those who had already read the contents. A faint, green-inked 'C' in the first row showed her that the Chief of SIS had seen it. She opened the cover of her own pink notebook to take notes. JTAC had just analysed the results of the data they had supplied and cross-referenced them with other information from various agencies and technical sources. They had analysed every MISR or CX report from every meet the CHIS (Covert Human Intelligence Source) called Flame, or 3036 had attended for the last twenty years. Every handler's comment had been noted and either validated or discounted. It made for interesting reading.

The MI6 strategist considered her intelligence problems in the same way she approached her favourite crossword puzzles, and the more complex and challenging they were, the more she enjoyed them. She picked up her fountain pen, removed the gold cap, and prepared to solve this one.

She smiled as she crafted another line of script. *This is good stuff.*

The good news was that the addresses of all the victim's mobile phones had been analysed and had supplied vital evidence for the murder inquiry. In today's spycraft, once you had a mobile phone number, you had virtually everything else you needed. The digital dust trail often included every cash point withdrawal, every social media post, and a record of every time a phone had locked on to a Wi-Fi signal. And once that phone was travelling in a car, you also knew when the owner had crossed a border or had their car's number recorded on a motorway camera.

When the POI, or Person of Interest, was walking around, you also knew where he or she could have been filmed on the CCTV systems of London or any other big city. All this detail could nail the subject's pattern of life. The bad news was that all this newly discovered data was now mixed with agent handling operations and three murder inquiries, which meant possible disclosure problems further down the line, with evidence gathered from methods that needed to stay secret to be effective.

Collette already knew that two of the murder victims were linked. Flame had been a source, and the other man, Abdulaziz Karimov, his declared sub-source, so it was very likely that the latest murder victim was also known to them both. All the traced mobiles were burner phones, and all the users had been identified as former Afghan intelligence officers.

She inscribed her thoughts in an elegant script in the way she had been taught. Her teachers at Roedean School had always called them *the interrogatives,* but her instructors at the Fort had simply called them *all the Ws: Who, What, When, Where, and Why.* Any key to unlocking a mystery ultimately involved all of these, and she would begin with Who.

So, who was it that was methodically butchering his way through former Afghan agents?

She knew that he was skilled in his chosen profession and had the means to locate, isolate and kill his victims. Which meant that he had tradecraft as well as combat skills. But the real question was:

Why was it happening now?

It was likely that the murderer knew his victims because he was apparently familiar with their patterns of life.

But what made the murders happen within such a tight timeframe?

Was it a shared secret perhaps made critical by NATO's chaotic withdrawal from Afghanistan, and was it time-sensitive?

And finally, where could those answers be found?

She thought they might lie somewhere shrouded in the past in that strange and troubled land. Collette considered the neatly scripted points. Maybe it was just conjecture or supposition, both hated words in her chosen profession, although she knew that her conjecture was moulded by twenty years at the sharp end of counterterrorism. Her pen flowed freely as she wrote her conclusions. First, what did they know?

The murderer was almost definitely ex-military and a highly trained assassin.

He knew London.

He probably knew his victims.

Could he have the same background as them - maybe a KHAD operative?

And she needed to identify the intelligence gap.

What did they need to know?

After his dinner date with Babushka, I hope Mac can fill in the gaps.

★★★★

Nobu, Park Lane.

Colonel Sokolov has an amazing smile. Mac wasn't sure that was an appropriate thought during an agent debrief, but he was also a bit of a dinosaur and therefore didn't care.

I'm a nearly extinct species as far as the woke brigade at Six is concerned!

Katya's smile remained, but her tone became more business-like. "We need to talk!" said the Russian agent as she lifted her bag from the seat alongside her. She felt quietly reassured by the extra weight of the silenced pistol she carried in her expensive fashion accessory, but she sincerely hoped she wouldn't have to use it on the man opposite her.

The gun wasn't in her bag because of him - it was there to mitigate a risk that the MI6 man was unaware of. But she hoped he would be aware of the joint danger they faced after her dinner date. Mac glanced at his guest and wondered what was spinning through her mind. The conversation had been elusive so far. He needed a bridge to ask her the obvious question in a way that would not unduly offend her.

"So, why come to London to talk?" Mac's tone was conversational.

"You've read my file, and I've read yours. What's your best guess?" the Russian countered.

The MI6 man thought this was probably his best chance to broach the thorny subject of betrayal.

"Can I give you a possible scenario that we would both be familiar with after our time as intelligence officers, albeit on opposite sides? Would that be a good place to start!"

"I'm fascinated," Katya replied in a 'coy girl' voice. A thought flashed through Mac's mind.

This is not going to go well.

Ahmad and Lou sat in the cover car. A soft rain was falling, allowing the swish of windscreen wipers to keep an occasional rhythm with Classic FM as they watched the Russian watchers. They had managed to park up in a surveillance sweet spot that Colonel Sokolov's minders had missed. Waiting is always part of an intelligence officer's life. They were used to it, but that never made it any easier.

They were far from a perfectly matched pair as a conventional watcher team, but that wasn't what this task involved. The observation of high-value targets was usually assigned to the experts of Department A4. They, however, were just doing the same job as the car they were observing. They were 'eyes down' on the restaurant and providing close cover for Mac on his date.

Two men parked up in a car was never ideal, but far from unusual in this part of London. The super-wealthy patrons of the Park Lane Casino sometimes arrived with both their drivers and close protection, and the burly black ex-Marine, with Ahmad at the wheel of a shiny black Mercedes S Class, fitted the profile.

Ahmad rolled down the window occasionally to get a blast of air into his lungs, to stop him from dropping off. Lou broke the silence.

"Those Russians stick out like a racing dog's bollocks." Sometimes making conversation made the time go quicker, but sometimes it didn't.

"Yeah, I suppose so," Ahmad smiled. "But they are far from the only Russian heavies in this part of town. Do you think the Russian Embassy provided them?"

"I doubt it, bro," Lou shrugged. "Why would Babushka go to all the trouble of doing the Harrods shuffle on the A4 team? No, I guess our Russian friends are her own Wagner people." "What - Wagner as in the Russian private army?" Ahmad asked - just as, by coincidence, *Flight of the Valkyries* started to play on the radio.

"Yep, we know the SVR uses them a lot." Lou again checked the target car.

"Private Military Companies are the perfect solution for plausible Governmental deniability, and Wagner supply that service."

"Yeah." Ahmad looked thoughtful. His Kurdish family had fled Saddam Hussein's tyranny in Iraq, and it had been Kurds who had sometimes been on the receiving end of brutal Russian military operations in Syria. "Although the Russian Government's policy sometimes stretches the concept of plausible deniability to its breaking point, mate. They seriously miscalculated things at Deir Ezzor."

Lou knew about the 2018 battle that his co-handler referred to. It was when a force of roughly 600 Wagner contractors, armed with tanks and artillery, assaulted a position held by the Syrian Democratic Forces, a largely Kurdish militia group. The Russians had not known that the SDC had US Special Forces embedded with them, with artillery, airstrikes, helicopters, and even an AC-130 gunship above. When the dust cleared, half the Russians were dead.

Lou was observing the Russian car through the rain-spattered windscreen as he replied.

"Yeah, not a great result for them, but lessons were learned on both sides."

"What, like don't fuck about with the Yanks and an AC-130 gunship?" Ahmad was familiar with the awesome capabilities of the AC-130 from his time down-range in Helmand on Herrick 9. It was a flying gun platform armed with 40mm Gatling guns that fired 200 rounds a minute and a 105 mm cannon. It was known in the US military as *Spooky* or *The Angel of Death*.

"Yeah, but it was also a bit of a warning shot to the West. The number of munitions needed to push back the Russian attack was awesome, including using that AC-130 with its Gatling guns. Remember that Deir Ezzor was a direct confrontation between Russian mercenaries and American troops, and both had much to prove. The American SF guys were surprised by the resilience of the opposition. Wagner held their ground for four hours, counter-attacked, and managed to break contact and withdraw in good order."

At that moment, one of the occupants of the Wagner car chose to open the passenger door, stand up and stretch. Lou had once been a Recce Trooper and sniper in the Royal Marines and had learned to accurately scale a man's height from a distance. He used the proportions of the target vehicle to assess the Russian bodyguard's frame.

"Fuck me, he's a big old lump!"

"Yeah, you wouldn't want to spill his pint," Ahmad said.

"No problems," Lou answered. "We have the technology!"

He pulled a heavy brass knuckleduster out of his coat pocket and showed it to Ahmad.

Ahmad laughed. "You are such a thug."

"Yeah, true, but you never know when you might need an equalizer, and I can't shoot the fucker." Lou smiled. "Yet."

Back in the subdued lighting of the restaurant, Mac moved the wine glass around the pristine white tablecloth in a circular motion, for no apparent reason, as he moved into his pitch.

"OK." He paused and tried to meet Katya's stare but lost his way in her eyes.

There was a further pause as he attempted to re-engage his brain.

"You all right?" The Russian seemed to sense his discomfort.

"Yes." Mac went for a regain. "I am just aware that things are not good in Russia now."

"And you think they are better in London?"

"Yes, I do, and that's why you've made your decision."

"Explain!" Katya said.

"I have looked through your file, and I think I know why you have become so disillusioned with President Putin's Russia. The situation in Ukraine is going critical, and you're here to talk because you don't want another generation of young Russian soldiers going to war. You are here to stop that happening, aren't you?"

Katya glared at him with the steely glint of a combat veteran's eyes. "What do you mean?"

"Please don't worry, we have made contingency plans, and we will look after you."

"How?" A glimmer of a smile began to play around Katya's eyes.

"I wondered why you made your presence known and why you don't want your embassy involved."

"And what does that mean?" Colonel Sokolov of the Russian Federation's SVR had realized that her new date was trying to proposition her, but not in the usual way.

"You are here because you need asylum." Mac paused for dramatic effect. "We can help you."

Katya straightened her back bolt upright and leaned forward. The smile was gone.

"Listen very carefully." She sought out Mac's eyes and engaged them with an unblinking stare. 'I am not, and never will be, a traitor to my country. You have jumped to a conclusion based solely on speculation and then reinforced it with your agency's combined groupthink. You British should learn to see yourself as others see you."

"What do you mean?"

Katya went on. "What do you imagine people in my country think when they see you Brits and the USA run away from a war and leave the people that helped you clinging to your planes at the airport?"

"The Soviet Union left as well," Mac countered.

The Russian spy supplied the riposte. "Yes, but Najibullah's government survived for three years after we did." The MI6 man then thought before he spoke.

"Yes, our withdrawal was shameful, and we are still dealing with the fallout. But in my country, the intelligence services can only advise against such folly."

"And do you think that the SVR is any different? Our advice is ignored as well. We both gather information to turn into intelligence which is briefed to politicians who spin it any way they like or even totally ignore it. Your own country's rationale for the Iraq war, and what your press called the 'dodgy dossier', proved that. So please don't lecture me on our foreign policy. I will always act in my country's interest." Katya then seemed a bit embarrassed by the heated exchange.

She lightly brushed back her hair with her fingertips while she regained her composure.

"But as you English say, we should let sleeping dogs lie. The past is in the past, so let's leave it there. If we let what happened affect the present, it shapes the future.

"OK, the pitch is over, and I have your answer."

As Mac replied, the Russian spy smiled. "Don't worry. A dinner date between two agent handlers will always end up with at least one of them pitching the other."

"So," said Mac, taking a sip of wine, "what have you got for me?"

"It's a story about when my own army left Afghanistan."

"I hope this will be more than a history lesson, Katya."

"Yes, it will be. If there is one thing that Afghanistan has taught both our countries, it is what your great Prime Minister Winston Churchill once said:

'Those that fail to learn from history are doomed to repeat it'."

Outside, on the street, the tall man leaned on a car and shivered slightly as he watched the British watchers observe the Russian bodyguards. As he pulled up the collar of his long dark blue overcoat and wrapped it tight around him, he felt inside his right-hand pocket for reassurance, touched the knife's hilt, and smiled.

I'm getting soft; London has diluted my soldier's soul. A hundred ambushes in the cold of the Hindu Kush, and now a gentle breeze makes me feel a chill. But the opportunity to kill always comes along eventually. It's only a matter of waiting long enough!

Chapter 9

There was a palpable silence across the table as Katya tried to decode Mac's best poker face. She knew that the quote from Churchill had piqued his interest and focused his attention.

"Ok, I'm listening," he said.

"But can I start with a question for you?" said Katya, holding Mac's gaze. He was again almost transfixed by the Russian agent's eyes. Eyes that seemed to be exploring his own and scanning him for any weakness.

"Have you heard of the Penovsky Foundation?"

"No, but there was a Soviet general called Vladimir Penovsky who ran the GRU in the late '80s."

"Yes, that's the same man. What do you know of him?"

"Is this an interrogation?" Mac smiled.

"No," Katya smiled back. "I just need to know what you already know to save time later."

The MI6 man shrugged his shoulders and reached across the table to pour more wine into her glass.

"Yes, Penovsky was the youngest General in the Soviet 40th Army and probably the most powerful. He was the man that controlled Spetsnaz operations and was very much a Kremlin hardliner. He was nicknamed Vlad the Impaler because he was supposed to have repaid the treatment given to the Russian dead, after an ambush in Khost, by leaving Afghan bodies arranged in the same way."

"Impressive knowledge," Katya said. "But do you know what his favourite poem was?"

"Unsurprisingly, no," Mac smiled.

"A poem from one of your own Afghan wars." Katya returned the smile and recited the first two lines of the final stanza:

*"When you're wounded and left on Afghanistan's plains,
And the women come out to cut up what remains …."*

Mac interrupted the recitation. He, too, liked Barrack Room Ballads by Rudyard Kipling.

*"Jest roll to your rifle and blow out your brains
An' go to your Gawd like a soldier."*

"So, he liked my favourite Victorian poet?" Mac raised his eyebrows as he spoke.

"Yes, we all did; Kipling's poems - in translation, of course - were very popular with the 40th Army. Most soldiers like the same things, no matter what country they fight for. Penovsky thought the poem summed up the brutality of that war. He also saw his Army's withdrawal as a betrayal, a stab in the back from the Politburo. He didn't want to lose a war against an evil ideology, and he especially hated the West's support for it. He wanted revenge. He wanted payback!"

'Payback!" Mac said. "What type of payback?"

"He organized a plot against the government of Mikhail Gorbachev in Russia and within the Soviet Army in Afghanistan."

"And where is he now?" Mac shifted uneasily in his seat.

"He's dead, but while alive, he was protected by other senior Afghansy. The plot failed to materialize and remained secret for decades. And when it was finally uncovered, Mother Russia had moved on, and it was then considered too damaging to reveal in public. The General had prospered under the Yeltsin regime to become a billionaire. He died last month, leaving behind his hugely influential Penovsky Foundation. His last will and testament revealed what our intelligence service calls 'The Penovsky Plot', or at least one of its most dangerous remnants."

"Remnants?" Mac asked.

"There is no easy way of saying this." Katya sounded almost apologetic. "All the Afghan sources working for you in London also worked for me."

"They were double agents?" Mac tried not to seem surprised.

"Yes, the dead men, including the first victim, were also linked to Penovsky."

"In what way?"

"They were his agents before they were yours or mine, and he was paying them a substantial sum to keep a secret."

"To avoid a scandal because of the disclosure of the plot, or maybe even blackmail?" Mac was thinking aloud.

"No, not really; the General wasn't the sort of man you could blackmail and expect to live. He was paying them because they were still working for him, and they knew of the plot because they were part of it. They had all been working on another highly profitable strand of the payback that Penovsky planned for the Western democracies who supported the Mujahedeen against us."

"The Afghan drug business?" Mac's body language signalled his surprise.

"No, he wouldn't have approved of that, but I think that was maybe a sideline they developed, mainly to supply pre-emptive intelligence on radical Islamist groups in London to your organisation and ours."

"We suspected that was the case, but we never confirmed it."

"Yeah, well, I can confirm it now." Katya's face was again emotionless. "But Penovsky's revenge on the West was far more subtle than that: it was a two-pronged assault on what you call liberal democracy."

"And what do the SVR call the concept of liberal democracy?" Mac countered.

"Weakness, as you proved last year in Afghanistan." Katya's smile was cold. "And the one measure was designed to undermine it, and the other was meant to pay you back for Russian blood in a more kinetic way."

"Kinetic - can you explain that first?" The word had grabbed Mac's attention.

"No, later! First, I will explain that your agent and his ex-operatives used the Foundation's money over the last ten years to weaponize illegal immigration into western Europe."

"Was that thought up by the SVR?"

"No. You must be aware that politics and our security services are much more intertwined in Moscow, so things are more complicated. I know how it works in your own country: your intelligence agencies sometimes, I think the English term is, fish in the same pond and compete with each other. Well, in my country, it's the same, only we have three competing agencies: mine, the FSB, and my old unit, the GRU. And the GRU was using Penovsky's money to finance the human trafficking gangs, and his agents had insider knowledge on weaponizing it. But it had to be kept secret to work."

Mac gave his dinner partner a sceptical glance.

"Afghans and a secret?" Mac had the experience of generating intelligence in Afghanistan and felt that the average Afghan couldn't really keep anything to himself. Katya knew what he meant: in Afghanistan, only the most intimate secrets are not shared with the tribe.

"But Penovsky's Afghan people were special. They were all trained in Russia and had all been deep-cover agents within the competing elements of the Afghan Mujahedeen. You guys called them the Peshawar Seven, didn't you?"

"Yeah, but I never realised that they were so deeply penetrated."

"The same way you thought your agents could not work for me?"

Katya was deliberately teasing him. She noticed her date's face flush slightly and decided to let him off the hook.

"Yeah, a senior man in the SVR summed it up for me when I found out. He said that Afghans will tell you one thing, think another, and then do something completely different!"

"That sounds about right," said Mac.

"It wasn't until Penovsky died that we discovered the truth."

"Is that why you had them all killed?"

"No, it was nothing to do with us. We now know that the dead men were triple agents, working at a low level for your agency and ours, but only as a form of cover. We think that they were only truly loyal to Penovsky and the GRU. We believe they shared a secret with whoever is contracting the circle of knowledge, one man at a time, and he is protecting the secret."

"What is the secret?"

"And that's why I'm here. In the early days, the Penovsky plot intended to pressure Gorbachev and get him to reverse the withdrawal decision. So, an arms cache was sent to be hidden in the Panjshir Valley."

Katya seemed hesitant and avoided eye contact as if she was a bit embarrassed.

Mac took over the conversation. "Any Russian piece of kit, RPGs, SAMs (Surface to Air Missiles), or even the US Stinger systems would all be outdated and useless after thirty years anyway! They've got much better systems now."

The weaponry developed in the late 1980s was now old technology. Mac also realized that the recent US withdrawal had ensured that the Taliban had lots of new high-tech US weaponry and very little use for the old stuff.

"No, Mac, it's a bit more serious than that!" Katya finished toying with the food and looked up. Her eyes had regained their steely glint.

"How serious?" He knew it would be bad news.

"We have three nuclear suitcase bombs that went missing in 1989, and we think they were lost in Afghanistan."

In the hum of the restaurant's background conversation, Mac composed his thoughts.

"Lost? What do you mean by lost?" He raised his eyebrows. "You lose your iPhone, not a nuclear weapon!"

"Or maybe stolen is a more accurate description," the Russian agent replied.

"Can you elaborate?" Mac nervously toyed with his napkin as he spoke.

"Yes, Mac." As she spoke, he could once again see the hard look of a combat veteran in her eyes. "I need to run a recovery operation into the Panjshir Valley. I need to locate the missing weapons, and I need to do it without the open involvement of my government." Again, Mac felt her gaze boring into him as she simply said, "We need your help."

Mac blinked. *I need to talk to Collette. Now!*

Chapter 10

A late-night meeting was far from unusual for Collette and her colleagues at what they called 'the Office.' She was still at her desk when she received the call from Mac. She had used the time to pore over the files on her desk and make notes in her pink notebook. The files had the highest classification and sported the usual red covers. One contained everything the security services knew about Mac's dinner date, and the other was titled The Penovsky Foundation. They made interesting reading.

An intelligence file is never a straight-line narrative and not a story at all. It's an odd mixture of known facts and comments compiled by different people at different times. The facts only emerge after analyzing all the available information and only when confirmed by other sources. The comments, however, are different. They are the written record of an intelligence officer's thoughts and sometimes only reflect the quality of the officer writing them.

Although the file compiled on the woman called Babushka was the thickest of the red binders, it was, conversely, very thin on fact. The difference in espionage between what you know and what you don't is called the Intelligence Gap, and that gap, in Colonel Sokolov's case, was a broad chasm. Collette had read the file with interest because it was like reading about the Soviet version of herself. Like her, the Russian agent had achieved her rank at the sharp end of her agency. She neatly inscribed her conclusions.

Colonel Katherina Sokolov: DOB 15-12-1970 (approx)

GRU (Spetsnaz) Captain, Afghanistan. Alpha Group and Zenyth Task Group. KGB First Directorate (Foreign Operations)

Decorations:

The Cross of St George.

The Order of Military Merit.

The Order of Military Merit to the Fatherland.

The Order of Zhukov.

Collette wasn't quite up to speed on Russian gongs, but she knew that the Cross of St George was the Russian Federation's equivalent to Britain's Military Cross. She then looked at one of the grainy photographs attached to the file. It looked like a snap from the Soviet/Afghan war. A young woman dressed in Spetsnaz summer camouflage lounged against the fuselage of a Soviet helicopter gunship with a heavily armed, dusty-looking group of soldiers, all dressed in a mixture of Soviet military and Afghan kit.

The girl wore the distinctive, blue-striped paratrooper tee shirt under her chest webbing and cradled a short AK74 assault rifle in her left arm as she smiled sweetly at the camera. The photograph had been copied many times and was black and white, but the dark stains that covered the camouflaged uniform looked like blood, and the smile indicated that it wasn't Katya's. The file had only just scraped the surface of the enigma that was Babushka, but it had given her MI6 opposite number a grudging respect for her.

She led from the front!

Collette moved from her desk to the large window, stared at the twinkling lights on the other side of the river, and wondered what the man who ran the Middle East desk had found out. Her thoughts were interrupted by a tap on her office door; she checked the monitor and pressed the door release. Mac looked up at the camera with a worried expression.

That's not good news, Collette thought as she closed her notebook and placed the cap back on her pen. Mac wore the same pained expression as he entered the office.

"Well, how did it go? Not that well?"

"It depends on how you measure success."

"Who debriefed who?" Collette had guessed that it had been one-way traffic.

"Yeah, not sure, really. It was a bit like a training session at the Fort. The one at the end of the final exercise where you're knackered with the DS is trying to make you do the double. So, I'm still not sure who was controlling the conversation."

"Start with a short synopsis, and we can expand from there. You OK with that?" Collette smiled.

"Yes, totally, but there are things that you need to know first."

"I'm listening." She brushed her hair back and smiled.

"She outlined a terrorist plot that our withdrawal from Afghanistan has just uncovered, and she suggested that we could work together to stop it."

Collette was silent for a moment and glanced down at her notebook. As she looked up, Mac knew she had already discounted the possibility of cooperation.

She smiled. "OK, Mac, so stop talking in half-riddles and tell me what you've found out."

Mac returned the smile "OK, so not a riddle but a question, to save time explaining. What do you know about the portable nuclear weapons developed during the Cold War?"

"That's an old-school question, Mac. And I'm not quite that old, but they were called suitcase bombs."

Collette had once been given a lecture on the subject by an elderly veteran of the Firm on a rainy afternoon during her training at Fort Monckton. At the time, most of the students thought that it was just one of those 'filler lectures' designed to give the DS, as they called the regular Directing Staff, time to set up the next hideous scenario on the final exercise. She remembered the students on either side of her doing simultaneous imitations of those nodding dogs that used to be in vogue in the back windows of cars in the 1980s She was now glad that she had stayed awake.

"I'm aware of that weapon system's capability and the way the Soviets intended to deploy them, but that's the total sum of my knowledge. Why the question?"

"Because the Russians lost some in Afghanistan."

Collette took a moment for thought. "Somewhat careless, don't you think?"

Mac knew that Collette sometimes disguised her concern with a touch of levity. "Yes, that's what I said to Colonel Sokolov."

"And her organisation is sufficiently worried to try and get our cooperation to get them back?"

"It seems so." Mac didn't elaborate further.

"The whole thing seems strange." Collette reflected his own thinking. "But I think that we should run the whole scenario past Spellcraft. What do you think?"

Mac was one of a select number of senior officers who were signed into Spellcraft and therefore knew of its existence. He thought that Collette's tone held a tinge of regret, and he smiled to himself; he knew the internal politics of MI6 and where her ex-husband was working. The early referral to a confirmatory source was a testament to her professionalism.

"Sounds like a plan, but what about the lost Soviet kit?"

"We need to find someone who knows all about it. Are you thinking of the same person as me?"

"Yeah, Danny Mac. He was the resident expert on all things nuclear and portable back in the day."

"Yeah, he is the man we need. Can you give him a call?"

"Sounds like an excellent plan," Mac agreed.

****

Baker Street, London

Danny McMaster was in the office early. He found that solitude facilitated productivity when it came to the more mundane tasks that running a security company entailed. He had a week to rework and reprice a bid for a multinational that wanted to develop its footprint in Mozambique, and he had to finish his security outline for the Qatar World Cup. He took a break and peered downwards at a rain-sodden Baker Street. It was still dark outside, and the large plate glass window reflected a face etched by the past, with each line representing a hard decision made during life in the shadows.

He had started his intelligence career in what he sometimes called his 'halcyon days,' recruiting sources in East Berlin and then in Northern Ireland. After that, as a Commanding Officer, he shouldered the responsibility for his boys and girls in the Defence HUMINT Unit while they ran agents during the twin military disasters in Iraq and the last Afghan war. He knew that his face was scored by both time and responsibility. It reflected the sadness of a life spent making close calls against deadlines and times when he had sometimes zigged instead of zagged, and his people had paid the price.

Danny's mobile rang and disturbed his reflections.

"Fuck!" Danny mouthed the word as Mac's name, and the work number flashed onto the screen. He never used Britain's most popular swear word in public. He was one of the very few people he knew who were interested in the etymology of words, and the one he had just uttered *wasn't even old fucking English,* but ancient German, or maybe Swedish, meaning to strike or move back. He had mouthed the word instinctively because, although Mac was a good friend and a call from him was almost always welcome, such a call on his secure-line mobile usually had ominous implications.

"Hello Mac," Danny answered brightly. "And to what do I owe the pleasure?"

"You say that as if I have motives other than just a pleasant catch-up with an old pal."

"Yep," Danny smiled; two former agent handlers 'having a chat' was always more than it seemed. "That's true. What do you need?"

"We just need some advice."

"What about?"

"About some old-school Cold War stuff. Weapons capability and that sort of thing."

He was being deliberately guarded in his reply, and Danny was intrigued.

"I'd be happy to oblige, my friend, but when?"

"As soon as it's convenient."

"Where?"

"The Office?" Danny knew that Mac was referring to VX. "I'll message you a time and meet you downstairs, pal."

"I'll await your text and bring a head full of history."

Mac laughed. "Thanks, mate, we will owe you one." And he hung up.

★★★★

The Binner

The electronic door swished open with what sounded like an intake of air, and the JTF boss stepped into her agent handlers' territory.

'The Binner' was the steel-lined and cyber-sealed room in which the Joint Task Force's agent handlers tapped out their source reports. The space was open, air-conditioned and bright, and occupied by modern computer workstations, with the obligatory standard MI5 pot plants that were supposed to lighten the mood. The space's focal point was a huge TV monitor that covered most of one of its walls. The Binner looked the total opposite of its nickname and appeared to have been furnished by a Swedish IKEA fanatic. Nobody now knew why that nickname had come about. It was supposed to have originated in the dark days of the 'Troubles' in Ulster and been coined by the once-controversial military intelligence unit called the FRU (The Force Research Unit).

Collette had arranged the crisis meeting in the Binner because the other conference rooms were block-booked by MI6's new cultural equalities unit for 'Awareness Training'. But a crisis meeting was never called that in the modern security services' lexicon. At the JTF it was simply termed a PCC, or planning case conference, but to the attendees, it was a crisis meeting in all but name. Collette moved to centre stage by the TV monitor and addressed her troops.

"OK, first, let's talk about Colonel Sokolov. We now know why she is operating under a true name cover in London. We will then discuss how we think that Flame's murder and those of two of his sub-sources are linked to her presence."

The team was all aware of what 'true name' cover was. The surveillance technologies of the twenty-first century, including the digital tracking of smartphones and watches, and the widespread use of biometrics with facial recognition, have made conventional spycraft all but obsolete. So, a 'true name' spy was now more likely to live their cover posing as a businessperson or an academic, with no obvious governmental links.

Collette looked towards Computer Chris. "Very well, let's talk about the target we codenamed Babushka. Chris will elucidate."

MI6's technical expert moved in front of the monitor. "First of all, guys, a disclaimer: please remember that the information we have on the target is only what she wants us to know. The Russian Federation's digital security is tight, and we only see what they want us to see." He smiled.

"So, this is what we know. Colonel Sokolov's true name cover is a senior partner in the Wagner Group. It is a large company. It has strong links to the Kremlin and has been its proxy for military business in Crimea, Ukraine, and Mozambique. Colonel Katherina Sokolov is an influential player in Moscow."

Chris glanced towards Mac to continue the download.

"It now seems we have a motive for her current activities and our agent and sub-sources getting murdered. I will ask Mac to explain."

Mac was sitting at the conference table. Lou and Ahmad looked on from their computer workstations. A recent surveillance photograph of a very smartly dressed and smiling Katya, holding a bag with the Valentino logo as she left the Old Bond Street shop, flashed onto the monitor.

"So why is she here?" Mac said as he pressed for the following photograph. "It's an interesting story. If it is true, we have a problem that needs to be addressed."

At the same time, the woman that the Joint Task Force was discussing was sitting in her suite at the Lanesborough and considering the same problem. She consulted her dressing room mirror and adjusted her hair while new possibilities flashed through her mind. She still hadn't quite worked out the full implications of the information she had gifted the SIS, as many questions remained unanswered.

The process an intelligence agency or intelligence officers use to extract the truth from the inherent falsehood of spying usually is data-driven. A spy agency uses what it calls the Intelligence Cycle to turn raw information into intelligence. The process has four stages: collection, analysis, processing, and dissemination. Katya also used a similar system, one that her first KGB instructors had called DADA, to solve any problem. She always collected the available Data, Analysed the content, and then made a Decision before she took the appropriate Action.

Such action kept you safer in the shadows, and she usually operated on the very edge of safety. She remembered a quote from Kurt Vonnegut, an American author she had once read:

"I want to stand as close to the edge as I can without going over. Out on the edge you see all kinds of things you can't see from the centre."

And it was only from that very edge, but shrouded by the darkness, that you could safely search for what was always out there waiting to ambush you. Katya always felt safer in the shadows. It was the first time in her long intelligence career that she had operated in the open. It was, therefore, a new and unnerving experience.

The other thing that worried her was a bit more personal.

Mac's remarkable similarity to the man she had fallen in love with as a young girl had spooked her, and she had found herself drawn towards the Englishman in an almost primeval way.

Was that just a coincidence?

Has he been chosen because he looks like him?

The presence of the abnormal always triggered her alarm responses.

Am I being told the truth? Or am I being set up?

Her latest deployment had been unexpected, but she was glad to get away. Her department of the SVR was, as usual, stuck in the constant internecine struggle between the FSB, Russia's domestic security service, and the GRU, the country's military equivalent.

They were vying for influence, money, and patronage within the decreasingly small number of politicians who found favour with the Kremlin's permanent Czar, Vladimir Putin.

The outcome of the scrap was close to call, but it looked like Colonel General Sergei Beseda of the FSB had the GRU's Admiral Igor Olegovich Kostyukov trapped on the ropes. The FSB had the inside track, reporting directly to the President. Still, the GRU boss had the outside advantage of having over 25,000 Spetsnaz troops under his command, and he was Putin's go-to person for some of his more extreme international interventions.

Katya knew both men and the Czar himself. She had protected herself in a way only a senior intelligence officer could do by gathering incriminating information on all of them. Meanwhile, she had been tasked with cleaning up a GRU mess in Afghanistan that had a particular resonance for her.

Coincidence?

★★★★

Colonel Sokolov's roughly opposite number in Britain's Secret Intelligence Service was back in her office at Vauxhall after the meeting at the JTF, considering everything discussed and the information gleaned from Mac's dinner date. A thought occurred to her:

Are we being set up?

Collette's long career had evolved through experience, and experience sometimes breeds doubt. In other words, in the world of intelligence,

Things are seldom what they seem!

She remembered a simpler time and her first assignment when 'mobile technology' was the latest car you could buy. Her first job for SIS had been to work out how she could infiltrate an organisation intent on genocide in the western Balkans. As she did now, she had started her plan with a pen and a blank piece of paper. From that blindingly white and blank piece of A4, she had mind-mapped a scheme to find her way into the heart of that group to obtain the secret information that the British government required.

Her first trip involved travelling under false flag cover with a false identity, which had taken her to places that she never thought she'd visit. It had involved many nights dark, dangerous corners, in whispered conversations with terrified agents that she won over with compliments and lies. She remembered the days conversing with rival militia leaders, involving the copious use of the local home-brewed alcohol she had applied as a type of truth drug.

Spying was much simpler then!

The modern security and intelligence services now faced what they termed Hybrid Threats, and they presented more complicated challenges. The twenty-first century's astounding technical advances have made espionage dramatically more complicated. But the principles were the same. No matter how high-tech things got, you sometimes still needed boots on the ground to get the information you needed. Infiltration and extraction were still the same, and you needed to get people on the ground as soon as you perceived a threat because it was only pre-emptive intelligence that saved lives. From the deepest recesses of her memory, she dragged up a thought:

You needed to be on the edge to see things that you couldn't see from the centre.

The MI6 officer allowed herself a wry smile.

Did I hear that quote at the Fort?

She considered her options as she quickly reviewed the neat script and reached for the desk phone.

"Hello, Collette? How are you?" There seemed to be a hint of surprise in the voice.

"Hello, Damian." Collette was trying to sound business-like but actually sounded sultry. *Do old habits die hard?*

"Business or pleasure?" her ex-husband quipped.

"This is the secure line; business, obviously." Collette was less than sultry this time.

"You have a short memory, my love - you've used it for sweet nothings in the past, haven't you?" The MI6 woman blushed slightly as she thought back to some of the near-pornographic late-night chats they had had back before love left home.

"Point taken!" Collette flicked her hair back and felt her face flush as a brief glimpse of their former lovemaking flashed into her mind. The power was strong then! Her former spouse could still both excite and confuse her.

"Business. Spellcraft." Her voice was firmer now; the intelligence officer was back in control.

"All right, when can we meet?"

"No meeting. We can talk over this means, can't we?"

"No, Collette, when you signed into Spellcraft, you knew its requirements."

"Must have been in the small print!"

"It may have been, Collette, but according to the document you signed, the only way we can discuss this is face-to-face and in a secure room."

"When?"

"How urgent?" Her ex now had the upper hand.

"Very!"

"Come down to small conference room Z7 on my floor." He glanced at his watch. "In two hours, at five. I have a deadline that I need to meet. Is that OK for you?"

"I will be there." Collette knew she had no other option. She was going to see her ex-husband for the first time in a year.

She placed the phone back on its cradle and hit the speed dial again. Ahmad was sitting at his desk in the full flow of conversation with Lou when his phone rang. He looked across at the big former Royal Marine.

"It's the Boss," he mouthed as he hit 'receive'.

"Can I be of any assistance?" Ahmad said in his most polite 'customer services' voice that he occasionally used with other members of the JTF.

"Yes, you can." Collette usually found it amusing, but she was having a bad day. "Have you got Lou with you?" She was terse.

"Yes, boss." Ahmad was more business-like now.

"OK, put me on speaker." The smaller guy in the handling team complied. Collette took a moment to collect her thoughts.

"OK, you're both listening?"

"Yep," the handlers said in unison. "Fire away," Ahmad added.

"I want you two to trawl every Afghan source, sub-source and CASCON (casual contact), to research any dormant connections to the KHAD, and anything you can find on the man the Branch scooped up, Talil Mohammad Dostani, and his connections to it."

"How long have we got?"

"72 hours, but he has political connections, so it will be hard after that."

"Anything specific?" said Ahmad.

"Yeah, we need to know the name of the other Afghan ex-KHAD operator that is trying to kill him."

"Can we have the arrest file?" Lou asked.

"Yep, it's on the way now."

"That's a big roger," said Lou, "We're on it."

Collette placed the phone down and was already looking at the speed dial for the second important call of the day. She had to arrange some in-depth cover for Mac and was ringing what MI6 called The Increment.

Any intelligence officer's overseas deployment to a hostile environment was always covered by an extraction plan and needed the people to make it happen. The dictionary definition of the word 'increment' was an increase or addition. It was a typically British understated codeword that suggested why the unit was formed but not how it was used. It was what MI6 called the permanently attached ex-special forces contractors who now worked for it.

In the past, backup would have been supplied by regular SF soldiers from either the SAS or SBS, but as global counterterrorism expanded and the Sabre squadrons became overstretched, the SIS was forced to recruit former special forces personnel on a permanent contract. The new unit was tasked to supply the appropriate level of risk management in situations that always required maximum discretion while operating in very dangerous places.

It comprised of suitably qualified members from across the spectrum of the SF and included not only former members of 'the Regiment' (SAS) or the SBS but also men and women from the SRR (Special Reconnaissance Regiment). The recruited contractors then received further intensive training in both Great Britain and the USA.

The Increment was tasked from a nondescript office in Slough, buried within a white-walled tower block of concrete and glass, along with other administrative functions that the Firm had outsourced from VX. The unglamorous location was compensated for by being only ten minutes from Heathrow Airport.

Ernie, a recently retired SBS major was struggling with his accounts. He was trying to organise the unit's monthly expenses as a Royal Doulton figurine of a British Bulldog, draped in a Union Jack eyed him suspiciously from the corner of his desk, as if the dog suspected him of cooking the books.

The phone rang. A quick glance at the secure line told him who was calling. He grabbed the phone just as the Excel program that he had been struggling with crashed without apparent reason.

"Fuck...bastard", he mouthed, followed by a polite "Collette, how can I help you?"

"Hi, Ernie. How's life in Slough?"

"A lot less stressful than Vauxhall, old girl." Ernie was the man who had recruited and set up the 'Increment', and he had once occupied an office at Vauxhall Cross. "At least here, I can put the phone down if somebody pisses me off, and I'm not tempted to strangle anyone." Collette laughed. Typical Ernie.

The former Shaky Boats (SBS) officer had once been a Sgt Major and had risen through the ranks over an eventful 25-year period. He was known to be conversationally very brusque, and he hadn't always got on with the new, liberally-woke breed at VX, but Collette liked him.

"What do you need?" Ernie was typically to the point.

"I need cover for Kabul, two handlers, for a possible exfiltration if things go wrong."

"And are things likely to go wrong?"

"Not that sure, but I need to consider all the options. What do you think?

"Yeah, if things are going to go noisy anywhere, it's over there."

Ernie had just updated himself on the latest intelligence on Afghanistan. The current Taliban government was not only facing food and fuel shortages but was fighting with elements of ISIS K outside Kabul and facing a new challenge from what used to be the 'Northern Alliance' in Panjshir.

"I've got a team still in place; in fact, you know one of them."

"Who?" Collette had no direct access to who was on the books of the Increment.

"Ricky Miller."

Collette smiled when she heard the name. Ricky was one of Lou's ex-sources who had been resettled as part of the Firm. The last she had heard of him was when he had just passed selection for the SRR. She guessed that this attachment to the Increment was part of his suggested career path.

"That works well; he's trusted. Who else have we got?"

"It's a good team." Ernie reminded himself by glancing at the team schedule on his office wall. "Three of my India guys and Ricky." Ernie used NATO's phonetic equivalent for the letter 'I' instead of the word 'Increment', which grated on him. To him, the codename sounded typically Oxbridge and, therefore, in his eyes, poncey. "They also have a local crew, available from the Triples, that worked well on the last job."

Ernie referred to members of the now disbanded Afghani GCPSU, or Police Crises Response Units. CRU 333 had been a commando force trained by Britain's special forces that were now outlawed by the incumbent Taliban government.

"How did that go?" Collette enquired.

"OK, but I'm still trying to get the Afghans' wages."

She knew what he meant. After the millions that the UK had wasted over the last twenty years in Afghanistan, mainly in bribing warlords and bent politicians, even the most straightforward intelligence task or source payment now had to be triple-accounted and explained before final payment.

"Good luck with that!" she said with a despondent sigh.

"Yeah, thanks!" Ernie's voice mirrored her doubts.

Chapter 11

Collette Brown thought the principal virtue of a practical education in the strange art of agent handling was its ability to inoculate you against surprise. Consequently, very little fazed the MI6 officer. Even so, after making three important phone calls to set up the Afghan end of the operation and only two hours before a SPELLCRAFT meeting with her former husband. She turned her attention to a murder mystery because she had a nagging feeling that they had missed something obvious. She would stop occasionally as if staring into a crystal ball and waiting for some magic to happen. It wasn't a bad analogy, as a life in the shadows had sharpened her intuition to an almost clairvoyant level. She knew the murders were about protecting a secret inside a finite circle of knowledge that contracted after each brutal killing.

Reaching across the desk, she picked up the preliminary police report and reread it. She finished, made some notes, and tapped her laptop to again study the link analysis schematic that Chris had provided. She then tapped the keyboard again and compared it with the link analysis from HOLMES that Special Branch had sent her. It was useful. The Home Office Large Major Enquiry System collected and analysed information on places, times, missing persons, and murder methods and was, therefore, particularly useful for identifying serial killers. The system had been developed after the botched Yorkshire Ripper inquiry in the 1980s.

When all the known data on the first murder was fed into its server, HOLMES had found links to two similar murders in the

UK and possible links to five other killings across Europe. Some of the victims also had a familiar profile. A Ukrainian scientist in Paris, a Belarusian politician in Prague - and always with a similar MO and a commando-type blade. A knife only made for killing.

Is the killer starting to emerge from the shadows? She thought as the desk phone rang.

"It's Chris. I think we might have something."

"Come up and see me some time." Collette gave her best Mae West impression and immediately knew that the joke was wasted on a man far too young to ever have heard it.

"When?" Chris predictably hadn't got the joke.

"Now!" Collette smiled, noting the confusion in the tech guy's voice.

The short trip up from his office, deep in the cyber-protected bowels of MI6, gave him time to gather his thoughts. Chris caught his reflection in the shiny steel as he stepped into the lift. As he adjusted his spectacles and straightened his tie. he mentally prepared a quick presentation for his boss. Sometimes, simple clues were missed in his strange online world amidst the vast jumble of data and algorithms.

He had just run a gap analysis on the Wireless Application Protocol, or WAP, of the individual mobile phones they knew about. He had discovered something important that he thought might identify the murderer.

Chris arrived before Collette's desk, looking a bit like a nervous schoolboy presenting his homework.

"What have you got for me?"

"I think we may have a way to find him." Chris's eyes shone with enthusiasm.

"Yes, you've just discovered what we older types call the intelligence gap." Collette smiled.

"What do you mean?" His initial enthusiasm had drained.

"I bet you are going to tell me that one of the phones was off every time somebody got killed. Is that right?"

Chris understood at that moment just how smart his boss was. He was used to being 'Computer Chris', the leading expert on technical methodology within the realms of the intelligence world, but he now realised that his mentor and superior also understood how digital profiling worked. "Yes, that's pretty much it, Boss." Chris again used his forefinger to push his glasses back into position.

"So, give me the technical version," she said.

"OK." Chris was deflated but not defeated. "We've run all the data again. The five mobile phones we have put through have identified that just before the dates of the murders the victims had been contacted by the same mobile number, and that mobile was off around the time of the murders. That same phone was used in the London area yesterday to try to ring one of the other numbers we had identified, but now it is switched off."

"And you think that whoever is on the end of that number is the assassin?"

"Precisely." Chris had confirmed her theory. The MI6 boss then knew she had an opportunity to find the killer and unravel the mystery by taking the next intended victim into protective custody.

"Good work, Chris. Get me a fix on that phone." Collette reached for the security line for the SO13 liaison officer whom she had nicknamed Bertie the Branch (although never to his face).

Bertram Bradshaw was a senior Special Branch detective who had been weaned on the IRA London offensive of the 1990s. He snatched up the phone and frowned. He knew that MI6 people only called when the shit had hit the fan, and they needed something quickly - and when they didn't get it, they were a pain in the arse.

"Collette, what can we do for you?"

"Bert, it's about our murders. I will have an address in about twenty minutes. We will need a short protective observation of a suspected murder victim, and then we'll need an arrest as soon as you can arrange a warrant."

"What charge?" Bert was talking while making notes.

"We will start with money laundering and go from there." Collette was deliberately vague. "And, if I can't make that happen in time, just a straight protective custody."

"I will get Terry onto this ASP." Collette smiled as Detective Inspector Bradshaw mentioned his colleague. In a private joke between her and Mac, she called Bertie the Branch's sidekick Terry the Twig.

"Very many thanks." Collette replaced the receiver. She checked her very expensive watch. She was nervous; her next meeting was in person and with Damian Brown from the Spellcraft team.

★★★★

Ealing, London, next day

The man the KHAD called White Death was doing what he liked best. He was stalking a victim. Like all his other targets, he knew this one well. In this case, though, the impending killing held a hidden bonus, because he had never really liked him. In the days when he could differentiate between likes and dislikes, or slight annoyance and clinically applied fury, Talil Mohammad Dostami had always irritated him. He was one of those colleagues who was always looking for the inside track. His time with the KHAD had been more rewarding than the killer's own.

His intended victim had gained wealth, promotion, and status from the Soviets and then was ready to betray them when he first got the chance. The killer, by contrast, had supported them until the end, and all that he had personally gained was a piece of Russian shrapnel inside his head, and, ultimately betrayal. He tried to stay low-profile in London while doing his job, but his target had done the opposite.

He was familiar with his stalking ground. Ealing was in the west of the city, where some spores of the Afghan diaspora had blown in and taken root. He had a sweet tooth, and his favourite Afghan dessert shop was on Uxbridge Road. He would sometimes enjoy an ice cream cone made by his fellow countrymen and then stroll in Walpole Park. It was his only real vice - apart from murder.

He smiled when he thought of it. His intended victim was now an advisor to the Labour Party's Shadow Minister for Immigration. It was, thought the killer, the ultimate irony, as Dostami had arrived in the UK illegally in the same articulated truck as himself. Yes, he was the next to die, and he would enjoy killing him! He had thought about how he would dress for the occasion. His favourite long black coat had been left behind in his extraordinarily neat wardrobe. The killer now wore a workman's dark blue donkey jacket and a high visibility vest. A black woollen beanie was pulled down to cover his hair.

He carried a tool bag and was waiting, along with a small crowd of workers, at a bus stop opposite his target's house on Church Road. His intended victim's normal pattern of life would have him walking from his house to the local Labour Party office. A bus stop was always a good observation post (OP)', but only until the last bus on the route had gone. That bus was the 22 and was due in another twenty minutes. If the target still hadn't left his house within that time frame. He would just board the bus and replan the murder for another day. He touched the inside of his left arm almost as a caress; the carbon-black killing knife felt good and was like his lucky talisman.

But something wasn't right!

He just felt that he was not the only person watching the house.

Where would I park up for a short-term OP?

He surveyed the street scene again, but this time with a more critical eye, considering intelligence tradecraft rather than ice cream and murder. There was a white Transit van parked on the opposite side of his intended victim's front door. It was on double yellow lines and out of place.

Something wasn't right, so it was wrong!

Just as the killer had decided to abandon his hunt and step onto the bus, two police patrol cars pulled up with an urgent screech of tyres outside the target's house. He instantly recognised the vehicle type and its intent. The large BMW X5s with bright blue and yellow markings were distinctive because they were both ARVs (Armed Response Vehicles) used by the Met Police's SCO19.

The bus arrived and obscured the killer at precisely the right time, as the armed police exited the vehicles and moved quickly towards the house door. The Afghan took a deep breath to calm his emotions. His brain injury had long replaced a pumping of adrenaline and a sense of enjoyment with the ordinary mortals fight or flight syndrome. In his case, as the fright dimmed and the blood slowed, the pleasure faded, and the flight part was entrusted to the number 22 bus. He considered the problem.

How did they know?

A plan to kill had to be flexible at times. But what had gone wrong?

Had he been followed? No, definitely not.

Had he been betrayed? No, nobody knew of his mission.

Had they run a trace on the target's Penovsky phone?
And came to a conclusion.
Yes, they had his number!

Vauxhall Cross

It was a bright wintry day as the taxi pulled up and delivered Danny just short of the large building overlooking the Thames at Vauxhall Cross. He glanced at his watch, a 1960s gold Rolex Oyster Perpetual; it was a handsome timepiece and, like himself, was showing signs of wear but functioning perfectly. *Ten minutes to spare.* He was early, so he took a moment to arrange his thoughts. He glanced at the river as it shimmered in the milky sun. He was at an age where he could appreciate the beauty in the ordinary while detesting the stupidity of the banal.

He was not looking forward to navigating the new security system they had implemented at VX. It was doubly irritating for him because his name seemed to initiate extra idiocy at the security desk. It seemed almost like inverted racial profiling: *this older man looks typically English and a retired British Army colonel; he must be dodgy.* He sighed, rechecked his watch, and strolled towards the entrance. Just as he had resigned himself to the ordeal, he beamed a smile as he recognised the figure walking towards him.

"Mac!" The man he was going to meet was meeting him.

"Danny," Mac smiled back. "I thought I'd head you off before the dreaded security check, pal. I know how much you hate it."

"Yeah, thanks." Danny was relieved, "You've saved me from that 'shoes off, belt off and scanner' ordeal, and it's a great day for an amble up the riverside while we chat, don't you think?"

Danny had worked with Mac on several projects in the past and was glad to see him. His company, Hedges and Fisher, had been the default security choice for both Five and Six since the hostage extraction under fire in Iraq a few years earlier. His happiness at seeing his old friend again was only slightly tempered by the fact that whenever the company worked for him and the lovely Collette and Six, his people usually ended up somewhere down range, with the rounds incoming and danger always close.

"Well, what can I do for you?" Danny broached the subject.

"Just some input and advice, old mate, on something you know about."

The two friends, both ex-British Army, were now talking and in almost locked step as they walked away from the SIS building. It was strange that, when two military men walked side by side, that normally happened. Danny deliberately changed step as he spoke.

"What?"

"Nuclear weapons."

"A controversial area for discussion. You are not thinking of joining the CND, are you?"

"No, but I did toy with the idea when I was in my punk rock anti-establishment phase."

There was a silence as Danny appeared thoughtful. "I never had much time for that lefty shit, but I have always known that a world without nukes would be a better place. Nikita Khrushchev summed it up back in our own long Cold War. He said that in the event of a nuclear war, *the living will envy the dead*. But can you be more specific? It's a broad subject."

"Yes, sorry, I will clarify that. Can you please tell me all about Soviet suitcase bombs developed during the Cold War? I know you worked against them in the 1980s."

Danny now realised that his earlier levity could have been somewhat misplaced.

"Yes, they were a real threat then and they are now. Although, technically, 'suitcase bomb' is only a term used for a low-yield portable tactical nuclear device. They were designed to be smuggled into an enemy's country before the opposition could hit the big red button. The Soviet Union had a lot of them when MAD, or Mutually Assured Destruction, was in fashion."

"Any figures?"

"No, we were good, but never that good." Danny shrugged. "Perhaps hundreds, a ballpark figure of maybe 250? And the worrying thing was they were not really under the control of the KGB. The GRU controlled the portable nukes, and it was even rumoured that they had lost some."

"How many?" Mac was steeling himself for the bad news.

"It's complex; the other added problem was that the latest version, the RA 115, was also manufactured as a dummy device that could be used on insertion exercises for GRU Special Forces. That was also meant to be a secret programme, but, like lots of secrets that too many people share, it wasn't really a secret at all. A Russian whistle-blower finally spilled the beans in the late 1990s."

"Who was he?" Mac avoided a puddle as he spoke.

"General Aleksandr Lebed, the former Secretary of the Russian Security Council, told the Clinton administration that up to 82 of the devices might have gone missing after the Wall came down."

"You've got to be fucking kidding me."

"I wish I was, pal," Danny said.

"And how big are these things?"

"Like it says on the label. It's a large suitcase-size bag, although a bit heavy for the average weekend break, and probably banned at the Premier Inn. The version we knew about weighed up to around 45 kilos and was designed to take out a small city of perhaps 100,000 people."

"Would they still be viable after a long time in storage?" Mac said.

"Give me specifics here, pal. What are you enquiring about?"

"The SVR tells us that three of these things went missing in Afghanistan at the end of the Soviet/Afghan war."

Danny glanced across at Mac. "Thanks for the heads-up. The old secrets are sometimes found in the most perilous places, and this ticks both boxes."

"Thanks, Danny. I now have a clearer idea of what I'm dealing with. What are the chances of a viable device after this length of time?"

"I'm not a nuclear scientist by any means, but it was my understanding that the device had to be wired to an electrical source and had a battery backup. I think thirty years would be pushing the boundaries a bit. But it's not impossible."

"One more question, mate before we grab a coffee. Have you any air assets that we could use in Afghanistan if needed urgently?"

Danny smiled. "Like all things to do with our unique working relationship" (he borrowed a phrase from the British Army's standard radio procedure) "that's difficult but workable."

Chapter 12

London

Collette left her office emotionally confused. She knew why she felt conflicted; it was, after all, a perfectly normal human response. According to psychologists, the emotional part of her brain, or limbic system, was wrestling with the decision-making bit called the prefrontal cortex. She knew the psychological reasons for her temporary bewilderment, but that didn't make it any less confusing. Her heart was racing, and her legs felt heavy as she entered the lift.

Pull yourself together!

She had avoided any direct contact with Damian Brown since the decree nisi two years before, even though they sometimes had to attend the same meetings. She checked her makeup in the shiny steel of the lift door. Her stomach fluttered as she pressed the button for the three levels below.

This is the last thing I want to do.

The lift tinged, and the door opened opposite a small conference room, though it wasn't Z7. The very familiar figure at the entrance of the room was Damian. The same broad shoulders, with his slightly-too-long-for-Six brown hair now just a shade greyer and touching the collar of his classic and expensive Hackett sports jacket. And she knew from bitter experience how much it cost.

It was his Christmas present in 2015!

Damian was applying a key card to the door. He picked up the scent of Collette's perfume as he spoke over his shoulder.

"We are in here, Collette. I couldn't get Z7. I managed to get this at short notice."

He still has that unnerving ability to almost sense my presence.

He held open the door for her as she glided into the room. The MI6 woman's ex-husband politely gestured towards the conference table set up for a large meeting but was now accommodating a more intimate one. As Damian sat at one end of the table, she walked to the furthest chair away from him and sat down. He smiled.

A nice bit of non-verbal communication, but she still uses the perfume I like, so the further away, the better.

"What can I do for you?" He spoke first.

"Nothing for me personally."

You've done enough already, you bastard! The angry thought flashed into her mind as she replied. "But I do have some important RFIs (Requests for Information) that I would like answered as a matter of urgency."

"How urgent and how important?"

"Very, to both."

There was a brief silence as Spellcraft's boss considered his options. He knew Collette was, first and foremost, a top intelligence officer who would not ask for anything from a closed-cell source unless it was vitally important.

"What do you need?"

"I need to check the veracity of a story regarding the whereabouts of some stolen nuclear devices in Afghanistan."

"Babushka?" Damian knew everything that happened at Six.

"Yes." Collette took a deep breath, "And I have people deployed, so time is of the essence. I have this for you." She skidded a memory stick along the shiny white wood table towards him. It fell onto the carpet.

Her aim was far better with crockery.

He subliminally felt for the scar on his forehead as he picked up the stick.

"This is everything we have so far." Collette flicked her hair back as she spoke. "When can you run this past your asset?"

"You are in luck, princess. We have something arranged. I can get some answers quickly." She hated him using his old term of endearment. She had thought it sounded condescending even when they were married. *I'm going to tell him, but...*

"Thanks." She decided to let it go.

"I will ring you ASP." Damian glanced at his watch as he spoke.

"Sorry, princess, I will have to leave you." He turned and left the room.

That's not so fucking unusual, was the final angry thought as her ex-husband and the last Christmas present she had given him left the conference room together.

★★★★

Dushanbe, Tajikistan, 270 miles from Kabul

Ricky Miller took a breath and surveyed the scene in the MI6 safehouse, including the kit on the table. He had another look around and muttered his verdict to himself. "What a shithole!" Not only that, but the intelligence training he had received so far led him to conclude that this safe house wasn't very safe at all! It had very little going for it. Its ingress and egress were limited, it could be observed from just about anywhere, and it was almost permanently in the shade. The grey monstrosity that rose above it also served as a depressing reminder of his past.

It was the same type of housing found wherever the Soviet Union had spread its influence in the 1970s, *and not so different from Frobisher House,* the 1960s grey granite tower block in south London where he had squandered his teenage years. He and three of the lads had been assigned the so-called safe house, and the young Londoner had nicknamed his three companions his *partners in grime,* as the house hadn't been cleaned for years. The team also didn't like being dumped in the rundown building on the poor, grimy outskirts of the capital while the MI6 case officer was lording it up at the Dushanbe Hilton. There were three operators at work in the shabby front room.

All busied themselves with the more mundane tasks needed towards the end of a deployment. Ricky smiled as he thought of how he had evolved and arrived in downtown Dushanbe. It had been a long, challenging journey for the refugee gangster from London's postcode wars, from becoming a source within ISIS to his present incarnation as a serving MI6 officer on attachment to the Increment. He had learned some essential lessons on the way and had changed mentally and physically. As the slim teenage boxer's frame had filled out, his mind had expanded to keep pace. It had been a long voyage of self-discovery.

He now understood not only more about himself but also about the job he had grown into. As he looked about the space he and his buddies inhabited while they waited to find out where they would go next, a saying from his training days at the Manor sprang to mind.

Waiting. Like it or not, it's a skill all operators must master.

The two other Increment men sharing the work in the small house had been on a more conventional career path. Tam was a hard-as-nails but extremely funny ex-British Army paratrooper who had arrived via Glasgow, 2 Para, and then B Squadron 22 SAS. The other team member was another tough man from west Belfast's equally hard Shankill Road. Carl Wright, nicknamed

Shiner, was a former Four Five Commando Royal Marines corporal who had left the Special Boat Service ten years earlier.

Ricky cracked on with his admin. He was the team's nominated technical expert and, therefore, in charge of all the communications and camera kit.

He had inherited the job from the last Special Reconnaissance Regiment (SRR) man on the team. He was checking a piece of kit that they hadn't used on the previous job, a Black Hornet Nano camera drone. Ricky looked at the gear the ex-Marines in his India team called his 'part of the ship. It was.' an amazing piece of equipment. It was a complete airborne surveillance system consisting of a military-looking chest harness containing a screen and a base station, with what looked like two toy helicopters laid side by side on the dusty table.

Carl was sitting on a box containing a British NLAW anti-tank rocket launcher made, like himself, in Belfast while he was cleaning his favourite weapon. It was a 7.62 L129A1 Sharpshooter rifle. He had fallen in love with the weapon type on a long hot, dusty day on Herrick 10 in Sangin, in Helmand, Afghanistan. It was reliable and accurate and took down Terry Taliban at 800 metres. He was handling it almost reverentially. The NLAW had been delivered via the British Embassy's diplomatic pouch, just in case the Tajiks needed a demo of its effectiveness.

He looked towards the youngest member of the team.

"Ricky, you could've left your fucking toys at home, wee man." The banter was a constant reminder that morale was high.

"Yeah, I would explain what they are, Shiner, but it's far too technical for a dumb Marine!" Ricky fired back.

"Hey mate, but give it a try," said Carl. Ricky then realized that the older SBS guy was either genuinely interested or wanted to check whether he knew his subject.

"We used the early versions in Afghan, but this looks a lot more compact."

"Yeah, it's the Black Hornet Super Nano, made by a Norwegian firm called Prox Dynamics."

The Belfast man almost lovingly propped the rifle on the floor on its bipod legs and walked across and snatched up one of the small drones.

"Whoa, don't crush it!" Ricky looked at the size of Shiner's hands; they had a team joke that he hadn't really needed a paddle when canoeing in the SBS, as his hands would have done the job.

"Hey, it feels like a toy." He was impressed.

Ricky went into instructor mode. "Yeah, it only weighs 13 grams and is 16 centimetres long." The small helicopter did look like a child's toy. "The whole kit only weighs 1.5 kilos and consists of this monitor" - Ricky flipped down a flap on the camouflaged chest harness and a screen appeared - "this base station and this hand control."

He pressed down on the plastic module, and it clicked open to reveal two separate charging bays for the drones. He handed the single control stick to Shiner.

"You can control the whole thing with one hand." Shiner held the control stick and tried the buttons.

Ricky continued, "The most amazing thing is its capabilities. It's a modular set-up, and the drones can be fitted with cameras for either day or night. The night cameras are electro-optic and have infrared and thermal imaging. You can't hear these little fuckers at 30 feet, and they have a range of about a kilometre, with 20 minutes on target. This latest version has sensors that allow it to fly inside a building."

Shiner was impressed, "A great way to do a close target recce (CTR) without the risk of it going noisy."

"Yep, it's a game changer; pity I didn't get to use it." Ricky sounded almost disappointed.

"Don't worry, Rick, these jobs don't finish until the debrief, buddy. There's time yet!" Shiner had been with the Increment for five years. "But that's the fucker I want to try," he said, pointing to the NLAW within its packing case.

The only member of the team not sharing the same cramped space that day was the team leader. Joe Reid was a sergeant in the Royal Marines who had served ten of his twenty years in the SRR. While Ricky was explaining the Black Hornet, he was 'one up,' or driving on his own, in his once-white, slightly rusted Land Cruiser, trying to negotiate Dushanbe's curious traffic system.

The place was laid out in a strange, circular, Soviet way, with concentric rings of minor roads that didn't seem to lead anywhere. It also had all the hazards you would expect in a city where health and safety rules were left for foreigners to worry about. He had only just braked the car hard to narrowly avoid a legless beggar on a skateboard who had claimed the right of way on the main road. Navigating the town was doubly confusing.

He was using an old street map with the original Soviet names, many of which had been changed after independence but were still informally used by the city's inhabitants. So, Gorky Street was now called Tehran Street but still known as Gorky Street by the people that lived there.

He was the team's Afghan expert and a fluent Dari speaker who knew Afghanistan as well as any Westerner could, but Tajikistan confused him.

And Dushanbe doubly confused him. Where else in the Islamic world would you ever visit an Irish Pub opposite a Kentucky Fried Chicken outlet?

The thought crossed his mind just before he swerved the Land Cruiser to narrowly miss a garishly painted truck that had just pulled out from an intersection.

Fuck!

Disaster averted again. He thought of what he had achieved that day.

Not very much!

His mission should have been an easy one. He had to drive into town, meet the case officer and discuss the team's final extraction while also trying to obtain some wages for the carload of tough-looking Tajiks that were now supplying his rear cover.

He had then been subjected to a full hour of form-filling, with various arguments about who would pay their wages and what budget would be used to pay them.

The Afghan Tajiks had been recruited as auxiliaries for the mission. They were all from what had been referred to as the *Triples*, former Afghan operators from 333, the commando cops that had been trained by the British SF and based in Kabul. They had been top-notch throughout the joint Foreign Office/Six job. It had been a tedious task at times, a cross between supplying overwatch for the India team and FCO man at the meeting point and supplying a Quick Reaction Force (QRF) to react to any possible attack.

The discussions were held at three different locations, including Dushanbe's Hilton Hotel. The meetings had been with the FCO representative, and an organisation called the *National Resistance Front of Afghanistan*. The Front was all that was left as opposed to the Taliban regime. It was led by Ahmad Massoud, the son of the late Northern Alliance general Ahmad Shah Massoud, who had been killed by Al-Qaeda two days before the 9/11 attacks. It also included the very smart former Afghan Vice President Amrullah Saleh and the former Deputy Foreign Minister Mirwais Nab.

The talks hadn't gone well. The NRFA needed financial and military help, and the 'Firm' had been, at best, non-committal. Afghan politics - a mix of gangsters, former warlords, and powerbrokers - was a hornet's nest of conflicting interests, and it seemed to be a case of the adage 'once bitten, twice shy.'

The main item on the NRFA's shopping list was an end-user certificate allowing them to buy the British Army's NLAW missile system. Their main military problem was the very sophisticated hardware that had been gifted to the Taliban by NATO and the US when they deserted the country in 2021. The Talibs could never produce anything as high-tech as an American MRAP (Mine Resistant Ambush Protected) vehicle. Still, they knew how to use them, and the ordinary Soviet-issue RPG7 had minimal effect on their armour. The FCO, however, had doubts about supplying the kit.

Not that I give a fuck!

Joe's only concern was getting his Tajiks paid. The case officer had a typical bean-counter attitude. Because he hadn't seen the Triples on overwatch and because they hadn't had to extract him in an emergency, he had queried the wage rate. Joe rechecked his mirror. The Triples were still visible, and two cars down in the traffic. Whoever had taught them mobile surveillance had done it well.

As his car crunched into yet another Tajik pothole, his phone rang. It was connected to the local MegaFon network, one of Tajikistan's more reliable providers, with the best coverage from the city to the border. He steadied the wheel with his left hand and lifted the cheap Nokia handset to his ear.

"You have a job, mate!" Joe recognised Ernie Pender's gruff voice, no doubt delivered from behind his usual vast mountain of paperwork. He needed all the immediate information. He needed to let his operator know that he had to get back and prepare for a crash move and redeployment.

"Where?" Joe said.

"Your old stamping ground." *That meant Afghanistan, maybe Kabul.*

"When?"

"Stand by to move." That told Joe that the move was imminent.

"Instructions?" The car bumped again, and he nearly lost the phone.

"In an hour, normal means. Is that workable?" That meant that Joe needed to be by his secure link and contactable within that time frame.

"Roger that, Ernie, that's OK. I'll wait out."

"OK, keep safe, speak soon."

Ernie rang off. Joe pocketed the mobile and checked his watch. He needed to make some progress through this traffic to set up the secure comms on time. He checked his rear and pressed his hazard lights, so they flashed three times to let the Triples know that he was speeding up, and then put his foot down.

★★★★

London

Collette was trying to sleep. She'd hardly had time to even visit her mews apartment in Pimlico since the first Afghan had been killed, and she was once again sleeping in her office. Sometimes working in intelligence just took over your life, and as one piece of the puzzle clicked into place, the search for the next chunk increased the pressure. This operation had pulled other elements into its vortex, and as it picked up internal speed, it seemed to be spinning out of control. The MI6 boss had already deployed a team into harm's way solely on information supplied by a Russian agent in London.

There was a lost nuclear device.

There was a murder mystery.

There was a shadowy organisation called the Penovsky Foundation; was it linked to Putin?

Resting never came easy when other people's lives depended on your decisions. She had just about given up on the idea of sleep when her work mobile rang. She looked at the caller and felt a gentle flutter of excitement in her stomach.

It was from him.

Her face flushed as she rationalized her thoughts and gave herself a talking-to.

You are not a schoolgirl. You are a senior MI6 officer. This is just a secure text message from another colleague relating to national security. A colleague who just happens to be your former husband.

She read the message and felt somewhat deflated. It was all the things a work text message should be: clear, concise, and delivered with brevity.

Re your client. I have some answers. Ring me! DB

Collette took a deep breath and made the call. It was answered on the fourth ring.

"Hi Collette." She took another breath and composed herself.

"Hi. What have we got?"

"Lots. When can we meet?"

"Tomorrow?"

"Can you meet now?" Collette looked at her watch.

"I make it midnight."

"Yeah, but it's important." Damian's voice was clipped and emotionless.

"Where?"

"Sophia's in one hour; you OK with that?"

Collette knew Sophia's was an MI6 safe house in Soho, used only by the Spellcraft team. It was in Soho for a reason: it was a part of town where people went for all types of assignments and where other people ignored them.

"Does that qualify under the terms of the Spellcraft protocol?"

"Yes, it's an emergency meet."

"Explain?" Collette felt a slight hint of panic. She did not want to be alone in a room with Damian Brown.

"I can't say until we meet. The meeting is covered under the protocol because there's a chance of a severe compromise to my asset." His voice sounded firm.

"And is there?"

"I wouldn't be calling otherwise." Collette realised that the ball was in her court.

"OK; one hour."

"See you in an hour. You OK with that?" Collette glanced at her watch.

"OK, see you then." She still had that fluttery feeling in the pit of her stomach as she hung up.

Chapter 13

The gravel crunched under the Land Cruiser's tyres as Joe pulled up to the rear of the safe house in Dushanbe. He switched off the engine, clicked up the small switch to disable the starter, and collected his canvas holdall from the passenger seat. The Increment cell leader then tapped out the code into the security lock on the back door, and as it creaked open, he shouted to the guys inside, "Hi, kids, I'm home and I have news and gifts!" He received warm greetings in return.

"What fucking time do you call this?" Tam said, looking up as he continued to prep his C8 carbine assault rifle. The C8 was the L117A1 variant and fitted with an underslung grenade launcher (UGL). It fired a range of 40mm rounds, including high explosive, smoke, CS gas, and white phosphorus.

"Hoofing for some, driving around the big city." Shiner was loading some mags for the Sharpshooter with heavier 7.62mm steel-tipped armour-piercing rounds. Ricky looked up from prepping the tech kit.

"Did you get the Triples their cash?" He had adopted the role of being the Tajiks' unofficial shop steward.

"No, bruv, but Ernie's still working on it. And in the meantime, I will pay from the team's budget and sort it out later because we might need them for the next job."

"Next job?" Shiner interjected.

"Yep, it looks like we have a job in Afghan." British soldiers invariably dropped the end of the country's name in conversation.

"Where?"

"Don't know yet, lads." Joe checked his watch. "But we will soon - Ernie's going to squirt the orders now, and it might involve these." Joe opened his Ops bags and removed two packages. "Here's the prezzies, lads, via the Embassy's diplomatic bag and straight from London. They're MX Rattlers." He chucked one to Shiner and one to Tam. They quickly unwrapped the black plastic bags like kids after an Amazon delivery at Christmas.

"Wow!" It was with a sense of reverence that Tam held the latest piece of hardware that Sig Sauer, the German arms company, had produced. A new weapon for a soldier is sometimes viewed as artwork. "We finally got them." He knew the stats. The Rattler was the smallest rifle on earth and only 19.3 inches in length. It had a 5.5-inch barrel that weighed only 5 pounds, and it could also be fitted with a suppressor.

"Top kit," Shiner said, placing down the Rattler and picking up his own. "But I prefer this." He lifted his Sharpshooter.

"It doesn't matter anyway, mate, as I think they are for the people we are picking up." Joe moved to the dining table. "But let's find out what's happening."

Joe opened the team's Toughbook laptop that nestled amongst the other kit on the table, sat on the ornate but faded chair, and switched it on. He took a USB stick from his pocket, plugged it in, and then hit the return key. The three other operators gathered around his shoulders to observe the screen as it came alive with a bright swirl of letters that solidified into the word *Rosetta*; it was the most advanced covert messaging app the FCO used, developed for global communication. It sent coded messages in a millisecond, using a set of cyphers changed after every transmission. It could also be used anywhere that had a decent mobile phone signal.

Ting

A text arrived on Joe's local mobile. A smiley face from Ernie told him that Rosetta was up and running. He then hit the return key again and another message was downloaded. It would contain the outline orders for the next mission delivered in the usual British military format. The sequence never changed. It was always *Ground, Situation, Mission, Execution, Service Support, Command, and Signal.* He then removed the USB with the cyphered download and inserted it into the team's MacBook Pro. The team then sat around the table and looked toward the team leader as he read the orders. The first part of the orders is always the Ground paragraph.

"OK, lads, Ground: it's the Panjshir Valley." Joe looked around the team. As he got ready to present the mapping and graphics, he noticed the team smiling.

★★★★

Back in London, Collette sat at her desk and considered the Ground paragraph for her meeting with Damian. Sophia's wasn't a house at all, but a room in a five-star hotel situated in the heart of Soho. It entailed an ostensibly simple journey, but life is never simple if you are a spy. It would only take six minutes to get the Victoria Line to Oxford Circus station, and it was another ten-minute walk to the meeting. The pressing time frame meant that the usual anti-surveillance (AS) measures she would usually use would have to be ditched. It was after midnight and in central London. So, Collette opened her desk drawer and removed her own equalizers.

She placed a CS gas spray and a small Vipertech stun gun into her Louis Vuitton shoulder bag. The United Kingdom's capital city still had a crime and knife epidemic, and it wasn't the best place for a woman to walk alone at night, even if she was a highly trained MI6 spymaster. She felt uneasy as she scanned the platform at Vauxhall tube station. Collette had never liked crash moves. She liked to plan, but emergency meets are also part of the landscape in the strange world of agent handling. One part of an intelligence officer's training in AS is to look for what is called a double sighting, or a person that you see at the beginning of your journey and, again, suspiciously, at some later point during it.

Skilled surveillance operators will always carry with them some way to instantly change their appearance almost instantaneously. A reversible coloured jacket was always a good idea along with simple props such as a pair of glasses or a change of hairstyle for a woman. The trick to identifying a tail was to find something on a suspected watcher, such as a distinctive scuff on a pair of shoes that could not be changed quickly or an existing physical feature that could not be changed at all.

It was late, and the platform was not busy, so she was able to make a quick assessment of her fellow travellers. Collette had the advantage of knowing the ground. She had been on this platform at the same time and everything seemed as it should be. She made a mental note of the other people on the platform, and she recognised three of them as admin staff from her building, but others stood out.

There was a courting couple of black-garbed Goths who were loved up and cuddling against the tube station wall, under a faded Covid poster reminding people to stay two metres apart. They were either demonstrating brilliant tradecraft or simply not in the game. Then, a retired, military-looking man with a moustache stood behind her on the platform. He was tallish and smelled very slightly of gin and cigar smoke, but his fine military bearing was somewhat offset by a certain unsteadiness on his feet, so she discounted him for the same reason.

A static OP in plain sight is called a *trigger* in surveillance parlance and is sometimes provided by operators disguised as the sort of people you tend to look away from. The surveillance experts at A4 sometimes used a trigger dressed as a tramp or a foul-smelling junkie, but a semi-drunk middle-aged Army type didn't fit the bill. Collette was pretty sure that she was starting her journey clean.

The tradecraft taught at the Fort covered all the obvious ways to thwart foot surveillance. These included the old classics like stopping abruptly, suddenly reversing your course, or stopping just after you had turned a corner. Or the ones that you see so often in the movies: watching for reflections in shop windows or entering a building and leaving immediately by a different exit.

When boarding a tube train, you are supposed to leave it until just before the doors close before you hop on, and that's precisely what she did. Collette exited the train, at the last second, at Oxford Circus, and again checked the platform. She was clear, and had 25 minutes to walk along Oxford Street into Soho. She checked her vintage Cartier watch. Only twenty minutes to the RV. She hurried along Oxford Street and intended to turn right into Wardour Street and then into Dean Street; that would give her an extra turn before the safe house, and that was all she had time to do.

Soho was not a great place to be alone at night, but there were numerous CCTV cameras, and the bright neon lighting everywhere was almost blinding. But muggers and criminals don't just operate in the shadows, especially not in twenty-first-century London. She reached into her bag and took out her spray. It was a mixture of pepper spray and CS gas that she had bought in Paris. The Firm only gave out the police issue stuff, which was not as good. She looped the small chain on the top of the spray over her forefinger and wrapped her fist around it. The spray was of a heavy metal-cased construction that contoured inside her fist and was also designed to be a type of emergency knuckle duster.

She felt safer as she looked towards her destination. It was in one of the more upmarket parts of the area, in a quiet mews that contained one of the few five-star hotels in Soho. She had known that it was one of the locations that Spellcraft had solely for its own use. It was typical of Damian, always pushing the boat out.

At £870 a night, the bean counters must still be in shock!

But she could see immediately why he had chosen it. It made good sense. It was positioned in a cul-de-sac and had an approach that could be easily monitored. It was costly and was off the beaten track to most of Soho's usual tourists and thrill-seekers. It also had the reputation of being the go-to place for sexual assignations between the very rich, which ensured a modicum of privacy because discretion was assured in a place where everybody needed to be careful. Collette paused and checked for surveillance for the final time.

She entered the mews, and the hotel's tasteful lighting gleamed from the end of the street. An impressive building, with an extended portico in marble, with miniature potted spruce trees on each side, and lots of smoked glass. The outline of a smartly dressed doorman moved behind the shiny steel frame of the front entrance. She reached into her bag and swapped the pepper spray for her mobile. She opened it and fired off a text.

ETA 2 minutes.

And then, ting, the reply:

RT, Room 28, come straight up.

Collette walked towards the hotel, replacing her phone.

Twenty-eight is his favourite number. The thought just seemed to pop into her head, *The same age as the girl he was fucking.*

She put the thought aside, and her mind was back on the job. But the fluttery feeling in her tummy had started again as she hurried towards the hotel.

Chapter 14

Collette walked quickly past the doorman, who hovered around the hotel's main entrance. He greeted her cordially but was professionally discreet. The hotel's foyer was as she expected, small but very upmarket. The main focal point was an eight-foot-high ceramic effigy of what looked like a rotund black cat by a Colombian artist Fernando Botero. The hotel foyer followed the Latino designer look: lots of shining steel and glass with brightly coloured, patterned furniture.

A large blond man she recognized as one of Spellcraft's's minders was seated at the far end of the foyer. She had seen him around the corridors at VX, looking like an eleventh-century Viking squeezed into a Marks and Spencer suit from their XL range. She could see him surreptitiously whisper into his covert comms as he reported her arrival to his boss. Room 28 was on the second floor. She waited by the large smoked glass and stainless steel lift and pressed the button. The doors opened with an almost simultaneous ting. As they closed behind her, she checked her appearance in the mirrored glass before she selected the floor.

She rummaged in her shoulder bag for her lipstick, applied it, and checked her hair with her fingertips. She replaced the lipstick with a perfume atomizer sprayed on each side of her neck and then thought.

Why am I doing this?

She pressed the floor button. The lift chimed as the second floor came up far too quickly for her. She took a deep breath as the doors opened, and she stepped into the corridor. Collette checked both ways; another hard-looking Increment guy was standing at the end of the corridor talking into his mobile. She guessed that he was outside room 28, and the big lump gestured towards the door and confirmed it. The man nodded as she approached and used a key card to open the door with a smile.

Collette felt a warm flush hit her cheeks. She had tried to keep him at a distance after the divorce. It had been painless and uncontested, as such things usually are when both partners are on career paths. She thought of her marriage certificate as just like a first-class boarding pass on a long-haul flight. It was a piece of paper that was incredibly important before you flew and great fun while on board, but useless afterward and not worth the paper it was written on. Apart from being a reminder of having a great ride, that is - and in Damian's case, that was true.

Her former husband was sitting at an occasional table by the window. The room was at the zany end of designer, themed in bright colours with lots of yellow and scarlet. He stood as she entered. She understood what had been happening in the room through the simple art of observation. The place smelled of fresh cigar smoke. The small occasional table had a half-empty bottle of Beluga Gold Line vodka in an ice bucket in pride of place. It was flanked by two shot glasses and an ashtray with the stub of a Cuban Montecristo cigar.

Scorpion has expensive tastes, she thought while reading all the signs that told her that Spellcraft's prize asset had only recently been debriefed.

Damian looked across and flashed a warm smile.

"Fucking Russians," he muttered. "I don't know how long my liver will last with this job."

Collette understood: a source meet can involve a social side, and with Russians, that meant lots of vodkas. "What have you got for me?" She tried to be emotionless, but a slight quiver in her voice betrayed her.

"A lot, so get ready for an intelligence avalanche, but please excuse me if my speech is slurred. I have been suffering for my craft." Collette knew that was true. Damian was a fitness freak and only drank occasionally. "But I need to get assurance from you before we chat."

"What assurance?" She was suspicious of yet another concession being extracted from the Joint Task Force.

"We need to work together," Damian whispered the phrase and looked into her eyes.

Collette felt her face flushing.

"What do you need?"

"We need you to keep a close hold on Babushka."

"Why?"

"That is what I'm just about to tell you. But I must have your cooperation before I do."

"Agreed."

"OK." Damian opened his small police-style notebook and quickly flicked through the pages before he spoke. "I will give you the headlines and then answer your questions." He smiled. "And I can guarantee this will be graded at A1, and you will get the CX as soon as I download it."

She understood the jargon, knowing that sources are graded from A to F and range from *Completely Reliable* to *Reliability Unknown,* while the information they provide is graded from 1 to 6. Therefore, this new A1 CX was the MI6 version of MI5's MISR. A grading of A (reliable) and 1 (confirmed by other sources). This was the highest grading that could be given and meant that the report was considered accurate. Damian looked again at his notebook and took a while to focus. Collette guessed that the vodka had taken its toll.

"The source knows who Babushka is and why she is here. He also knows she has been lured to London as part of a plot to kill her. Colonel Sokolov and six others are implicated in a plot to remove Putin and are now on his kill list. Her department was responsible for the initial feasibility study for a short and limited war in Ukraine. She reported that the war would be neither quick nor limited and advised against it. She also has another disadvantage in the increasingly polarised political atmosphere of Moscow. Sokolov is a Ukrainian Cossack name, and to ultra-nationalist Russians, that's a consideration.

When she became aware that some elements of Putin's inner circle still intended to advance into Ukraine and what she considered a potential meat grinder, she became involved in an FSB plot intended to replace Putin. She also knows too much about the kickbacks to the arms industry from the Kremlin, and she has the evidence. So, Colonel Sokolov has been sent on a fool's errand to London so she can be killed, with the killing blamed on the West."

"If that's the case, why don't we tell her?" Collette said.

Damian raised his voice slightly. "Because she wouldn't believe us." The ice clinked as he picked up his vodka. He swirled it in his hand as if in thought. "How can we get someone like her to trust us? We need to know what she knows. She has access to the advanced planning for when the tanks start rolling on Kyiv. So, how do you get someone like Babushka to trust you?"

Collette smiled. "Are you thinking of a honey trap scenario?"

"I think she's a bit too wise and Moscow Centre to fall for that one." Damian was dismissive of the idea.

Collette paused," Maybe, but let Mac run with it. He can be very persuasive, and I think they may have a mutual attraction anyway."

"So, what's the plan? Recruitment?"

"Yes, but we need something else we can give her." Collette closed her eyes as if thinking. "Does Scorpion have access to the GRU's Penovsky files?"

"I can ask him. Why?"

"If we could find where the original nuclear cache was meant to be stored, she would have a start point for what she is looking for."

"That's a long shot after all these years. Do you think she actually believes the suitcase bomb story?" There was a sceptical edge to his voice.

"No, but I think she has another reason to get back there, something more personal. Maybe a precise location would supply her motivation to go to the valley. Can your asset go through the files and find a grid reference?"

"Maybe, but he will need time."

"Then let's run it by him," Collette said. "Could he get the location quickly?"

"How quickly?"

"By tomorrow?"

"I'll try." said Damian, "But I'm a bit confused as to why she couldn't gather this information herself. I'm sure her position in the SVR would guarantee the same level of access as my friend has."

"Can you just run with it anyway? If you like, it will provide Mac with something to cement the relationship - a reciprocity thing.?"

"OK, I will ask him."

"Thanks. Meanwhile, I will brief Mac and make the arrangements."

"Sounds like a plan." It was Damian's turn to smile. "Now, I have an excellent bottle of Chilean Sauvignon Blanc in the fridge. It seems a shame to waste it."

Collette took a long breath. Work was over for the day, but she knew by the tiny flutters in her tummy that she had to refuse.

"When can I get the CX?" She was work-like and professional again.

"As soon as it's on my system and before departmental release."

As Collette glanced across at her ex-husband, visions of their former lovemaking flashed into her mind. "And when will we know if Scorpion can get details of the LZ?"

"I will REVCON him tomorrow." Damian used the handler slang for a reverse contact procedure. "That's the safest time."

"OK then, just one drink." The phrase popped out of her mouth almost before she thought about it.

Maybe not a good idea?

Chapter 15

The killer knew that his mission was compromised and that his time in London was over. He had made the appropriate arrangements. As soon as he had realised his mobile phone was blown, he had destroyed the sim, smashed the handset, wrapped it in baking foil and awarded it a watery grave in the Thames. The new target was not an easy hit. There was a part of him slightly in awe of her. She had been one of the people he had known in Afghanistan. He knew that killing her meant getting close - and with her, being close was dangerous. He had moved to a safe house in Luton while he thought about his options.

He had always been good at planning at both the tactical and strategic levels, but now he had to start from scratch. The basic tradecraft you needed to recruit an enemy agent was the same that any killer needs. The most important element was having a POC or point of contact.

The POC would come from his employers as soon as they could establish it. They had access to her movements, and she was unaware that they wanted her dead. The first thing he acquired was a new burner phone. That was easy to arrange in London, via TOR on the dark web. The service was expensive but reliable. The new burner phone, stolen and set up with a new sim, could be dropped to a suitable dead letter box and paid for by Bitcoin. It would be organized quickly, to be delivered at a place of his choosing when he was in an overwatch position to receive it. He had selected a rubbish bin in Brentwood Park; it was a public space and only twenty minutes' walk from the safe house.

He went early and gave himself enough time to conduct some anti-surveillance on the way. He had only waited ten minutes when a young Asian lad on a moped, the criminal version of Deliveroo who specialised entirely in guns, drugs, and burner phones, dropped off his package. The phone came prewrapped in baking foil and had the sim installed. Now he was again in touch with his handlers and with only a day missing from his call schedule.

The next decision to make was the type of weapon he needed to complete the job. Knives are very effective against the unwary but unadvised against the pre-warned. It was a difficult decision for him. He loved killing with his knife. It was the closest he felt he came to sexual fulfilment. He loved the feeling of slicing in and penetrating his target's body. It made him feel excited and special, almost omnipotent. He especially would have loved to kill her with his knife. To feel her drift away under his blade, with that sweet sticky smell and the delicious tang of fresh blood ... but maybe a pistol and a silencer made more tactical sense. He would prepare for both.

He knew that the chances of him obtaining a suitable POC in London for his next victim were slim. She would be protected by concentric layers of security and would always be shadowed by the British. His time might not come until she was back in Afghanistan. After all, he thought he knew where his probable POC would be. He thought that the Russian woman would try to find the place in Panjshir where he and Jalaluddin Haqqani had killed and dumped the bodies all those years ago.

★★★★

Collette looked up from the hotel bed and observed her half-naked body in the mirror above. She hadn't noticed the mirror the night before and she doubted that Damian had, either. Their lovemaking had been frenzied, with a desperate edge to it as if both were capturing the moment. It was exciting, quick, and shameful, but also very sexy and satisfying. She had not wanted it to happen that way. But it had! The cobwebs of two years of enforced celibacy had been blown away by primeval longing for a meaningful sexual connection. Damian had supplied that connection and she had happily accepted it. Collette collected her clothes from places scattered throughout the room.

She found her La Perla knickers resting on the empty wine bottle beside the bed. But she didn't feel bad about it, even though her former husband had done his usual disappearing trick. She took a deep breath and resolved to get back on track. She had a source report to read and she also needed to get Mac and Babushka to Afghanistan. She did feel used and as tacky as the mirror above the bed. It was yet another cliché within a cliché: the ex-wife bedded by her former husband. But the only thing she truly regretted was the fact that she had indulged herself while her people were in harm's way. She needed to regain her focus.

How would she get Babushka to Panjshir?

As Collette considered the problem, Colonel Sokolov of the SVR was resting on her bed at the Lanesborough. She had suffered a sleepless night thinking about her problems and some possible solutions; both were using her subconscious like a wrestling ring. She knew things had changed. She presently occupied the position at the centre of the intricately spun spider's web of the former KGB, the most feared and, some would say, most effective foreign intelligence service on earth. As a former director of the SVR, Sergei Lebedev had once said:

"There is no place on the planet where a KGB officer has not been".

She had been at the centre of that global web of agents, informers and sub-sources, and now she was detecting the first shivers of the malign intentions vibrating towards her. At first, it had not been anything in particular, just an occasional unanswered email or maybe a strange login failure to a site she needed to access. There was also a disturbing rumour in the Western press that a senior FSB man had just been arrested in Moscow.

She thought she knew who that might be.

She had hoped that the Panjshir mission would give her time to gain some closure from the previous war while she distanced herself from the plot to stop the next.

Putin's yes-men had wanted another conflict because they had forgotten the last one. But Colonel Sokolov of the SVR hadn't. She still remembered the boys they had lost in Afghanistan. She remembered what had happened every night at airports throughout Mother Russia. The sealed zinc coffins were unloaded from giant Antonov An-12 transporter planes bringing them home to their families. They were told that they had died on patriotic duty, but that was a lie and now history was repeating itself. She remembered her young love from all those years ago. His body had not come back. He was still lost.

This feeling of loss and her last assignment had led to her soul-searching. It had been a straightforward intelligence task. Her department had been asked to assess the strengths and weaknesses of the Ukrainian Army and its likely response to the attack, but her conclusions had not been well received by the Kremlin. The research had been thorough, as the lives of young Russian servicemen were at stake. The first thing they had done was to buy ten British NLAWs on the open arms market for evaluation. She felt that this was a critically necessary step since the Ukrainian Army had recently received considerable numbers of these cutting-edge anti-tank missiles, after being trained in their use by British and other Western troops.

The GRU had run the tests and the evaluation had not gone well from a Russian perspective. The Spetsnaz major in charge had started by watching a video on YouTube that explained the weapon. The results had proven just how vulnerable even the latest Russian T14 Armata tank was to what the manufacturers called Overfly Top Attack or OTA. The NLAW was designed to strike and penetrate the less heavily armoured upper part of the tank and had an excellent kill rate. It was also a disposable 'fire and forget' missile that was ideal for the countryside, and it could be fired perfectly from within confined spaces, so was also ideal for urban warfare.

The Russian SVR colonel knew more than she had told Mac. She, after all, had researched the battle plans very thoroughly and then produced evidence to support her reservations, but that had not gone down well at the Kremlin. She knew the proposed timings for the invasion and the outline of the attack. Russian paratroopers and Special Forces would try to take Kyiv Airport in ten days, starting on or about the 24th of February, but the tanks would roll over the start line at precisely the wrong time for armoured warfare in eastern Europe, when she knew that the countryside would be mired in mud.

She would have to use Mac. She needed him on her side. She needed somewhere safe to run. She felt strange, she felt helpless. Her eyes filled from nowhere. She felt a single tear roll down her face, and then remembered something she had heard somewhere:

"Tears are the words that the heart can't express."

★★★★

Collette urgently needed a shower, some time on her own and some rest and recuperation before returning to the office, but she had too much to do. Her initial plan to grab some time at her apartment was scuppered by a ting on her mobile phone. It was Damian.

Sorry I had to leave early.
The thing you wanted is on the system now.
General release in two hours. D xx

She was sitting at the same desk she had occupied three hours earlier as she accessed the CX that had just been loaded onto the internal Spellcraft system. The document could only be read by MI6 personnel signed into the protocol. It would be further sanitised before it went onto the main server. She studied the computer screen as it gave up its secrets.

A source meet generates two documents in MI6, the CF or Contact Form, and the CX. A CX was the SIS's version of MI5's MISR, essentially the same thing but with a different name. It was usually considered the ultimate sin to put a CF with the corresponding source report, but Collette had access to both. The CF was just the document that allowed the analysts to quickly upload the basic data associated with the agent meet. It contained the grade of the information, in this case 1, and the location of the meeting, and how long it lasted. It also told others how many times the source had been met and gave a grading of all the reports thus far. The CF was written in an almost formulaic and precise way.

It also contained arcane terms used only by agent handlers. For instance, it never rained in agent handler land, but the weather was sometimes inclement. An agent or source was always called a CHIS (Covert Human Intelligence Source) So, for example, 'the agent decided to arrive by taxi because it was raining' became 'inclement weather caused the CHIS to take an alternative mode of transport (black taxi/hackney cab).

Likewise, in handler land, an agent didn't walk to a location but went Foxtrot or FT from point A to point B. But once you knew how to write a CF you never really forgot it, and Collette had written and read hundreds. She now studied the document that contained the extracted information.

SIS CX 196-02
SCORPION
Source number 6664
22.00 hrs 12-02-22
Handler: Damian
Location SH 91
Cover Increment Team 06
AS-A4

AS-A4 meant that the anti-surveillance serial to protect the agent had been provided by the A4 department of MI5. She then read the document's preamble and the bullet-pointed text.

Source Scorpion was met by the handler at safe house 91 and the debrief was conducted safely, securely, and without compromise. He seemed to be agitated when greeted and was offered alcoholic refreshments to calm his mood. He had important information to impart. A summary is bullet-pointed below with handler comments.

Scorpion is worried about his security.

CHIS Info: There is a witch hunt at home. Anatoly Bolyukh, the deputy head of the FSB, is under suspicion of being involved in something organized against Putin. Bolyukh and Colonel Sokolov are known to be opposed to any action in Ukraine.

CHIS Comment: I believe Sokolov's presence in London had brought unwelcome attention onto me.

Case Officer Comment: AB is a prominent Afghansy (Afghan war veteran) and is thought to be plotting to depose Putin.

CHIS Info: Katya Sokolov is under threat. She has been accused of providing intelligence reports that seriously overestimate the capabilities of the Ukrainian Army and are seen as both "defeatist and cowardly" (Putin's words). She is also thought by the Kremlin to be implicated in the above Bolyukh plot. She is currently in London and trying to get help to recover lost Soviet ordnance of some kind from the Panjshir Valley, in Afghanistan.

CHIS Comment: I am not aware of the details of her curious mission, but I suspect that she has been given it as a way of both reducing her influence in Moscow and allowing unnamed non-state agencies to eliminate her on foreign soil, thus allowing Moscow plausible deniability. I'm not sure how this would happen. Maybe an attack that they can blame on Ukraine, killing two birds with one stone, as it were.

Case Officer Comment: Colonel Sokolov is hugely influential in Moscow and is feared by many in the corridors of power both for her contacts and her operational abilities. A possible false flag attack in the planning stage.

A CX always finished the same way, abruptly, with just the date/time group and the handler's details.

Collette took a deep breath and logged off. She stood up and turned away from the computer to think. *Maybe that's what this is all about. The alleged lost nukes are a ploy to distract us from what is happening on the Ukrainian border.*

The phone disturbed her thoughts. It was Damian.

"Hi. You read it?"

"Yeah."

"What do you think?"

"Interesting."

"You could say that."

"What's the next step?"

"We need to introduce some distance; my source is at risk as long as Babushka is in London, and she is even more at risk. Can we move her?"

"Maybe, but we have two main problems. First, to protect her against Moscow she needs a cover story, and second, to get her cooperation she also needs to know that she's under threat."

"We can't tell her that. It will compromise Spellcraft."

"What are the options?"

"I have an idea. It's a bit extreme and it could mean political problems with the Kremlin."

"You mean that we arrest her?" The idea had also occurred to Collette.

"Yes, precisely, and we can do it under existing immigration law. We can claim that her paperwork was incorrect on arrival." At the other end, Damian's eyes lit up as he had another idea. "Or maybe play it by the book and issue an Osman warning - you know, one of those Threat to Life warnings. That could get her on side."

"And then?" Collette felt the conversation seemed somewhat surreal. The ex-husband that she had just had sex with was now just another senior colleague.

"We could use that as a pretext to get her to cooperate with the only viable cover story to get her back into Panjshir. That would give Mac time to recruit her."

"Yes, that might work. When?" Collette asked.

"ASP, but any idea how we can get her and Mac to Afghanistan while she is supposed to be banged up in Belmarsh?" Damian knew that Collette's forte was operational logistics.

"Danny said he could help. He has contacts in Tajikistan."

"Ideal," Damian said. "Whose budget?" Always a thorny question between department heads.

"Your source, your information, your need, your money."

"Roger that; let's crack on," the SIS man agreed.

Collette felt deflated. He had not mentioned the night before. It had just been business. She felt that she had whored herself for information, that she was an espionage slut. But then *ting!* It was her own phone. It was him again, a text message this time.

Hi. Sorry, couldn't say much - works phone and all - but I enjoyed last night. I hope you don't feel that I planned it to happen, but I'm glad it did. I miss you xx

Collette didn't know what to say. She tapped out *I miss you xx.* And smiled. Then there was another flurry of thumbs.

I've got work to do, Mr Brown. But do you want to do it again some time?

She got an immediate reply.

We definitely will Princess. Damian xxx

Collette immediately reached for the phone to call Danny McMaster, who was having a mare of a day. Just about everything that could go wrong had gone wrong. The commercial side of his business sometimes threw up more bear traps than the intelligence and covert operations side; commerce could be more cut-throat than espionage. The intelligence landscape was always harsh and murky, but at least you could trust some of the people some of the time.

A junior manager in his Newcastle office had secured himself a better position with a rival company by disclosing every piece of paperwork the company had about his costing and final quote for a consultancy for the Qatar World Cup. Six months of work had evaporated overnight, and Danny knew his bid would now be undercut. A lot of ex-intelligence types now inhabited the commercial side of life, and research was still research whether you were doing it for your country or yourself, and all the techniques were the same.

If you wanted to recruit another firm's employee you still needed a regular POC, a recruiting agent and, most importantly, MICE (Money, Ideology, or in this case Influence, and some Coercion) and of course the self-motivation that often lurks in a prospective agent: Ego. But money was usually the principal motivating factor, and that's what had happened in this case.

Danny slumped back into his chair and looked up at a particular unit plaque that hung alongside others on his office wall. It featured a Roman gladiator armed with a trident and net. In Roman times he would have been called a Retiarius. He was outlined against a green background with the words Fishers of Men scripted underneath. It was a biblical allusion to Mathew 4-19:

And he said to them, "Follow me, and I will make you fishers of men".

It had been the motto of his agent handling unit in the 1980s, the Force Research Unit. Danny thought about his old team and smiled for the first time that day, because that was the last time that he had felt at home. He was still smiling when the desk phone rang - the secure line only used by the security services.

"Hi, it's Hedges and Fisher; how can we help?" He recognised Colette's voice as soon as she spoke.

"Hey Danny, we need a favour."

"Is it a favour-favour or a paid-at-the-usual rates favour?"

"It's a usual rates favour." Collette suppressed a giggle.

"What do you need?"

"I need to get two pax to the Panjshir, safely, securely, and without compromise."

Danny smiled at the familiar handler speak. "When?"

"ASP."

"Roger that, I will ring you back." He paused and made a quick calculation. "It will be via Tajikistan. It will be safe and secure and without compromise, but it will also be expensive."

"Fair enough. Send Six the bill."

"Roger that, Collette, I will work on it now."

"Thanks, Danny." And Danny started planning the insertion.

Chapter 16

Spying is like acting but on a more dangerous stage, and spies, like actors, should always be in the appropriate costume for the role. Katya was looking through her suitcase trying to select the right tools for the job. She had baited a few honey traps during her early career in the old-school KGB, but that was a long time ago. She turned and looked towards the dressing room mirror and opened her hotel dressing gown and let it fall. She smiled; the flush of youth was gone, but her body was still firm and toned and she still possessed the vital equipment. The baseline kit was the easiest to select. She had assessed the target as an old-school alpha male and heterosexual with a capital H, so she selected the silk combo that she had bought at Agent Provocateur in Harrods with its basque corset, black stockings and suspenders.

The outer layer was harder to choose. She needed to look smart but not too available. She pulled a Max Mara cashmere coat in oatmeal from her wardrobe and matched it with the Hugo Boss mid-length dress in dark blue wool. Her shoes were the hardest choice. She loved her Jimmy Choo heels but they were not the most practical choice for a walk to an agent meet. She opted for a pair of lower heels by Louboutin that matched her other accessories.

Watch: by Coco Chanel, this was a beautiful steel and diamond tank watch, a present from Wagner Group. She checked the time. Two hours to go!

Bag: her favourite Coco Chanel Bottega Veneta in black.
Lipstick: red (Rococotte) by Louboutin.
Perfume: Katya smiled as she placed the perfume on the dressing table. She had bought it at Harrods and it was called Bond Number 9. Seemed appropriate for a meet with an MI6 man.
Knife: The Kizlyar foldable covert combat knife in black.
Pistol: Her silenced 7.62 mm MSS Vul.

As she walked towards the shower to prepare, she considered her position. A quote from the German philosopher Friedrich Nietzsche came to mind:

The best weapon against an enemy is another enemy.

Mac was waiting in the bar of the Dorchester, glancing towards the door while turning his lucky coin in his right hand. Not that he should need luck. The source meet had been rushed but well planned, and the location was ideally suited to the plan. It had the right profile for both parties, and it was only nine minutes' walk from the Lanesborough. It gave Babushka ample time to pass through the counter-surveillance box on Park Lane provided by A4. So far, everything had gone to plan.

Katya had obeyed all instructions. She had walked her given route bang on timings and had stopped when required to stop. She had left the hotel carrying her bag over her right shoulder; if she switched to her left, it would mean she knew, or suspected, that she had been recognised. She had been professional and compliant. Mac thought maybe she knew that things had changed.

The Dorchester bar was a famous London landmark. It was where the capital's richest people sealed deals, made alliances, and shared secrets, and where a quiet conversation generally went unnoticed. The MI6 man looked around the place. His eyes were drawn to the red glass spears of an art installation around the bar that sparkled flame-like in the ambient light. Impressive, but it wasn't Mac's type of place. He looked at his coin from Panjshir and smiled. He was happier when in the open air, and happiest at the top of a mountain. He would sooner be in the clean cold air of the Panjshir Valley than the Dorchester's unique scent of urban affluence. It was a subtle blend of expensive cocktails and even more expensive perfume.

But a good spy always adjusts to his or her environment.

As he glanced around at the bar's upmarket occupants, he ran a quick visual assessment and tried to guess their back-story. The far corner was occupied by a large Arab gentleman of rotund proportions and what Mac assumed to be his very expensively dressed and bejewelled blonde girlfriend. They talked in whispers and smiled as lovers should do. At the opposite end of the room, a Savile Row-suited business type was in discussion with someone who might have been his lawyer. The legal was taking notes and asking questions. The worried look on the suit's face told of his woes; it didn't look like good news. The central table was occupied by a quartet of Chinese tourists in heterosexual matched pairs who were talking excitedly in Cantonese in what he recognised as the distinctive, almost British, twang of Hong Kong.

Under the shining red spears, a group of American corporate types chatted over expensive whisky. They joked loudly with elbows on the bar. They all seemed slightly tipsy. Investment bankers, thought Mac, involuntarily recalling the related cockney rhyming slang. In another corner was Mac's close cover, a hard-looking Increment guy who was dressed for the part in a very expensive dark blue cashmere overcoat, a bit too snug for his frame. Six had its own wardrobe department, but it always struggled with the bigger sizes.

As he scanned the room, Mac was listening on his covert earpiece to the two teams conducting the CS. He was concerned: it was only a nine-minute stroll for Babushka, but it could be a dangerous one for his new Russian friend and recruitment target.

A Trojan callsign from the Metropolitan Police's SCO19 firearms unit was also on standby to cover the move. Mac heard them give the odd colour-coded location.

"Trojan 2, that's X-ray at Blue 2 intending Green 3." The X-ray was Katya. Blue 2 was Park Lane and Green 3 was the hotel he was sitting in. *Within the next five minutes.* He checked his watch.

Did she know what was going on in Moscow?

He thought she probably did. She was an experienced operator who should have picked up some warning signals from Moscow. But did she know the scale of the threat?

He had the ultimate handling task. He had to try to convince her she was in danger without being able to tell her how he knew about it. He also had to persuade her that being arrested was the best way to ensure a viable cover story. Would she think she was in enough danger to go along with the plan?

"That's X-ray at Green 3," Mac heard in the small pea-size receiver in his ear, as Katya glided through the door of the bar. Mac looked towards the Russian and smiled; she was a beautiful woman and was noticed by just about every male eye in the room. There was a low whistle from the Americans at the bar, and one of them turned as if to walk towards her. The Increment man stood up in his bodyguard role and glanced towards him. The American seemed to comprehend and turned back towards his friends as Katya spoke.

"Hi, Mac." She sounded sultry and relaxed. She noticed the glint of the silver coin in his hand before Mac conjured it into his waistcoat pocket.

"Hello, Katya," Mac said, as he stood and gently shook her hand. He moved around behind her and pulled the opposite chair out for her to sit on.

"Is that a silver thaler?"

"Yeah. A keepsake." Mac seemed almost embarrassed.

"From Panjshir?"

"Yes, from Ahmad Shah Massoud, for saving his life."

Katya's eyes glittered. "What a coincidence - I planned to kill him, many times." She smiled sweetly.

"I'm glad you didn't. He was my friend."

"But when your friends were killing mine ..." She was still smiling.

"I accept that." Mac was now sitting opposite the SVR agent. He felt he was almost losing himself in her eyes again. They were a bluish-green opal colour of radiant beauty, but, like the Panjshir itself, tinged with sadness.

The eyes of a soldier, not a killer.

"But at least you could negotiate with him, as your people often did." Mac could remember one of the locally negotiated ceasefires arranged with the Soviets, for pragmatic more than political reasons.

"Yes, I was involved in some of those negotiations." Katya's eyes flashed. "He was a good man, but still my enemy. You were in my valley then, weren't you?"

"Your valley?" Mac looked puzzled.

"Yes, I was born in the Valley of the Five Lions."

"Where?"

"Outside Charakar, on the Salang side. My mother was a Tajik and my father a Russian colonel from Ukraine." He noticed that Katya was now whispering the information as if she were trying to protect a secret.

"Does that make things difficult for you?" Mac said.

"How would it?"

"Split loyalties, maybe?"

"No Mac, my loyalties are very much intact, although some people's perceptions of them might have changed." Katya looked

144

away. The MI6 man knew from the body language that he had hit on a sore subject.

"Whose perceptions?"

"It's not something I want to discuss at this moment."

"Your father worked at Bagram?" Mac changed the subject, but he had noted the tiny chink in her emotional armour. Bagram had been the main Soviet air base when Mac was in the valley.

"Yes, and he was a good man as well."

"When you see what's happening in Panjshir now, you realize that a lot of good men died for nothing."

"Yes," she agreed. "It's called warfare; it's what politicians do when they run out of other ideas."

Mac paused and considered her statement. He knew it was true; he had been a paratrooper before he became a spook. A quote sprang from the deepest recesses of his memory to justify his time in the valley with Six. It seemed to fit.

"When the forces of oppression come to maintain themselves in power, peace is considered already broken."

"Bravo!" Katya's face lit up. "A quote from Che Guevara to a Russian spy."

"But isn't it true?" Mac tried to establish eye contact; Katya looked away.

"Isn't that what an occupying army does? Yours, then ours, then yours before you ran away?" the Russian fired back. "The Taliban are now the oppressors in Panjshir, and you've left the population to it."

"Touché." He knew that was true.

"So, Mac, why have you asked me out? And I hope it's not just work," she pouted.

"I think you know why!"

"Explain."

"I have asked you here with all the proper precautions because I believe that your life is in danger."

"Mac, as you know, my life has been in danger since I was a child, and as time goes by little changes."

The Russian colonel's face was impassive as she slowly moved her fingers through her hair with her right hand. Mac noticed how small and delicate it was. He also noticed her immaculately manicured nails. At that moment she looked vulnerable.

"But many have tried, and they've found that I'm hard to kill." The glint of steeliness was back in her eyes.

"Nevertheless, your life is in danger." Mac had rehearsed this part. "And, under our rules, I must give you an Osman warning."

"Osman warning?"

Mac handed Katya an envelope.

"The name is incidental, just someone whose family sued the cops when he was murdered. But it's a serious document. It's an official Police Threat to Life Warning. Open it up now, please."

Katya quickly scanned the room and then opened the official-looking letter and read it. It had the Met Police crest at the top and a header that said RESTRICTED.

Threats to Life Warning Notice
Katherina Sokolov (Russian National)

I am in receipt of information that suggests that your safety is now in danger. Our research suggests that the threat is credible, but I stress that I will not under any circumstances disclose to you the source of this information. I have however no reason to disbelieve the account as provided. You are advised to revise all your security arrangements. The Metropolitan Police have a duty to ensure that you know about this information and will take all the steps we can to minimise the risk. We cannot however protect you on a day-by-day or hour-by-hour basis.

I also stress that the passing of this warning by me in no way authorises you to take any action that would place you in contravention of the law (e.g. carrying weapons for self-defence, assault on others, breaches of public order).

Katya looked at her very expensive designer bag. *Maybe the gun wasn't a good idea!*

She glanced back to the letter.

I, therefore, suggest that you take any action that you might see fit to increase your security measures, cancel any planned meetings, and always carry your mobile phone.

This document has been drawn up as a reference according to Metropolitan Police procedures where such threats have been identified or alleged.

Chief Inspector B Bradshaw Metropolitan Police Service (SO13)

14-02-2022

"A nice Valentine's Day gift," Katya said, as she refolded the letter and placed it into her bag. "I suspected as much but couldn't be sure. Was it from a source report?"

Mac just looked at Katya and shrugged. "You don't expect me to answer that question, do you?"

"You already have, Mac." Katya shrugged back.

"Listen to me very carefully." Mac leaned across the table and whispered. "You are in extreme danger. Three people have died already, and we think you are next. I can help you and I do have a Valentine's gift for you."

Mac handed her a red envelope. Katya opened it. The card inside said Happy Valentine's and had a series of numbers that she recognised as a set of GPS coordinates.

"Is this what I think it is?"

"Yes."

And it's somewhere in the valley?"

"Yes," Mac repeated. "That's the last known location of one of your M1 24 helicopters. We think it was the same one that was carrying your stolen weapons."

"I tried to locate it before I left Moscow, but I couldn't. How did you get it?"

Katya lied easily; after all, that was her job. She had already read the Kremlin's files and knew not only where the helicopter had gone down but also the possible location of the weapons hide.

"You know I can't tell you that," Mac said with a smile.

"Are you going out there to look?" Katya asked.

"Of course, it's all arranged. Do you want to come?"

"I thought you'd never ask." The SVR woman smiled.

"We have a cover story for you that will protect you."

"Let me guess - you are going to arrest me."

Mac was again surprised by Katya's capacity for forward thinking. It was almost clairvoyance. "Yeah, a very public arrest by our Special Branch at your hotel."

"Can you escort me back there so I can pack?" Katya smiled.

"Yes Colonel Sokolov, it's all arranged."

"Please Mac, not so formal. After all, we are Valentines now, aren't we?"

Mac's face flushed a little as he clicked his radio comms four times to summon the car.

★★★★

The Lanesborough

The MI6 man's heart was racing as he stepped into the lift behind the SVR spy. He felt the opposite of scared; he felt elated. The pitch was going well. She was hooked, and it looked like all he had was to reel the Russian in. He also didn't feel bad about it: after all, he hadn't lied, and in espionage, that was what you usually needed to do. Mac deliberately turned away from Katya in the close confines of the lift. He was too close to trust himself. Her perfume seemed to fill the space, and he noticed the outline of the suspender belt under the clinging dress. He was looking at the floors flash by on the lift's digital display when he thought he heard a slight intake of breath behind him. He turned, and Katya was facing the shiny steel corner of the lift with her head down. For once, the legendary Babushka looked very vulnerable.

"Are you OK?" he whispered.

"Yes." Her voice was low. "It's just hard to think this is the end of the road for me."

"Maybe it's the beginning of the road." Mac looked at her reflection in the mirror of the lift. She was tearful.

"Everything I've worked for has gone."

The MI6 man didn't know what to say. A trite "Maybe it's not that bad" was all he could think of.

"Mac, I'm under threat from my side. What do you mean, not that bad? It's a disaster."

And then Mac committed a cardinal sin for any intelligence officer. He moved across to Katya and touched her shoulder gently. The Russian SVR colonel turned and just melted into his arms. Their warm bodies pressed together, and their mouths met.

Katya looked over Mac's shoulder as he kissed her neck. She saw her face reflected on the opposite side of the lift, and she smiled. *Got you!*

Chapter 17

In Tajikistan, Joe, the Increment's team leader, was considering all the options for the trip to Panjshir. It meant 367 kilometres, or 228 old-fashioned miles, of dodgy roads and perilous terrain, but that was what they were used to. The planning phase hadn't stopped at Orders. It also included those elements under the heading of Service Support and what the others knew informally as the What-ifs. What if a car breaks down? What if we have a casualty? What if we have a full-on contact? Any soldier who has worked in Afghanistan knows that any plan needs to be super-flexible to survive the dreaded *Alpha Foxtrot Foxtrot*, or 'The Afghan Fuck-up Factor,' and to survive contact with the country's inhabitants. One of those requirements is verisimilitude.

He smiled when the word came to mind. He hadn't had a clue what it meant when he had first seen it. In an email from his former Ops Officer when he needed extra money on his white sheet for Haji kit (Afghan clothes) in Helmand. The major concerned was a black belt third-dan lover of the English language, and it simply read:

Your need for verisimilitude is considered and appreciated.
APPROVED. $100 limit.
But budgetary restraint would be even more appreciated.

Joe had thought at the time: verisimilitude? What the fuck is that? He quickly checked the dictionary: it meant the appearance of being real or true, and that was precisely what you needed when you were straying into Terry Taliban's backyard.

The team all wore the unique combination of tribal and Western clothes used by Panjshiris in the winter: the ubiquitous woollen pakol hat and tribal-style scarves, with a variety of patoo shawls, or shoulder blankets, draped loosely over their regular clothing and kit. The exceptionally Shankill-white Shiner had to apply some old-style camouflage cream to his face to blend in, but the darker Tam and the even darker Ricky didn't need to bother. By the time they had loaded the vehicles, a film set's wardrobe department couldn't have made the team look any more Afghani. At least at first sight. The cars were also chosen to blend in. All three would be the universal white 4x4s used by both aid agencies and bloodthirsty Afghan warlords.

As the three vehicles set off from Dushanbe to the border, the first stretch would involve the most challenging roads but would be less dangerous. After that, they were in enemy territory and would need that degree of verisimilitude.

The drive to the border was along the Pamir Highway and followed the ancient trading routes of the Silk Road. It twisted up from tarmacked roads and soared into Parmir's rocky mountain passes. At times, the road would plummet downwards on little more than drivable tracks to strange-sounding villages with names like Kalal Khumb and Kharag before they arrived at the border crossing at Ishkashim. They had encountered the odd police or military checkpoint on the Tajik side, but the paperwork supplied by the NRA leadership had ensured that they breezed through with just waves and smiles after a quick chat with the Triples. The latter had also handled the negotiations at the border post on the Afghan side. In this part of the world, bribery was king, and the more you gave, the brighter the smile. The team slipped across the border and made good progress, and they were soon driving through the Wakhan Valley. Now for the dangerous bit.

Joe reassured himself by checking the C8 CQB carbine tucked alongside him in the recess of the passenger seat. It was covered by the same well-used shemagh (tribal scarf) he had owned since 45 Commando RM on Herrick 14 (Afghanistan, 2011). He quickly checked the Glock 20 car pistol stowed in the covert door holster. It had an extended 33-round mag, effectively making it ideal for a car drill.

Sometimes a mag change isn't a great idea in an ambush!

The Glock 20 used a heavier 10 mil round and therefore had more stopping power, but he needed the shortened C8 assault rifle for any contact over a hundred metres. He squinted into Afghan's winter sun and concentrated on following the small winding white dot on the horizon that contained his Triples doing their lead scout thing. He then checked his rear-view mirrors for the reassuring presence of the rest of the team in the other white Lexus 4x4.

The former Afghan commandos could talk their way through most problems up front, and his teammates at the back would handle things if they went nasty and noisy. It had been a long, hard drive with all the usual perils associated with the Tajikistan road system. In any third-world country, especially one with the syllable 'stan' at the end of its name, it was always better to use a three-car convoy. His Afghans were about a kilometre up front, and he was in the middle, controlling things. The rest of his guys were further back but within striking distance should either of the cars in front have any trouble.

Communications between the cars were established by the old Special Forces radio system. You 'sent' by depressing a small button by the gear lever and listening with the usual pea-size covert earpiece. It was the '90s - or more like the '80s - technology developed for 'the Det' (14th Intelligence Company) and the FRU in Northern Ireland, but it was Afghan good enough for this job.

Joe also had a '90s-style compact disc in the Land Cruiser, still considered a state-of-the-art item in Dushanbe. He was playing a bootleg copy of Motown Essentials. The vocalist was murdering the song *Once, Twice, Three Times a Lady* by the Commodores in English while trying to sound American, with an Asian accent. He smiled and thought:

Turbo Hoofing (Royal Marine slang for excellent).

"Hey Joe, we need to break trail." Joe's earpiece interrupted the Chinese Lionel Richie. He had long since given up trying to teach the Triples radio procedure, as they usually used Dari, and only one of them, Farzin, could speak good English. But Farzin loved American cowboy movies so much that he sometimes sounded more like John Wayne than an Afghan commando. The other three could speak some English, reinforced by a vast array of British swearwords and Royal Marine slang, because they had been trained by the Special Boat Service.

"Roger that. Tea?" Joe had been working with Afghans long enough to know that they drank tea nearly as much as the British.

"Yes, boss, we're fixing to find a hoofing place now." It was said in a cowboy voice, and he smiled; the Triples were good guys. Where else could you get a mixture of cowboy and RM slang in the same sentence?

"Roger that, Farzin. India Two, this is India One, OK with you?"

"Tea sounds good," Ricky said. "Can I have mine with six sugars?" Which was the only way the Triples ever drank it.

"I'll see what I can do!" said Joe.

Ricky was driving the QRF car. The road was getting icier as they went into the Wakhan Valley, the road was getting icier, but the Lexus had been fitted with winter tyres and held the road well. Tam was in the passenger seat, riding shotgun with his C8 tucked neatly beside his leg. In the back of the car, one of Shiner's big paddle hands rested on a brightly coloured Afghan blanket that covered his 7.62 Sharpshooter rifle with its 6x scope. He reached into his small backpack on the back seat and rummaged around. Alongside some L109 frag grenades, some smoke, and a couple of Flash Crash stun grenades were some tea bags.

"I've brought our tea bags lads - Thompson's Punjana, the best Belfast produces."

"I prefer Tetley's," Ricky said from the front.

"No, Thompson's tea, made in Belfast and goes down a treat."

"Just like the Titanic?" Ricky quipped.

"That's cruel! But funny," the Ulsterman laughed.

"Hello, India Two - the Triples are turning off now."

"Roger that," Ricky said.

"India One, LUP in ten, lads."

"India Two, roger that, out." The team understood what needed to happen. Both vehicles would pull off the road to let the Triples check out a Lay Up Position (LUP) at a secure location.

Joe selected a place to stop. To his right, a hill climbed upwards into a mountain; the road dropped away into a deep crevasse to his left. He glanced up at the snow-topped peaks and caught a glimpse of Afghanistan's beauty. The white mountains reflected a translucent blue sheen as they glittered in the cold winter sun. He checked the GPS. The scenery distracted from the reality of the situation; in another two hours, they would be inside a war zone.

The last couple of months had seen heavy fighting in the Panjshir Valley. Now, the Taliban government in Kabul had dropped all pretence of reform. The women shuffled around, shrouded in the burka. The girls' schools were shut. And the subjugation of the local population had begun in earnest. Most of the Taliban foot soldiers were Pashtun fighters from Helmand Province, and for them, the struggle was tribal, hate-filled, and personal. They saw the Tajiks as the betrayers who had helped NATO bring down the previous Taliban regime, and they wanted payback.

The Tajik NRF fighters, under the leadership of Ahmad Massoud, son of the famous 'Lion of Panjshir', had fought for the valley and lost. The Taliban's superior numbers, and the advanced weaponry unintentionally gifted to them by the hasty US withdrawal in 2021, had quickly taken the valley that had previously defied the might of the Soviet Army. The NRF now only controlled some strategic points on heights atop the mountains while they tried to reorganize during the winter.

Ting

Joe's local mobile sounded. It was a message from Ernie at Control. He glanced at the screen: *MC and SITREP, 5 mins.* The team leader understood the brevity code; it meant

Mission Change and Situation Report in 5 minutes.

Joe had five minutes to set up the Rosetta comms system and get any changes to their mission. He reached for his laptop and hooked up the OOA (Out of Area) transceiver.

He had only just managed to extend the thin wire aerial when the usual 'smiley' face tinged onto his phone as Ernie squirted the feed. Joe removed the cyphered thumb drive and slotted it into the other laptop. There was a brief explanatory note followed by mapping and a complete set of orders. The note was like Ernie himself, terse and straightforward.

Mission change. Proceed to agent contact at GPS Latitude 35.29559° or 35° 17' 44" North: Longitude 69.50077° or 69° 30' 3" East.

DTG: 16/02/22 0200 to 0400

2 x Pax

ZAP CM1022

ZAP 777777

Heli insertion and LUP. ID as per SOPs.

Joe quickly looked at his GPS, checked the coordinates, and then double-checked with his mapping. He fired up the Firm's tablet and waited for the satellite live feed. He soon had a better idea of the terrain. A GPS can give you a precise location, and a map can give you an overall appreciation of the ground. Still, contour lines and spot heights couldn't convey the incredible ruggedness of the terrain as well as a live satellite feed. Joe knew how vital the live feed was likely to be. He would try to pick up the incoming case officers in a hostile environment, in the mountains, and in winter.

And winter in Panjshir was unique.

The live satellite feed spotlighted the difficulty. He touched the screen, moved it, and focused it on the target area. The valley looked like God's hand had just scooped it out of the ground. It had been carved by glacial movement rather than erosion. Joe knew average temperatures on the valley floor could reach over 20 Celsius during the day but plummet past minus 20 at night. The lush green on the screen was the verdant valley in the middle bisected by the fast-flowing Panjshir river. That meant that, once they entered, they were channelled along the only drivable road in winter in enemy territory. The river that flowed so swiftly and brought life to the valley also brought difficulties because whoever controlled the river controlled the Panjshir.

There were four green dots grouped together that indicated their present position. Each Increment team member had now activated his tracker. He scanned the tablet out and got an idea of the scope of the task. The quickest and most direct route was down the narrow metalled road of the Wakhan Valley before the mountains and valleys blended in the target area. The agent RV was deep in the Panjshir and also on high ground.

If it was a Heli-insertion, would the chopper land at the RV, or would the case officers have to climb up to it?

He again looked at the message and decoded it. The Firm issued ZAP numbers chronologically and consisted of the agent's initials and his operational number. 1022 was an old number, an old-school agent, and the second ZAP was all the sevens, which meant that it was someone from outside the Firm.

Maybe the CIA?

Joe tapped the steering wheel in time to the latest track on the Chinese version of Lionel Richie an assessment. The three other lads had tucked their vehicle in behind him. There was still a lot he didn't know. That was the problem with a rushed deployment. It was always done in a hurry.

What comms? Will they have trackers?

Ricky kept his C4 tucked into his side as he walked towards the driver's side of Joe's wagon. The Increment's team leader looked in his wing mirror and smiled as Ricky strutted towards him. He could tell it was him by just the way he walked. It was that 'don't give a fuck' rolling gait typical of all inner-city lads from hard working-class areas. Joe opened the armoured door.

"What's up, bruv?" Ricky was scanning the other side of the valley but with the C4 still out of sight.

"Yeah, brief this SITREP to the others, mate. We have eight hours to get past the Talib checkpoints at the beginning of the valley and pick up two case officers. They'll be inserted by chopper and on the ground before we arrive. The agent ID will be as per SOPs (Standing Operating Procedure)."

"We should get a confirmation of the approximate drop zone soon," Joe added as he showed Ricky the tablet. He was the tech guy and had been worried about cloud cover interfering with the satellite feed. One small blue triangle indicated where the team's locator beacons merged. Joe knew they would depend on this advanced technology to tell them when other friendly forces arrived on the plot.

"How's it working?" Ricky asked.

"Top notch." He scanned the screen outwards and gave it to him.

"Amazing!" The tech stuff had always fascinated Joe.

Ricky played with the screen, panning out to the mountain tops in what was left of the Wakhan and then zooming in to the start of the Panjshir.

"That's not good." Turning the screen towards his team leader, he panned the satellite image into the main Taliban checkpoint at the valley entrance. A stolen US MRAP (Mine-Resistant Ambush Protected) vehicle stood sentinel. The heavily armoured MRAP had been developed as the US Army's solution to the Taliban IED threat but was now supplying the enemy with an excellent fighting vehicle almost impervious to the older RPGs that the NRA possessed. The checkpoint was busy. It was a brick building with crenellated walls that stretched across the road and looked just like a small castle with a large arch at its centre. He tried to assess the enemy's strength. Two Taliban fighters manned the barrier, with at least another six resting with their weapons in the shade of the MRAP.

The MRAP at the checkpoint was mounted with one of the most effective pieces of American firepower ever invented. The awesome and iconic US issue Browning .50 cal machine gun has changed very little since it was first patented by John Browning in 1918. He then scanned past the chicane of blast walls that served to channel and slow down any approaching vehicles and looked along the only road by the fast-flowing river. He immediately spotted two other Taliban vehicles that looked like Ford Ranger trucks. He ran the live mapping further down the road towards Kabul and the Salang tunnel and murmured, "Whoa, not good." His eyebrows crinkled. "Could be a game changer, mate."

"What are we seeing?" Joe could see the worry reflected on the younger man's face.

"Troop reinforcement, and a major one by the look of it." Joe realised that the two Ranger trucks were just the lead element of a large convoy consisting of MRAPs, more Ford Rangers, and even US Army trucks. They seemed to stretch forever along the valley floor; they were all full of troops flying the plain white flag of the Taliban.

"How many?" said Joe.

"Fucking hundreds!" Ricky replied with a smile.

"Right." Joe made a quick assessment, "Situation change, mate. Let's close up to the Triples and make a new plan."

Ten minutes later, the Increment men parked the two wagons at the bottom of what appeared to be a rugged granite cliff face in the general area of the GPS fix that the Triples had supplied. While Tam and Shiner provided area security for the cars and equipment, Joe looked upwards and spotted Farzin waving down from a rocky outcrop above. It could only be accessed by a steep goat path that twisted 100 metres from the valley floor.

When Joe and Ricky arrived, the Afghan commandos were already sipping sweet green tea and in their natural element. After all, they had been born and brought up in these mountains and knew them far better than their British colleagues ever would. Joe now had to harness that knowledge to develop a workable plan. The four Tajiks had positioned themselves inside a defendable position, a natural hollow amongst one of the Wakhan valley's characteristic rock runs that provided both cover from view and fire. The Triples squatted in the usual Afghan manner, nearly impossible for a Westerner, unless a gymnast or Yoga exponent, with their M4 rifles balanced across their knees.

They casually sipped tea from small glass cups and told jokes while they observed the surrounding mountains for the enemy. They had positioned themselves into the loose outward-looking circle that the British Army calls all-around defence. Joe's Dari was good enough to understand that they were telling jokes. They were usually the Tajik version of the old British 'the bishop and the actress' stories, but the bishop was now a mullah, who was always stupid - and a Pashtun.

They had arranged a small picnic for themselves on a blanket behind them. It was laid out for the Brits and looked like a great way to spend a day. Joe recognized the first course. It was a local Panjshiri specialty of plain yoghurt and a flatbread made of corn meal. The main course was wrapped in a white cotton cloth and smelt like another local delicacy: chicken, goat kebabs and pilau rice. Pilau was Joe's favourite, a white rice dish mixed with carrots, raisins, and nuts. Farzin beamed a smile and stood as Joe and Ricky reached him.

"Howdy partner. Pretty hoofing LUP, eh?"

"Yeah, hoofing, partner." Joe used the same Marine/cowboy mixture of slang; it was easier. "An excellent choice, but I don't think we've time to eat. The Taliban are starting a big operation in the valley."

"There's always time for fucking scran, boss," Farzin replied matter-of-factly. "And the best time to hit the first Talib checkpoint is after last light."

"Explain?" Joe asked.

"Hombre, we've made a plan," Farzin said.

"What sort of plan?" Joe and Ricky knew that the Tajiks were the only real experts on their home turf.

"Like all good plans, it's a simple one." Farzin opened a black plastic bag by his feet and took out what looked like a couple of dusty white sheets. Joe noticed Arabic written on them and recognised them immediately. They were the only flags the Taliban were allowed to fly, the white banner emblazoned with the Shahada, the Muslim declaration of faith and one of the five pillars of Islam:

There is no god but God, and Muhammad is his Prophet.

"I was a-fixing to fly these on our cars," said Farzin in a cowboy drawl. "I guess you Brits call it hiding in plain sight, no? Farzin winked, and Joe and Ricky squatted down to hear his plan. But even as he listened, Joe knew that the mission had become far more complicated, maybe even impossible. If a significant clearance operation was underway in the valley, then their chances of achieving a successful extraction had just plummeted. He would have to let London know about the change of circumstances and wait.

Could they cancel the insertion?

He looked at his watch. The insertion was going in 'comms dark'.

No, it's too late!

Chapter 18

Mac's head was spinning almost as fast as the rotor blades on the Mi 17 helicopter that was now flying at 200 kilometres an hour and low over Tajikistan. It had only been 36 hours since they had left London. The arrest operation had been a very public affair, with the woman MI6 called Babushka playing to a gallery of wealthy hotel residents and staff. As she was bundled into an unmarked SO15 car, she knew she would end up at RAF Northolt, the nearest airport, where a private plane was already organised to get her and Mac to Dushanbe.

As soon as they had hit the tarmac, an official from Tajikistan's equivalent of MI5, the SCNS or State Committee for National Security, had boarded the Learjet and transferred them by car to the former Afghan air force airframe sitting 'burning and turning' on the helipad. The Mi 17 or Hip chopper was flown by a Tajik Air Force crew who had flown this mission many times before. The old Russian helicopter's cover story was that they were flying in US food aid to the rural areas of Afghanistan, but its real purpose was to supply logistical support for the insurgent NRA. The two passengers sat opposite each other on either side of three pallet loads of what looked a lot more like ammunition than food. The crewman had supplied each of them with a communication headset and a black Molle military rucksack. Mac knew it was the standard MI6 issue Increment kit for a cold-weather deployment.

Someone had thought ahead.

The old helicopter vibrated in the way only a Mi 17 could as Mac listened to the chatter of the crew. He wasn't worried about all those extra tolerances the Russians used when engineering their weapons; they were built into everything Russian, from the oldest AK47 to the latest tank. It was kit that was designed to survive both battle damage and poor maintenance. From the cabin, there was a step up to the crew compartment. He could see the pilot's boots through a shabby green curtain; the co-pilot was wearing bright white Nike training shoes. There was a strong smell of cigarettes from the cabin.

Not much health and safety here.

Another glance confirmed his thoughts. He looked at the front of the helicopter, where a mass of wires curled down from under a ripped colour poster of his friend from the mountains a lifetime ago, Ahmad Shah Massoud. The wires were bound in black masking tape and held together with cable ties. It wasn't pretty, but hopefully functional, although it did little to inspire confidence. The Tajiks had inherited some of the working practices of the Russian air force.

If it's not broken, don't fix it!

But the Mi 17 was a sturdy aircraft and the workhorse of many other air forces in poorer mountainous countries, including Nepal. The airframe used the uprated Klimov TV3-117MT engines that were ideally suited to the stresses and strains of high-altitude flight. Mac found the vibrations strangely reassuring as the engines demonstrated their functionality. He looked across at Katya and wasn't at all reassured by her attitude. She had been cooperative and polite but had spoken very little since leaving London. Mac was confused. But then, from his own experience, he found all women slightly bewildering.

How could someone be so hot-blooded and amorous one moment and so cold the next? He knew that he had made a grave professional error. He had cynically thought that the sexual act would cement their relationship, but he now felt that he was the only one who seemed to be firmly attached by it. She looked across as the aircraft banked hard to the right. She seemed controlled, unperturbed, and in an almost trance-like calm. He couldn't work out what she was thinking, even when she made eye contact and smiled. Mac remembered the way he had described her to Collette.

One cover story is always hidden within another that fits perfectly inside the next. With Babushka, you never really knew who you were working against or who was running whom. She's an ace manipulator, and, in this game, she knows she's got the upper hand. What is she really thinking?

The Russian agent was thinking about what had happened in London. She had enjoyed it. In Moscow, the higher you progressed up the espionage food chain, the less you could enjoy the essential life-enhancing nutrient of sexual satisfaction. Apart from being involved in the occasional - and sometimes sexually strange - KGB 'Kompromat' operation, or honey trap, as it was known in Britain, she hadn't the time for sex or even the inclination. She knew she had been immediately attracted to Mr. Christian McCann, and he had not disappointed her. She secretly wished they hadn't met as adversaries, *but they had*. Espionage, in general, and agent handling are all about lying and manipulation. A spy must always have a certain amount of ethical flexibility to shape another person's behaviour to his or her will.

Now, he had the advantage because she needed him more than he needed her. Katya needed closure; she needed resolution. Her problems with Moscow had clarified her feelings. She had always considered herself a child of the old Soviet Union. The young idealist had thought of Communism as a global movement for good.

The young girl had committed herself to the Communist cause, but the older SVR colonel realised that it just didn't work, and her beliefs had been shaken apart in the valley they were flying into. They had been told that the Soviet mission was to educate and empower the religiously backward Afghan proletariat. But as soon as she had lost her first friend and killed her first man. She had learned what war was all about. Just a struggle to the death. The military intervention had failed back then, and it would do so again in Ukraine because of that same stale mindset inside the Kremlin.

Nothing changes. Actions have consequences.

She knew Mac was telling the truth when he told her life was in danger. She knew that Moscow doubted her loyalty. A half-Tajik, half-Ukrainian SVR intelligence officer who knew where the Moscow elite had hidden their money. *Why wouldn't they?*

She was now sure that they wanted her dead. Was it Putin or the Penovsky foundation that was coming after her? It made no difference. She must protect herself. She also yearned to discover what had happened all those years ago in the remote part of Afghanistan that had become her young lover's final resting place. The key to both those mysteries lay in the Panjshir Valley. And the man in the helicopter opposite her was the only person who could get her there. The tanks would start to roll across the border in less than a week. Colonel Sokolov, the experienced spy, knew that the most valuable type of intelligence was pre-emptive or before enemy action happened because, after its sell-by date, it was often just history.

I *need to talk to Mac. I have information to trade, but I need assurances.*

After decades of service to her country, the Kremlin elite had finally forced her to think about herself.

★★★★

In the Panjshir, a killer was thinking about her as well. He half-remembered a saying that drifted in from his subconscious:

The two most powerful warriors are patience and time.

He had always found that to be true. He had been waiting, looking down at where that Russian helicopter had landed all those years ago. He used his US Army-issue M25 binoculars and scanned for movement in the surrounding terrain. The memories from that day drifted through his mind with a strange, slow, and exhilarating clarity. It was as if it were yesterday. The giant shape of the gunship almost blocked the sun, and the air was tainted with the scent of aviation fuel as it hovered and then landed in a squall of dust on the hillside in front of them. There was a brief period of quiet as the dust settled and the helicopter's doors opened.

And then that moment of individual internal silence that every member of an ambush experiences before the teeth of the trap spring shut. When his finger is lightly touching the trigger and just needs to be depressed. When the thirst for vengeance stretches discipline to breaking point.

They had seen the Russian soldiers fan out from the aircraft to form a protective perimeter, as twenty pairs of Afghan eyes on both sides of the war machine watched them with shallow breathing. They waited until the older Russian, and the warlord were out of the killing zone, and then the slaughter began.

He remembered the look of surprise on the pink face of the turret gunner of the Soviet MI 24 gunship as two RPGs howled in from opposite directions. The scream outlined on the face of the pilot as the Russian paratroopers tried to fight back. The stream of bullets changed them instantly from living and dangerous warriors to the dead. And then it was over.

He remembered capturing the pilot and felt a shiver of excitement when he recalled the way he had killed him. He had taken his time; Haqqani had wanted information, and he had supplied it. The man had been tied to a makeshift cross and tortured. He had been alive and naked when the killer had flayed him with his favourite knife. *He had suffered marvellously!*

There was the same near-abandoned village opposite that seemed to be cascading down the valley's slope. The stone houses scrambled up to the snowline like precariously balanced playing cards. It looked like if the one at the top were to collapse, the whole village would tumble into the river. The same markers were in place. A large skull-shaped boulder of silver-grey granite sparkled in the winter sun. The upturned T54 tank on the valley floor was destroyed all those years ago and left as a warning to others, whose rusted barrel pointed towards the entrance to the old emerald mine, secreted by thick vegetation and the low scrub of stunted juniper trees. The thick rolls of barbed wire placed to protect the local children from the miles of dark underground danger had now almost rusted away.

He scanned the village. No military movement. He occasionally spotted a shambling figure crossing a street, but most of the inhabitants had left. It had once been an epicentre of Tajik resistance, so the Taliban had declared it an exclusion zone. He flexed his fingers and looked at his hands as he tried to get the circulation pumping to his fingertips. They were getting old now, but back then, they had been the same age as the fighters, now sharing his refuge against the wind. The man smiled.

It was a lifetime ago when I waited with Haqqani's Mujahedeen. They were wearing only what they had salvaged from dead Russians, and their only uniform was a woollen pakol hat and a dark brown patoo (blanket) to wrap around themselves when the gunships were hunting.

The newer Haqqani men were dressed in the latest equipment the USA could supply. The uniforms were the same as those used by American Special Forces. Each of the fighters wore Protek helmets. Some wore the wraparound ballistic sunglasses for a super-cool look, with their bodies protected by US body armour. All were armed with the latest variants of the US M4 assault rifle. Although they looked like a US Army recruitment poster, they were fighters from the Haqqani Badri 313 Battalion, the warlord's special forces trained by Pakistan's own intelligence agency, the ISI or Inter-Services Intelligence.

How times have changed! It's progress, I suppose.

The former Afghan Army military post in which he sheltered showed signs of more recent violence. The smell of fear still pervaded it, a pungent fusion of the strange metallic scent of blood and the odour of recently expended ammunition. The small piles of shell casings around the base of the sandbag wall bore testament to a fierce firefight until the ammo had run out. There were still dark pools of dried blood on the ground and a bloodied shell dressing snagged on some barbed wire that signalled surrender in the cold mountain breeze. The Badri 313 men had finished them off with knives. To preserve ammunition.

Now it was only a matter of time. He was sure she would return to find what they had hidden all those years ago. But he needed to move. His team needed to set up in the hillside village guarded by the silver skull. That would be the only way he would ever get close enough to kill her in his favourite way. He touched the sharpened carbon steel resting in the leather scabbard on the inside of his left arm and felt a thrill as he thought of its power over life, history, and function.

The knife was part of him, and *he was the knife, and we will be waiting for you!*

Chapter 19

Collette was back at her desk. She felt like she had been glued there for days, as so much had happened in such a short time. She was physically and emotionally exhausted, but she was old-school MI6 and was used to it. She remembered one of those quotes from some leadership seminar at VX in the early days, before training became dominated by the prevention of sloppy pronoun use and the heinous dangers of 'misgendering':

When you become a leader, you give up the right to think about yourself.

She opened the first folder on her desk. It was in dark Special Branch blue. It outlined the circumstances of the arrest, caution, and initial questioning of Talil Mohammad Dostani. At the time of his interview, he hadn't yet realised that he had been next to get kebabbed by a serial killer. He was full of umbrage and outrage and boasted about being a political big wheel. He had been in custody for under 24 hours. He would get a visit from Lou and Ahmad within the next 12 to ensure he was put in the picture, or as Lou in his cockney parlance would say, *'Rembrandted .'* That would give 'Computer Chris' a chance to fully exploit any 'Techint' from his computers and thumb drives that the Branch now had in its custody.

It would also allow him to exploit any recent traffic on Dostani's mobile phone. The number was already identified in the earlier link analysis diagram for the murder inquiry. So, it also gifted them another bonus. The phone's MAC address had traced its precise position and allowed it to be linked to CCTV coverage at specific places, with timings. That allowed the footage to be searched for the assassin's image, and forensic video enhancement did the rest. She took the A4-size images out of the folder and placed them side by side on her desk.

Some were still somewhat blurry, but Collette knew that all depended on the pixel definition of the camera, and the cheaper, or older, the camera, the worse the image. One picture featured a tall, black-garbed wraith-like figure that seemed like a comic book version of an evil killer. Another photograph was a face shot. It was clear. The man was looking up, his eyes seemingly blazing, his face white and death-like. It looked like a glance of evil, a glimpse of the Devil. She felt a shiver run along her spine.

Scary bastard!

Her thoughts were disturbed by the distinct ring of the secure line. Ernie's number flashed up. She knew that he wouldn't usually phone her unless they had encountered some problems.

"Hi, Ernie."

"Hi, Collette. Not good news, I'm afraid, although it's an operational worry rather than a compromise." The Increment boss added the latter to allay any immediate fears of casualties or deaths.

"Fire away.".

"It looks like my lads are shut out of the valley due to an ongoing Taliban operation. We have a satellite overview, and it looks like they have arrived in strength. Our friends in Tajikistan think it could be an attempt to dislodge the NRA from strategic points on the high ground."

"Have we any other tech coverage that would let us know?" Collette was aware that over the last twenty years, all Taliban phone and radio comms had been gathered and rigorously examined by GCHQ (Government Communications Headquarters).

Ernie released an exasperated sigh, "No, they pulled the plug on that as soon as we bugged out."

"OK, I'll check to see if the Cousins still have access." Collette used the MI6 nickname for the CIA. "I won't ask you how long it will be before your lads can proceed, but you know how exposed Mac is going to be, don't you?"

"Yes." Ernie was quiet for a moment as if in thought. "I think he and his guest will be on their own for quite a while, at least until the Taliban disperses."

"I can't let Mac know until he opens his comms on insertion. Can I give him a time frame?" There was a hint of concern in her voice.

"No." Ernie was emphatic, "He's on his own until my guys can get in. They've got a plan, but no hope of making it work until Terry Taliban goes yomping (hiking)."

"Roger that, Ernie, and understood. Just keep me in the loop." Collette rang off.

It was now her turn for a moment of thought.

If two people were going to have to survive in the Panjshir, they couldn't have been chosen more wisely. Both knew the valley as well as any foreigner on earth. If they couldn't hide there, nobody could.

Chapter 20

Mac looked out through the scratched Perspex window of the Mi17 and wiped the plastic with his gloved hand. The light was slowly bleeding away from the mountains, and they now seemed like ominously sombre shadows below, with only the odd twinkling light for company before the black darkness of night set in. As a paratrooper, the night had always been his friend, but on this mission, it did little to comfort him. He had always planned operations with great care. He liked to do what he would call, as an ex-para, *'test and adjust'*, but the rushed timeframe had prevented that. The mad dash from London had meant that many possibilities and maybe some better options had remained unexplored. To give it a military analogy, this felt more like a bayonet charge than a recce patrol. Another military saying sprang to mind:

Fail to plan, and you plan to fail.

He looked down again at the large inky blots of peaks and mountains and hoped that, somewhere down in the pitch black below, an Increment team waiting to meet them. He knew the Panjshir, and it wasn't a place where you could make mistakes. The Valley of the Five Lions in winter was cruel and left no room for error.

He looked across at Katya, and she glanced back and raised a thumb. She could now feel the old helicopter shift downwards as well. The pitch of the aircraft's twin engines peaked, and they shook as they dropped quickly towards the LZ (Landing Zone).

The slight popping of ears told the passengers that the chopper was corkscrewing downwards to the valley floor. Both knew the final approach would be at low level and maximum knots.

"Two minutes." The pilot broke the radio silence. The loadmaster moved from the aircraft's rear to the pallets in the centre of the cabin and started to unfasten the straps.

"We have one drop before yours." The pilot spoke clearly in what seemed like American English.

"Roger that," said Mac, while the Russian spy gave the thumbs up and adjusted her seat belt. The Mi 17 levelled out, and Mac caught the moonlight glittering off the silvery slash of the Panjshir Valley. Then he felt the aircraft pull back sharply as it gained height rapidly. Both passengers felt the increase in G forces as the old helicopter's engines lifted and then screamed upwards.

"One minute!" The pilot said clearly, as Mac looked towards the small set of lights by the crew door and saw the red light turn to amber.

He just had time to think *the drop-off was on high ground* as the green light came on, and the aircraft bumped heavily into the LZ. A helicopter resupply is always like a moment of organised mayhem. A forest of hands reaching in, the shapes of fighters dragging kit and crewmen pushing it, and, in a moment, it was all over, and they were flying again.

Two minutes later, the pilot barked, "Stand by!" Mac and Katya looked at the lightbox. "And thank you for flying with NRA airlines." Mac then realised that the pilot was actually an American. "Thanks," said Mac as he looked at Katya and removed his comms set. Katya mimicked his actions and again gave the thumbs up.

"Much appreciated." Mac removed his headset.

Then the lightbox went from red to amber and green as the helicopter bumped into their drop-off. Both operators slipped easily out of the airframe's gaping door, with the crewman heaving out their rucksacks and equipment after them. Then they ducked down and huddled together as the mad tornado of rotor blades, heat from the engines, and the scent of aviation fuel assaulted their senses. It was over in an instant, and they were on their own.

The two stayed huddled together until the sound of the aircraft faded into the darkness. The new visitors to the valley then uncoupled and in a slow, almost balletic movement, slithered onto their stomachs and, lying in opposite directions, listened to the night. This was the most dangerous part of the insertion when they found out whether their noisy arrival had attracted any unwelcome attention. Breathing was controlled, and ears strained to hear any noise that might indicate misfortune or betrayal. The pitch darkness seemed to lighten as their eyes gradually became accustomed to the dark. Mac looked to his front. They had touched down on slightly high ground but were still on the main valley floor.

The only sound now was the gentle whistle of the wind and the rumble of the fast-flowing river. Mac rolled onto his back. Looked up, and a thousand stars looked back. This was how night over Panjshir had always been, with each star wanting to outshine the others. To the ex-para, it always seemed that the more dangerous the place, the more beautiful the night sky. He moved soundlessly back onto his stomach, activated the tracker button on his watch, and quietly dragged the nearest rucksack towards him. He unclipped the two nylon bags attached to its side and removed the first lump of lethal metal nestled inside. He smiled when he recognized the weapon's aluminum, carbon steel, and polymer.

An *MX-M13 Rattler.*

Both weapons were already assembled and only needed to be loaded. He pulled a full 30-round mag of 5.56mm from the side pouch of the pack and fitted it as soundlessly as possible, with a barely audible click as the mag secured itself. He fitted the suppressor onto the weapon's five-inch barrel, then repeated the process with the second carbine and moved towards Katya.

"Your present from MI6," he whispered, handing her the MX butt first. "It operates just like a Yank M4. You OK with that?"

Katya was smiling in the darkness as she accepted the gift.

"Yes, I'm very familiar with your inferior capitalist weapon systems." She suppressed a giggle. "More gifts; you're spoiling me," she added. Mac watched as she quickly checked the weapon. She familiarized herself with the safety catch and selector, then soundlessly cocked the MX. She then checked and tightened the suppressor. "It's nice, thank you."

"You're welcome." Mac knew by how she handled the weapon that she was good-to-go and then went to retrieve the other rucksack.

Katya looked across the valley and tried to work out where they had landed. A sliver of moonlight now gave the undulating valley floor some shape, and there were some gentle twinkling lights on the opposite side. Not the rude bright neon of a city but the soft, muted lights of a rural village. She conjured up the names of the little villages she had known in her Alpha Group days - maybe Khanez or Jangalak, or even perhaps Malaspa, all in Bazarak Province, one of the many places where she had been operational. Mac moved up to lie beside her and whispered.

"I've turned on my tracker. It looks like a no-show for our reception party. We'll wait until we get off the LZ before I flash up the comms. We will make for high ground and some cover." Katya raised her thumb as she continued to observe through her optics.

"We'll patrol tactically in the dark and then change before first light. You OK with that?"

Katya raised her thumb again to confirm. She was aware of how things worked at night in the valley. *At night you fight. In the day, you* hide. It had been the same in the Alpha Group times. *It was enemy territory then, and it is now!* She held that thought while still scanning through the optics of the rifle. She could feel danger out there in the darkness.

"Moving in two," Mac whispered, and Katya took a knee and shouldered her rucksack. She quickly adjusted the straps and waited for Mac to give the signal. A gentle hand tapped her shoulder, and the MI6 man stalked past her and took the lead.

Just like old times! The Russian smiled and patrolled after him.

★★★★

Collette was looking at the live satellite feed on her desktop computer and having a pang of operational regret. Mac's tracker was the only lonely bright blue triangle in the whole of the Panjshir Valley, and there was no update from Ernie. She had started the mission without all the usual checks and balances in place.

Sometimes fortune favours the brave, but sometimes it doesn't.

The only thing she was sure of was that she had selected the best man for the task. Everything now depended on the Russians. The political situation in Ukraine was worsening, and tech chatter picked up by GCHQ at Cheltenham indicated that the Russian Army was gearing up for what they called a special military operation. Collette's secure line rang to disturb her thoughts. It was Computer Chris.

"What have you got for me?" She spoke first. Chris understood by the tone that she was multi-tasking, as always. "Some very interesting results from the laptop and phone that SO13 seized from Dostani, and he's up to his neck in it!"

"Explain that?" Collette picked up her pen and opened her notebook.

"Too many strands to discuss over the phone, but it seems he was working directly for the Penovsky Foundation, smuggling people and drugs across the Channel. The tech analysis shows strong links to the Afghan drugs trade and the Albanian gangs that sell them."

"If he was making them money, why would the Foundation want to kill him?" The inquiry had a sceptical tone.

"Because he knew too much?"

"Yes, makes sense. Have we got evidence of the drugs thing?"

"Yes. Cheltenham has deciphered numerous emails, and he is looking at at least a ten stretch."

"OK, give this to Ahmad and Lou. We've enough to pressure him, so let's get him pitched."

"Straight away, Boss," Chris said.

"And Chris" - Collette then smiled for the first time that day - "good work!"

★★★★

Mac led Katya up a steep rise. He had to look for cover before he could tap his sat phone's encryption codes. He also wanted to use some light. They climbed to what looked like an ideal spot, a semi-circle of boulders above a grassy hillock that had overwatched the immediate area. Mac moved into a hollow amongst the large slabs of granite and took a knee and removed his rucksack. The Russian woman took a knee facing the opposite direction. Mac smiled as he unfastened his pack and said very quietly, "You've done this before, Katya."

"A few times." She pressed the wire-framed butt of the MX into her shoulder. "But it was a long time ago." A glimmer of moonlight outlined a wistful smile. Mac used his rucksack to block out the light as he flashed up the sat phone. He then tapped in the cypher and waited. The phone beeped as it acquired the uplink. He tapped in a speed-dial number.

"Mac!" Collette sounded relieved.

"Hi, Collette. You will never guess where I am."

"Yep, I've got a good idea, and you're feeling lonely."

"Yep."

"OK, Mac, I will explain. You are on your own because there is a major Taliban offensive about to kick off in the valley. Tech chatter indicates that it's an operation to clear NRA forces off the mountains."

"Roger that; what are the options?"

"The ball is in your court. You are the man on the ground. You only need to give me an approximate LZ, and the Heli that dropped you off will get you on their next run, or you can crack on, hide, and wait for the extraction team. Your call."

He turned and looked at the SVR woman. She was scanning to the rear of them, weapon in the shoulder. Maybe this was the chance to get closer to her. He smiled as he thought: *is that work-related or personal?*

Katya scanned the optics over the ground to the rear and then to her left. The veterans of down-range shooting wars sometimes survive because they have developed a sixth sense of survival. She had that uneasy feeling that someone was watching her. She also knew that sometimes, as you peered the darkness. Someone from the darkness was looking at you.

She heard Mac's calm voice whisper into the sat phone and felt more assured.

"OK, Collette, we will stay. We are going to lie low somewhere until the boys arrive. You OK with that?"

"Yes, Mac, more than OK, but just be careful and remember who dares doesn't always win."

Mac smiled, typical Collette. "OK, I will comms check you when we are in cover." " "Right but stay safe."

"That's a big roger." Mac finished the call.

★★★★

Tariq would not have seen the strangers if he had not felt cold. He had only awakened to wrap yet another blanket around himself before returning to the ambient warmth of his flock. The goats had now been finally tethered for the night. They were far more vulnerable when tied together, not only from the wild dogs roaming the hillsides but also from Panjshir's hungry inhabitants looking for food. He only had his family's old rifle, a knife, and a wooden staff for protection, but his determination was usually enough to keep unwelcome callers away.

The helicopter had travelled just over his head and fast, and the noise and downdraft had scared his goats before it flew over the low hill to his front. He had cursed bitterly as he gathered them in again. It was only when he was pulling out the last one, a young doe entangled in thick bracken, that he had seen them. They were just two figures outlined against the skyline at first. They were carrying backpacks, but when the front person stopped and knelt, the figure immediately behind knelt and faced the other way.

These are foreign soldiers, and that means danger.

They had weapons, but they were small and nothing like the ancient rifle he had slung over his shoulder. He frowned. He was old enough to remember when the Russians had arrived in the valley; they had stayed a while, killed people, and then gone. These seemed the same.

Mac talked over his shoulder to his patrol partner.

"Can you smell that?" The wind had shifted, and the sweet, pungent smell of goats' shit now drifted across their location. Mac quickly stowed away the comms kit and shouldered his pack. Katya helped him with the final strap and checked that the cover was properly secure.

"Yeah, goats," Katya agreed.

"And where there's goat shit, there are goat tracks, and that's what we will need to get into the mountains quickly. We need to get out of the valley, so we will push the pace a bit. You OK with that?"

"Good idea," she agreed. Mac was already up and moving, so she followed quickly. They picked up the goat track just before the ground started to steepen.

★★★★

The Badri 313 patrol had been in the valley for months and knew it well. All four Muslim 'brothers' were from the same place, a little town called Spera in Khost Province, and were proud Pashtuns from the Zadran tribe. They had come to the valley to fight the Tajik idolaters six months before, and they were still doing so on the night the helicopter flew low over them. The patrol leader, Haji Azmaray, was performing *wudu*, his ritual washing before prayer when the dark shape of the aircraft flashed overhead. He knew exactly what it was. They had been expecting it: a weapons resupply for the accursed NRA.

Azmaray's thoughts switched from prayer to revenge as he thought about his nephew, martyred in the fighting the week before. He reached for his M4 carbine and saw the others doing the same. Within minutes they were patrolling into the darkness, with only the general direction of the aircraft's flight path and Allah for guidance.

Chapter 21

Acton Police Station. London

Lou and Ahmad had not been given a time frame for the interview of Talil Mohammad Dostani that they intended to transform into an interrogation. The Metropolitan Police no longer called the room they occupied an interview room. It was now referred to as an interview suite. If the name change had been meant to make things sound comfier, it had failed miserably. Gone were the good old days of Paddington Green, when domestic and Islamist terrorists could have their own space to discuss their murderous activities.

Now they had to share space with ordinary criminals, drunks, druggies, and grime-rapping gangsters. The room, therefore, smelled of stale cigarette smoke and poor people, tinged with the faint tang of urine. The magnolia walls were blank, with nothing to distract the room's occupants, but badly needed repainting. The focal point of the room was a plain wooden table just wide enough to stop a seated policeman from reaching across it. The seating arrangement was standard: two straight-backed chairs for the prisoner and his counsel and two equally uncomfortable ones for the cops. All furniture was securely fixed to the pale green linoleum floor. An ancient-looking tape machine was likewise permanently screwed to the desk.

Not that anybody's going to steal that heap of shit. Whatever the Old Bill's budget is spent on, it's not new tech kit, thought Lou.

The solicitor's chair was empty for the time being but was in danger of being filled soon, so the two agent handlers were frustrated with their progress. So far, they had presented the evidence gathered from the phone and laptop, and Dostani had only smiled. Even when they had shown him the Osman warning, informing him of a credible threat to his life, he had only smirked and repeated the standard phrase, "no comment".

"But we really are trying to help you here," said Ahmad, as he bent down to retrieve something from the briefcase by his leg. "And we are trying to protect you!"

"No comment." The Afghan's initial shock of capture after his arrest had gone, and he seemed to be quite enjoying the experience. But that was about to change.

Lou reached over and turned off the interview tape. "Oops! The machine seems to have problems." The big ex-Marine had been silent until then. He had just let Ahmad do the talking and concentrated on looking menacing, which he was pretty good at.

"You're not allowed to do that!" There was a tone of alarm in Dostani's voice.

"No comment!" said Lou.

"We've something to show you that we only want you to see, and we don't want others to hear," Ahmad added as he put the photograph face up on the desk and turned it slowly towards him.

"Do you know this man? Because he's the one trying to kill you."

A dumbstruck Dostani looked at the grainy photograph while the colour slowly drained from his face. He gasped as all the confidence seemed punched from his system. The killer's face had done the trick. There was a long silence before he muttered: "Belaya smert" (the White Death). The almost mournful phrase sounded like the whine of a frightened man.

Ahmad looked across at Lou, who was smiling. Agent handlers are trained to find and pull the lever that opens the door to a man's soul and ensures cooperation, and that lever, for Mohammad Dostani, was fear.

We've got him! Ahmad smiled as he pulled out a digital voice recorder and switched it on. Lou raised his voice as he glared at the terrified Dostani. "We can only save you if you cooperate." The Afghan looked away as he said, "What do you want?"

"Everything." Ahmad clicked on the digital recorder and gave his co-handler a nod.

"Just start from the beginning and tell us everything, and you can get your life back."

Lou picked up the photo on the desk and stood up. "Or you can face ten to twenty banged up in HMP Belmarsh with a good chance of meeting your old mate." The ex-Marine held the picture up to Dostani's face.

It took only an hour to debrief the terrified new agent. The police interview that became an interrogation ended up with a new source making a voluntary statement, with a handler's voice only interjecting occasionally to ask a question or to clarify a point. The Security Service's latest source spoke quickly, clearly, and rapidly as if his life depended upon it because he knew it did. Two hours later, the report and the recording were loaded into the central server. Ten minutes later, the printed version and an encrypted thumb drive containing the audio were lying in a red file folder marked 'SECRET UK EYES ONLY' on Collette's desk.

Collette opened the folder and, over the next hour, read and listened to its contents. It was more of a story than a conventional source report, as it was written as a verbatim transcript of the conversation between Dostani, now known as agent number 1664, or *Shark,* and his new handlers.

Although it sometimes disintegrated into the ramblings of a terrified man, it traced Dostani's involvement with the Soviets in Afghanistan during the occupation. He had been a HUMINT handler with the KHAD, with assets within the hardline *Khalis* faction of the Peshawar Seven, when he had been recruited as a double agent. He explained in detail how he had become the linkman between Jalaluddin Haqqani of Khalis and Pakistan's ISI, and then how he had started to work for General Penovsky of the GRU. He described his treachery as an accidental bump in the road. All three groups, in his opinion, had different but equally powerful motives for cooperation. Haqqani, above all, wanted power, while the senior officers of the ISI wanted to keep the money flowing from the West, which was funding Pakistan's nuclear programme. And Penovsky just wanted to keep the war going because he saw the planned Soviet withdrawal as a betrayal. He had also offered to sell the Soviets' latest nuclear device to Pakistan, to sweeten the deal. It had been an unholy trinity of combined but competing interests to keep the war going.

And then there were the victims. Dostani's voice became emotional when he talked about what had happened all those years ago in Panjshir. He explained that Penovsky had been double-crossed, the helicopter transporting the device to the Panjshir Valley destroyed and his soldiers killed. The only two Russians to survive the ambush, the officer with the nuke and the pilot, had then been tortured to death. The conversation on this part of the tape was the most interesting.

Ahmad (A): "Why kill him if he'd arrived with the nuke?"

Dostani (D): "Because he hadn't."

A: "Explain."

D: "Penovsky had only supplied the dummy version that the GRU used on its military exercises. He wanted to test the waters to see if the ISI could be trusted."

A: "And they couldn't."

D: "Precisely."

A: "So what happened?"

Collette heard a nervous quaver in Dostani's voice as he described the events.

D: "The Russian helicopter set down inside a carefully prepared ambush. Haqqani wanted Massoud and the Tajiks to get the blame He had arranged ceasefires and truces with the Russians that had weakened the Khalis faction."

A: "Did anybody survive?"

D: "Only the Russian officer with the dummy nuke and the pilot survived the initial ambush."

A: "And what happened to them?"

D: "Skinned alive by the man in that photograph. He was in the KHAD as a killer named Igor Kalash."

Collette heard the fear in the man's voice.

A: "Why?"

D: "The older officer because they wanted to find out about Penovsky."

A: "And the pilot?"

D: "Just for fun! The man who did this enjoyed doing it. You could hear the screams from deep inside the caves as he worked on them. There's something else you should know." There was another tremor in his voice.

A: "What?"

D: "He's not human. He's pure evil, and if Igor the White Death is sent to kill you, you die!"

Collette then opened the other folder on her desk. It had been supplied by the Spellcraft team and was for her eyes only. It was a thin one with only a few densely typed pages and a head and shoulders portrait photograph of a young man in the dark brown uniform of the KHAD. It looked like a picture taken at the end of a course or period of training. The man in the photo posed with his Soviet-style peaked hat held formally in his right hand, and his eyes turned towards the camera. She recognised him immediately as the scary bastard in the CCTV footage. The face had changed - it was lined now - and the blond hair had faded into grey, but the eyes reflected the same glow of fanaticism.

Nature or nurture, she thought. *Are you born a killer or are you moulded into one, by training or circumstance, or both?*

She began the read the notes. They were extracted from a secret Soviet file hidden inside some dusty drawer in the GRU archives that should have been burned but which had proved itself every bit as resilient and hard to destroy as the man whose name was typed on the first page.

IGOR DUMO KALASH

Born. Nuristan, Afghanistan

DOB. Unknown

Igor had no family. They had been killed in tribal fighting when a rival clan had raided his village. He was twelve years old, lost in the mountains and frozen close to death when he wandered into a Russian firebase in the Wakhan Valley. His formative years had been spent with or around the Soviets; he had received military training in the Caucasus and eventually became a specialist killer used by the KHAD. Collette continued to read, almost spellbound. The file traced his killing career, from his first successes with Afghan intelligence to working as a contractor in Baghdad for Saddam Hussein's feared secret police, the Al-Amn al-Khas. The list of the dead was a long one.

This man was horribly good at what he did.

Chapter 22

The killer looked at an old Soviet map and tried to work out the approximate grid reference of where the 'crocodile' had touched down all those years ago. He still referred to the old Soviet MI 24 gunship by the nickname the Russian soldiers of the 42nd Army gave it. They called it the crocodile because it was both heavily armoured and killed people very easily. But that was when it was flying and not ambushed on the ground. The grid reference of the ambush had never been recorded, but anybody in that part of the valley at that time would know about it.

Mujahadeen did not do grid references much; they just knew their piece of the battlefield better than any interlopers. But he, as a former KHAD officer, had needed to read a map. He looked at where it had all happened. Sometimes the little piece of shrapnel in his skull confused his numerical reasoning, but he eventually thought he had identified on the map the hillside village with the large skull rock. The entrance to the old emerald mine was nearby, and the destroyed tank was another reference point.

The killer drew a rough resection on the fragile map and then marked it. That was about where the helicopter had landed. He wanted to write the grid down but again was confused by the sequence of the numbers. He had learned to map-read in Russia, where the grid was in a different sequence, and the NATO system temporarily confused him. He wanted to make sure that his quarry could reach where the Russians had died, but he also needed the rest of the Badri 313 operators in the valley so that she could not escape.

★★★★

Haji Azmaray knelt and sighted his M4 and looked through its Trijicon ACOG sight, and the night became less opaque. He could now clearly see the folds in the ground and the gentle slope that became a mountain. He still sometimes marvelled at the advantages the kuffar pigs had had over him and his other Muslim brothers during the long struggle to free Afghanistan from the infidels. They were shooting at him with this piece of American devilry when he was shooting back over the iron sights of his AK47. How he had survived only Allah knew, and only He had willed it.

The three other brothers were covering his back as he made his assessment. He could see the slightly darker shade of what looked like a goat track snaking off into the high ground. He scanned his weapon over the middle distance and found what he was looking for. The outline of a single human figure amongst a flock of goats. Haji had been a farmer before he became a warrior. He knew that a Goatherd was the guardian of his flock. And therefore, the eyes and ears of anywhere his goats roamed. The Badri commander lowered his weapon and scratched his beard in thought.

I will ask the goatherd.

★★★★

Collette rechecked Mac's location. The small blue triangle that represented his tracker had made some progress. The MI6 man had put 6.5 kilometres between him and where he and the Russian woman had touched down, but their pace had slowed over the last hour. She guessed they were now fighting the gradient and the elements and heading into the mountains. She checked the Increment team's trackers. They were still static. The situation was far from ideal. Both groups were isolated and unable to support each other in a place that was about to become a battleground. She needed more help, but that was difficult. Her Majesty's Government had decided not to support the Tajik resistance, but she knew the CIA had retained some assets in the country. But she knew they wouldn't share them for fear of compromise. There was only one person she could think of that might be able to help, so she reached for the secure line.

Danny heard the mobile ringing from within his desk and picked it up after the second verse of Elgar's *Land of Hope and Glory*. It was the encrypted mobile that the Security Service had given him. He swiped the phone.

"Hi, It's Hedges and Fisher, Danny speaking. How can we help?" He used his best customer service voice.

Collette smiled. "I hope you can."

"Whatever and whenever."

"The whatever is happening in Panjshir, and the whenever is now."

"How can I help you, Collette?"

"I believe you have some unofficial contacts with the NRA in Dushanbe."

By using the word unofficial, she indicated that the whole conversation was outside the scope of the usual permissions she would need to elicit from the Foreign Office.

"Yeah, I can talk to somebody reliable who could talk to somebody who can make decisions." Collette knew that Danny had direct access to Amrullah Saleh. The Tajik resistance leader had once been Ahmad Shah Massoud's intelligence chief, the former Vice President of Afghanistan, and the head of the NDS, the former government's domestic intelligence service.

"What do you want me to do?" Danny asked.

"Can you arrange some help for Mac and the India callsign?"

He checked his elegant 1960s Rolex and calculated the time in Dushanbe.

"Give me a couple of hours."

'Thanks, Danny." She felt relieved as she said, "We owe you one." And she put the phone down.

★★★★

The Badri patrol had no problems finding the goatherd. He was a simple man, and like all simple men, he did not understand the importance of the information he had passed. He first thought that the four Taliban fighters were Americans by how they dressed, and he was relieved to find that they were Afghans. He could not read or write and did not understand politics. He valued only his family, goats, and religion, and outsiders could not take any of these precious possessions from him. He had therefore volunteered the information freely and politely, even after they had held him at gunpoint and taken his prized British Lee Enfield rifle. Haji Azmaray then killed him only because he wanted to test the suppressor on his new American M4 and, of course, because he was a Tajik. The goatherd was a simple man and did not understand politics, so he died.

Haji pressed the trigger on his short-barrelled M4, sent an aimed double tap between the goatherd's eyes, and turned smiling to the rest of the patrol.

"See, my brothers, hardly any sound." The other Badri men nodded sagely in agreement.

★★★★

Joe and the team had waited for twelve hours, and the time was hanging heavily. They had done their best to hide the vehicles, but it was difficult in a bare-arsed valley. They were parked in a slight depression and hidden from the valley floor by the berm of raised earth that had once been a Russian patrol base. They had moved on foot to an overwatch position and now got colder while they waited. Joe was accustomed to the cold. He had done his mandatory three winters in Norway with 45 Commando and was used to the mountains, including the wind chill factor, but that did not mean he liked it.

His Afghan Triples hated it even more, not because of the climate but the enforced inaction. Joe knew they, unlike the rest of the Afghan National Army, had joined to fight. As they waited, they thought of their comrades already in the hills with the Tajik resistance who were taking the fight to the Taliban. It was, therefore, a welcome relief when his local mobile tinged with a message from Ernie in Slough. It was just the 'smiley face' emoji letting him know to set up his comms. The cyphered message came five minutes later, and Ricky decoded it.

Situation change. The team has permission to use local friendly forces to extract case officers. Good luck.

There followed the GPS coordinates for a possible RV, a graphics download to help with planning, and a local Roshan phone number with the name *Ghazi*, who Joe thought might be the local NRA leader. He put a new sim card into the phone and tapped it in. He then walked across to where the Triples were on watch. It was always unwise to not include the new troops in the plan.

After all, it was their country!

Farzin was looking depressed when Joe arrived. "What's up? A long face but no horse!"

The Afghan commando smiled and told himself to remember the pretty cool saying. "Just waiting here isn't good for my guys when we have bad fuckers in the valley." He repeated the sentence in Dari just so his team knew what was being discussed. They all nodded in unison.

"Remember that the Panjshir is our home, and they are killing our people." Again, he repeated the sentence for the 333 Commandos.

"Yeah, I understand that." Joe reached into his pocket, pulled out the phone, and flashed up the name and number of the resistance leader he needed to call.

"We are joining up with the resistance." He showed the name and number to Farzin.

"Well, fuck my old boots," he blurted out. Joe couldn't help smiling. That was an expression Farzin had learned from his SBS training team rather than from cowboy movies. The Afghan commando leader frantically checked his phone and compared the numbers. "Is that what he is calling himself these days?"

Joe responded with a confused look. "Sorry, Joe." Farzin was smiling broadly now. Ghazi was an honorific title given to a great warrior. It was originally an Arabic word for a Muslim who fights infidels.

"When me and this hombre were at school, his name was Mohammad." He beamed another smile. "We called him crazy, Mo and he's, my cousin. He's a good fighter but a crazy fucker."

The familial connection didn't surprise Joe. "You ring him, then!" he looked at his G Shock watch. "And let me know what the plan is. Orders in one hour. OK with you guys?"

"You betcha, partner," Farzin said in his cowboy accent as he made the call.

Chapter 23

Once Haji had the direction tracking the new visitors to the valley was easy. The Badri patrol leader had farmed in a similar place before he became a hunter, and farmers can pick up the slightest change in the terrain. They followed the general direction the Tajik goatherd gave until they came to a depression in the snow-sprinkled grass where the helicopter had landed. He tracked the two sets of boot prints that led towards the mountains. One person heavier, one lighter, wearing the same type of boots with distinctive tread. Maybe a woman?

American boots?

He also detected where they had halted in the goats' shit and waited. The area was still free from frost, and he could see the outlines of two bodies. He felt the ground. It was cold now.

They moved over an hour ago.

The patrol used the goat track as their highway into the hills. They moved quickly but patrolled carefully. After an hour, Haji halted, took a knee, and examined where the grass became rocks. There were scuffs and boot prints on the small granite boulders. They were not easy to notice, but he had lived in the mountains and knew how to track. He knelt and felt the little piece of moss that had been dislodged.

We are near!

★★★★

Mac knew that he was being hunted but didn't really know how he knew. There was that almost primeval soldiering instinct that years in the Paras and the SAS had inculcated in the ordinary young man he used to be. It was not something that is taught, but something that is learned over hard years of being hunted. The main thing about being a Para is that you nearly always operate amidst the enemy, so you are always surrounded. His time in the SAS had reinforced this perspective: there are no enemy lines when you are trained to operate behind them. It was a strange feeling, almost like that sensation, that tingling in the back of the neck that tells you that someone is staring at your back. It was probably what had kept Neanderthal cavemen alive. Mac was maybe a wee bit Neanderthal himself, but it had kept him alive in Panjshir, Baghdad, and Helmand, and he felt it working now.

Katya was still patrolling behind him, occasionally turning around to use the rifle's optics to scan the route they had taken. She tapped Mac on the shoulder and pointed to the ground with an outstretched hand, palm down, the infantry signal for 'Go Firm'. She had felt the same; years of ambush patrols in the same valley had shaped her survival instinct as well. Both operators knelt and looked and listened. The Russian woman strained her ears as she observed through the scope. There was a glimmer of moonlight that cast shadows over the snow-flecked valley. All she could hear was a low whistling of the wind over the rocks that sounded like the whispered wail of '*No*'. It sounded, in her imagination, like the Russian dead of Panjshir trying to communicate with her.

They whispered, and she listened!

In that instant, thinking about the possible deaths of young soldiers in Putin's war, she finally decided to tell Mac her secret as soon as possible. And then she saw something in the far distance. At first, it was just a tiny blob outlined against the sliver of the moon as a man broke the skyline. Then another, and then two more. She clicked up the light intensifier on the scope, and now she could see four soldiers patrolling tactically behind them. She turned and closed up to Mac and whispered in his ear.

"We have company."

"How many?"

"Four."

"Distance?"

"Not sure, hard to assess; they were sky lined and before the last hill, maybe over a kilometre."

Mac ran a quick assessment in his head.

"We need to set an ambush. You up for that?"

"Yes." Katya's voice was icy calm.

"OK, let's go."

We need to get to higher ground and find a good ambush position.

★★★★

Fear is very motivational; it produces adrenalin that flushes the blood around the body and brain and helps you move faster and think more quickly. The two spies from the opposite side of the ideological divide were now bound together by the fear of death. Mac surged ahead, with Katya always within a tactical bound. He wanted to gain more height as he searched for the ideal ambush position. They needed to get the enemy very close to ensure first-time multiple kills. As taught by the SF, a textbook mountain ambush should leave no survivors. They needed cover from view and protection from high-velocity bullets if they came the other way. They also needed to be concealed but did not have time to prepare hides. His legs ached now with each stride as he scanned for the ideal position.

The goat track opened out into what looked like a snaking, well-travelled village path. It meandered ever upward between ominous-looking gravestone-like pillars of rock, and then there was a sharp left turn. Mac then knew. *This was it!* He turned towards Katya, knelt, and ushered her forward. Katya knelt with her right ear, almost touching his mouth. Mac whispered. "We have to take them here."

Katya looked around the prospective killing zone and smiled. "Looks good." She had made her own assessment. The surrounding rocks offered an ideal ambush position, with cover from view and some protection from fire. The sharp turn in the track meant that the Talibs would be committed to the open ground directly below her and Mac. Once they were engaged, they had nowhere to go.

"We will hit them from the rocks." Mac pointed to the sighting system on his Sig MX Rattler. It was a standard ACOG Trijicon, ACOG standing for Advanced Combat Optical Gunsight. But he realized that, no matter how advanced a gunsight was, it still needed to be adjusted to suit the soldier using it to hit a target.

"These things aren't zeroed. So, you need to go for low centre body mass and close."

"How close?" Katya was conflicted; the last time she had had to personally kill another human being was over thirty years before. She had been a soldier then and, therefore, a killer, but it scared her a bit to think she could revert to type so easily. But Afghanistan had always been a place where no mercy was either asked or given.

And self-preservation is marvellous motivation.

"We will be together. I will let you know."

She just had time to say, "OK, Mac," as the MI6 man stood, turned, and clambered up the rocky outcrop to find the perfect place to wait and kill.

★★★★

The American and British troops that Haji had spent the last twenty years fighting had unwittingly taught him many very useful lessons, some tactical and others painful. The infidels had arrived and stayed for a while, but they were always replaced by another group who did not know his fields as well as he did. The foreigners stayed and fought for maybe six months before returning to their sin-ridden countries, but he was always there waiting for the next lot to arrive. As one of the brothers had said,

They had the watches, but we had the time.

The new troops would always make the same mistakes, and Haji was always there to supply their opportunity to do it. But he, Haji Azmaray, had been fighting for twenty years and didn't make mistakes.

He took a knee and scanned ahead with his ACOG sight, breaking the ground up in the far distance using the moon's illumination and the intensifier on his scope. The quarry was harder to track now as they moved over rockier ground, but he could still pick up the spore. The faint footprints and boot scrapes on a scattering of white snow showed him that the two they were following had increased their pace, with the stride patterns wider, even though they were on a gradient. Twenty years of combat experience told him

They know they are being followed.

He turned his head slightly, so his words would carry easily to the others waiting with him. "We must be careful, brothers. They know we are here."

The two intelligence officers were close together. They selected their firing positions and then sat back-to-back on their rucksacks with Mac forward, waiting to sight the Talib patrol. Mac felt the heat of her back on his. He wrapped a dark brown patoo blanket around them for warmth and camouflage. Here they blended easily into the darkness of the rocks and were protected from the wind chill. It was deathly quiet, with only the slight whistle of the rocks as they connected with the light mountain wind.

"How long will we wait?" Katya was the first to speak.

"Until they come." Mac knew that they could not outrun them. "I have a good view of where they will start to climb our track, and then we just wait until they are within thirty metres before I initiate the ambush."

"That sounds like a good plan." Kayta's accent, for once, seemed to have a Russian edge. "And I have something to tell you, just in case I can't later." Her voice sounded sad as it drifted along the wind.

"What?" Mac was hoping that it was going to be something affectionate.

"I have the start date and the plans for the invasion of Ukraine."

The MI6 man tried not to sound too surprised.

"When?"

"Soon, in a week, on Thursday, February the 24th."

"Why didn't you tell me fucking earlier?" Mac's whisper was almost violent.

"Why do you think I didn't?" Katya was straightforward. "I do not want to be responsible for the deaths of Russian soldiers. A week is enough time to warn the Ukrainians, to save lives but not enough time to organize a bloodbath."

Mac could see the logic.

"OK, just tell me what you know, and I will remember it."

Katya turned slightly towards him.

"I will start with the general plan for Operation Thunder. The plan is to encircle Kyiv with simultaneous special forces attacks, to kill Zelenskyy and install somebody else."

"Sounds feasible, but will it work?"

"No, it won't. I have carried out the research, and I know it won't. I think it would be best if I just tell you the whole plan, and then you can ask questions afterwards. If we have time before the wet work?"

"Fire away." Mac smiled - not a good thing to say in an ambush position. "Metaphorically, that is!" he added.

"How long have we got?"

"Until they arrive," Mac said.

Katya then told him everything she knew.

★★★★

Haji knew something was not right because it felt wrong. His long years fighting the infidel had taught him that. He had ambushed enough people to know that you could get bumped yourself when you least expected it. He looked up from the track at the rocks on both sides and thought.

This is where I would set an ambush!

The art of ambush turns the hunter instantaneously into the prey; he had seen it happen. He stopped again to examine the tracks. The two they were chasing were moving more slowly now.

Maybe they are looking for an ambush spot or a hiding place!

The Taliban patrol leader turned to make a hand signal, and the patrol started moving tactically in pairs. But he remained kneeling, scanning the rocks above him as the man behind him moved past.

Katya examined the face outlined in her ACOG. The illuminated line of the sight bisected his body, with the small red triangle of the tip hovering over his combat helmet. The image was not what she expected. The NATO standard weapons and equipment initially confused her. She also noted the tactical movement expected from special forces-grade soldiers. The only obvious difference was the large shaggy beard that burst from under her target's helmet. He was at 100 metres and looking up at the rocks that separated her from Mac.

He then touched the top of his head with a hand, scanned with his M4 in his shoulder, and waited until the other men moved past him. As the other fighters moved, Katya acquired the next target, and the ACOG was full of a different head and body. A younger man. She was stalking the targets on the right. Mac would be tracking the two on the left.

Mac's scope was acquiring the head of the fighter on the opposite side of the track, with one patrol member still unsighted. All four Talibs would have to be in the killing zone before he could trigger the ambush, but the tactical patrolling had made his job harder.

These guys are good!

The killing zone was almost directly below them and fifty metres from where they lay in wait. He could hear the scuffles of their footfall now; he could almost hear their breathing.

Or is that me? Another twenty metres.

Mac watched from the shadows as the patrol stopped just short of the open area on the path. He tracked the leader's head with his ACOG as he turned towards the others. Mac now had his whole scope filled with the back of his helmet. A whispered conversation in Pashtun drifted in, amplified by the frozen rock.

He's giving orders.

Katya caressed the trigger on her MX. Her sight picture was complete, but the target was still too far away for her to ensure a first-time kill. She felt a tear roll down her cheek. She did not want to kill another enemy. But this was Afghanistan. *Nerves!* She dismissed it and inhaled deeply and concentrated on controlling her respiration. Now every nerve in her body stretched as she continued to fill her scope with her primary target while preparing to switch to her second intended victim. The big man with the beard stopped, turned, and seemed to look straight at where she was hiding. It was a heart-stopping moment.

Has he spotted me? The first glimmer of the winter sun was beginning to break on the rocks behind her.

The big Talib scanned the area through his scope and walked past the rock Mac had placed as a marker for the ambush zone. When the last man patrolled past, he would spring the trap. Katya was now listening for the muted sound of Mac's suppressed MX. There was near-total silence now. Just the sound of the Badri men as they moved into the killing zone. Katya was again tracking the patrol leader. She dropped the sight picture from his head to the centre of his body mass. The tip of the graticule was now hovering over his chest.

Katya fired a split second after hearing the distinctive *phut, phut, phut* of Mac's MX. The patrol leader was hurled back as the force of a double tap slammed into his chest. She switched target - the other Talib had come on aim, his face masked with panic. He loosed off a long burst in the general direction of their hiding place. The sound of the Talib's M4 in the tight confines of the gulley resounded with deafening intensity and ricochets pinged dangerously over the rocks around her. Katya hit him with a precise three-round burst, and he cartwheeled over. Mac had engaged all his targets by the time she had finished firing- And then there were just the mountains and silence.

Mac whispered, "It looks like we've pulled it off," as both operators continued to watch for movement. The MI6 man was the first to climb from his hiding place to examine the dead. The Russian covered him from her firing position as he clambered to the gulley floor. He reached the ambush site and signalled for Katya to follow.

Haji thought he was dead, but then his eyes blinked open, and he looked at the start of a new sunrise. *It was Allah's will that he should live,* not the US-issue body armour. He was now lying on his back, trying to keep still as he heard the shuffling of feet and a muted conversation in English that he did not understand.

"Check for extra ammo," Mac said. "These lads won't be needing it."

CHAPTER 24

It was just before dawn when the Resistance arrived. And they did not come quietly. They owned this part of Panjshir, and they knew it. A Roshan mobile rang another Afghan number, and within thirty minutes the great Ghazi was hugging his cousin. Both had been in 333 Commando, and both had been born in Massoud's home village of Bazarak. The Increment team sat and drank tea while the new visitors caught up on their war stories and discussed ancient family ties.

Joe knew that was how things happened in Afghanistan: hospitality and tribal catchups could never be hurried, even though he had his case officers to meet. Any intrusion would be interpreted as a slight, and he did not want to piss off the men he could be fighting alongside. Ghazi was eventually introduced, with Farzin beaming hugely. "Ghazi, my brother, this is my boss, Joe. He's with MI6." Joe smiled. *Afghans don't do Opsec the way we Brits do*, thought the former British Commando.

Ghazi was a big man with a big smile, wearing a pakol hat, the soft, flat, rolled up, round-topped men's cap made of wool and goat hair typical of the area. The wild, long black hair was pushed inside it, with a haywire beard at the other end. He reminded Joe of Blackbeard the Pirate. He was dressed like the other NRA fighters, in just about anything functional for mountain living that they owned or could steal. It was a mixture of military and tribal, with an emphasis on warmth. Joe noticed that the former Triples still wore the Afghan National Army patch and 333 insignia, the white dagger on a blood-red background with the word COMMANDO on a black patch.

The group was armed with an array of weapons, the ex-commandos with M4s and other older fighters with AK47s. One older man, who looked in his fifties, had a sheepskin jerkin over his loose traditional kameez top, held in place by an old Russian RPD machine gun with two bandoleers of bullets as accessories. Only three fighters accompanied Ghazi, with four others perched on the ridge above, performing overwatch. The NRA leader had taken precautions just in case of a set-up. Joe was impressed.

"Hi, Joe. My cousin said that you were in the British Commandos. Do you know Lee Starkey?" The big Tajik's English was as good as Farzin's but without the cowboy accent.

It was a strange thing, especially about the Royal Marines, that in random places and at some odd times, a total stranger would expect you to personally know a man in a four thousand-strong military organization. But, in this case, he did. Lee Starkey was a legendarily hard Royal Marine who had been involved in the initial training of 333 Commando. "Yes, Ghazi, we were in the same Commando. Great bloke!" Joe could almost feel the ice break.

"Yeah, as you say," said the pirate, "a hoofing bloke. What can we do for you?"

"We must get into the valley and extract some of our people. Can you help us?"

"Yes," with another pirate smile. "But you will need to help us in return."

"With what?" Joe knew that everything now depended on what they could supply. The British Government had not recognised the NRA, so their advisory and military options were limited.

"We will attack the Talibs in the valley while the rest of them are in the mountains looking for us. We will kill many." Joe looked around the Increment team and saw the same expression on their faces that said, *"How the fuck do we get out of this?"* "So, what's the plan?" It was all he could think of saying in response.

Ghazi sat down on a rock, pulled out his traditional peshkabz hunting knife from his chest webbing, and started to inscribe lines in the ground in front of his feet. It was the rough outline of the Panjshir Valley. "This is the village of Khosdeh-Rutya," he said, marking a cross. "And this is the checkpoint on the road at the beginning of the valley." He carved another in the earth. "Our first objective is this checkpoint, and then we take out the Taliban strong points in the village." Ghazi beamed another smile. "And this is how we do it!" Joe realised they were now being given orders for the equivalent of a Commando raid.

London isn't going to let this happen.

★★★★

Haji waited. He had always been ready for death. He tasted blood in his mouth and knew the body armour had not prevented all the damage. He silently checked that he could feel his body's extremities. He moved his fingertips and felt for any movement in his toes as he silently felt for his Pakistani issue combat knife. His hand enclosed it like a meeting of old friends. He felt stronger now.

We have God's work to do!

His ambushers were moving along the gulley, checking the men that he had led to their deaths. He could hear them talking in English but did not understand the language.

"Just grab the extra mags and comms stuff." Mac was emptying the ammo from a young Talib's chest webbing. The 30-round magazines were interchangeable with the MX system. He picked out a grenade from one of the pouches and unhooked the Motorola radio from the front of the harness. "And these might come in handy." Mac checked that the pin in the grenade was correctly splayed and wiped the blood away from the radio before he stowed them both in his rucksack.

Phut-Phut! He heard Katya's MX put two rounds into the man she was about to search on the other side of the ambush.

She doesn't take any chances! Rule Ten of the Spetsnaz combat manual: When you search the enemy dead, make sure they're dead!

He then moved towards the older man with the beard. Mac came up on aim and sighted his rifle on the Talib's head, and then the head moved as Haji sprang to his feet with lightning speed, and suddenly Mac was fighting for his life. In a millisecond he was on his back, pinned by the big Talib and held with what seemed like maniacal strength. The MI6 man's left hand had gripped the Badri man's right wrist, where a carbon steel combat knife glinted in the early sunlight.

"ALLAHU AKBAR," the Talib shouted, as Mac felt the blood from the man's mouth connect with his own chin as he gasped for breath. Haji's face was a mask of fury as he pressed the tip of the knife toward Mac's left eye. And then she was there. He could see her on aim within five feet of the struggle as she moved forward and placed the suppressor of her MX into the side of the big Talib's neck.

Phut-Phut. Two silenced shots sent blood splashing from his carotid artery against the granite of the gulley.

"Thanks." Mac could think of nothing else to say as he pushed the dead Talib away. "You're welcome." Katya could not think of anything smart to say, either.

"That's another one transitioned to Jannah (Paradise)," Mac muttered, as he stood and checked his weapon.

"Yeah, I hope it's as good as he expected it to be." Katya started emptying the Talib's chest webbing. She prised the knife from his dead right hand, checked the blade, approved it, and placed it in her rucksack with the ammo.

★★★★

"They want to do what?" said a worried Collette.

"My lads on the ground reckon it's the only way to get the NRA to help," said an equally worried Ernie.

"Surely not. That's tantamount to Her Majesty's Government sponsoring an act of war." Collette was thinking fast. "Can we get Danny's contact to fly in some money?"

"I don't think they have anywhere to spend it in the mountains. They are motivated by revenge, not reward. So, what's the answer?" Ernie was brusque; he was a soldier, not a politician.

"Give me a few hours, and I will get an answer," Collette said.

"Roger that," Ernie said as Collette finished the call.

Collette knew what she had to do. She rang her former husband of the MI6's prized Spellcraft team and downloaded her problem. Damian Brown listened carefully and then came to the same conclusion.

"You've got to be fucking joking!"

"I wish I were." Collette was somewhat enjoying his discomfort.

"What are the options?"

"Not very many." She was looking at her laptop, showing how far the precious blue triangle of Mac's locator was from the Increment team. "We can ask Mac to E and E (escape and evade) with Babushka, but that's a really long shot with the Taliban push into the mountains." Collette's tone conveyed her doubt. "And it was our idea to try and recruit her. We need to look after them, don't we?" She put the ball right back into her former husband's court.

"Let me think about it, and I'll get back to you."

"OK." Collette took a deep breath. "But the clock is ticking, and we started this."

"Understood." Damian looked towards the secure line on his desk. "I will ask C."

Damian was referring to the man in charge of MI6.

★★★★

Mac was tired. The adrenaline rush you get from combat is often replaced by tiredness that makes every molecule of your body ache. He had pushed the pace to get away from the unburied dead. He was nearly at the end of his endurance. They had walked all day on a rocky uphill track on the slopes of one of the highest mountains in the Hindu Kush, and Qulah-y-Shakarow in winter proved itself as merciless as ever. And the higher they climbed, the colder and thinner the air became. A lung full of pure mountain air now came at a premium; your body had to work much harder for it. A thought occurred to him from his past:

I'm fucked! It's like the long walk on Selection.

Mac glanced back after each turn to check on Katya. She was always there, as determined and alert as if she had been born in the mountains. And of course, she had. Mac was impressed.

How can this be the same elegant woman I dined with at Nobu?

Mac was now looking for a place to rest. And as soon as he envisaged it, he spotted it. It was a small stone building looking down onto the goat trail. Mac knew that such places had been used by travellers in the Hindu Kush for a thousand years and more.

The Islamic world is as big on hospitality as it is on vengeance.

He stopped by the battered wooden door and signalled to Katya, who was already scanning her rear for any signs of trouble, with her MX Rattler on aim.

Mac opened the door a couple of inches and ran his hand along the inside of the frame to check for tripwires. Satisfied, he slowly pushed it open, to be assaulted by the concentrated stink of goat shit. It was a small space filled with animal fodder and the detritus of its previous visitors. Mac looked at the soft bed of straw and immediately felt even more tired. Katya was still standing at the door, covering the track they had walked along. "What do you think?" Mac said.

"Convenient." She turned and made a thumbs-down gesture.

"But not safe!" Mac understood; he knew his fatigue had affected his judgment.

"Yeah," he sighed, "I guess we sleep further up the mountain, then?" He remembered that his last visit to this valley had been as a welcomed guest, not an enemy.

"Yes." He knew that the Russian operator had worked in Panjshir in different circumstances, as a special forces soldier being hunted by Mac's Mujahadeen friends. "I think it would be better to overwatch this hut from up there." The former Spetsnaz woman pointed towards the rocky ledge above.

"Sound tactics," Mac said.

"But let's make ourselves comfortable." Katya picked up an armful of straw.

"Never hesitate - insulate?" Some of his training with Mountain Troop, G Squadron, 22 SAS was flooding back.

They moved further uphill to find cover from the cold of a mountain night. Mac knew his main priority was to send the intelligence gained from his pre-ambush debrief with Katya. He was already composing the CX in his head as they searched for shelter. The Russian Afghan veteran soon found the ideal place. It was a deep nook in the rocks with a view of the track and stone hut. The pair lined the bottom of their nest with straw and shielded themselves from the cold using the lightweight sleeping bags from their rucksacks. With fatigue slowly permeating his whole body, Mac set up the comms kit and squirted off the report to London,

Then the two comrades camouflaged their new hide with patoo blankets, pushed up close to each other for both warmth and reassurance, cuddled, and tried to sleep. Katya's hair smelled of blood, sweat, and goat droppings. Mac smelled the same. Haji's blood still clung to his skin, the last reminder of a brave man who had fought to the end. He felt the Russian woman's body warming his own. It felt natural. Just him, her, the wind, and the mountains. Just before he slept, he heard her whisper. "You do take me to the strangest places, Mac." Mac smiled and drifted off.

Chapter 25

Collette was asleep in her office when the report came through from the duty operator. She had been confined within its walls, being bombarded with constant demands from the Government to find out what was happening in Ukraine. The mainstream media, aided by Russian disinformation, had reported that Putin was standing down the forces he had gathered on the Russian side of the border. Collette thought that was very unlikely but had no evidence either way. The Spellcraft product was indicating that Putin was going to invade soon, but it had given no timelines. Decisions at this stage could only be made by conjecture, and VX needed accurate intelligence to feed the Whitehall beast. And then the secure desktop pinged.

It was a flash report, which was intelligence-speak for a top-priority signal of urgent intelligence bullet points. Collette smiled for the first time that day. Mac had hit the jackpot.

SIS CX 166-01

BABUSHKA

Source number NYA (not yet assigned)

23.00 hrs. 19-02-22

Handler: Mac

Location: Mobile

Cover Increment Team - NYA

FLASH SECRET UK EYES ONLY.

1. The armed forces of the Russian Federation will commence a short-term special operation into Ukraine at 0400hrs on 24-02-2022.

2. The following formations will take part. 2nd Guards Combined Arms Army. 15th Separate Motor Rifle Brigade. 21stGuards Motor Rifle Brigade. 41st Combined Arms Army. 55th Mountain Motor Rifle Brigade. 41st Combined Arms Army. 90th Guards Tank Regiment.

3. The following Special Forces units are to seize key infrastructure and Kyiv airport. 8th Directorate Spetsnaz GRU. 2nd Guards Spetsnaz Brigade. 3rd Guards Spetsnaz Brigade. 10th Spetsnaz Brigade. 14th Spetsnaz Brigade. 16th Spetsnaz Brigade. 22nd Spetsnaz Brigade. 24th Spetsnaz Brigade.

4. Enemy targets, axes of advance and detailed intentions will be debriefed when location and timings allow.

Collette rang Damian's direct line. "Did you see the report?" she said.

"Yes. This stuff is intelligence gold dust."

"What next?" Collette was staring at the single blue triangle of Mac's locator. It had not moved for hours.

"I think we'll get permission after C reads this."

"I know that you'll try your best." Collette replaced the phone with a worried look on her face.

★★★★

A worried look was also reflected on the face of the killer who, Collette knew, was Igor Dumo Kalash, or 'White Death'. Not that he ever really worried that much about anything when he was working. His main priority was to finish his assignment and move back to Europe, a target-rich environment for a professional contract killer.

It was a simple matter of market forces and supply and demand. You could never get properly paid as a killer in Afghanistan, because people there usually got murdered for free.

He looked around at the young men that had been assigned as his bodyguard by Haqqani. They regarded him with both fear and respect. Fear engendered by the aura of death seemed to hang around him like an evil halo, and a cold glance from his bright blue eyes could freeze a man's soul. And also because he was a Nuristani, a tribe distrusted by Tajiks and Pashtuns alike. It was the mountain warrior tribe rumoured to be either the last genetic traces of the army of Alexander the Great or the lost tribe of Israel, depending on who you talked to. The Nuristanis had been the last hill dwellers to convert to Islam and were therefore still known colloquially as Kuffars. The respect came because young Afghan men tended to admire and listen to their elders more than their counterparts in the West. And, after all, to them he was a Mujahedeen war hero.

But with White Death, the respect was a one-way thing. He had known many young men just like them over the years and he thought they were all the same. Whether it was the Mujahedeen of thirty years ago, or Al Qaeda in Iraq or ISIS in Syria, they were all killers, but of a much more dangerous type for mankind. They were ideological murderers and therefore the evilest type of zealot. But the Nuristani killed as a professional and did not care who killed whom in the valley. It did not worry him, as he had no real feelings one way or the other. He only knew that he worked for money and that they paid him well. And he knew his target must always die, because his reputation was at stake. *He had never yet let one live.* That was his ideology. He liked killing, and the more elusive the target, the more he relished the chase.

He had just heard over the Badri 313 radio net that one of the patrols had not reported in. He had checked their location when they had reported a low-flying helicopter and a possible supply drop to NRA insurgents. He thought that both incidents could be linked.

Was his target returning to the place where a Soviet aircraft had been ambushed all those years ago? That's where I will find her!

He thought of the cold dark place where he had tortured and killed the Soviets, and felt a dark rush of pleasure course through his body. He smiled!

★★★★

There are occasional situations in the service of your country that are somewhat strange, and Joe could remember quite a few. This one seemed completely bizarre but strangely satisfying. The message from London had arrived with a *ping* on his secure comms and it gave permission to:

Cooperate with local community stakeholders to extract British citizens and associates from the Taliban-controlled areas of the Panjshir Valley.

He had worked with the Increment long enough to know that what was said in an official communication between the Firm and the field was always disguised with MI6 spook gobbledygook, even on secure means. It was linguistic body armour against any subsequent internal enquiry. Every message was masked by vagueness, so that every sentence examined could later be moulded, if necessary, into plausible deniability. Joe read that message as:

The Op is a go, but don't fuck it up!

There was some more that made him smile.

Direct armed contact with either the armed forces or the representatives of the Islamic Republic of Afghanistan is forbidden. It is suggested that your role is only to supply support to extract the case officers and is solely advisory.

That meant: *Get it done, don't get caught or killed, and please don't fuck it up.*

Joe made his way to the circle of NRA fighters that were already readying weapons and loading ammunition.

Ghazi smiled his pirate best and said, "Well, can you help?"

"Yes," Joe said, "we are in. What do you need?"

"A couple of RPGs would be a good start, my British brother." Ghazi was short of those.

"We can help you, but we will need your help as well."

"What?" Ghazi shot him a quizzical look.

"We need to get to our people."

"Do you know where they are?"

"Yes. I know exactly where they are. I have their GPS location."

"Can you show me?" Joe flashed up the Firm's device and showed the NRA leader the small blue triangle nestled halfway up a mountain.

"Show me on the map." Ghazi did not seem to trust the technical kit.

The Increment leader unravelled a map from his pocket and indicated the position.

"Yes, that's not far from some of my people." Ghazi said

"We can get them."

"Have we a deal?" Joe said.

"Yes." Ghazi made an assessment. "We can get to them within three hours."

"Then we have a deal," Joe said.

Ghazi smiled in agreement.

"Hey!" The Increment team leader called across to Shiner Wright, the big Belfast man, who was checking his Sharpshooter rifle. "Hey mate, have we still got that NLAW in the back of the wagon?"

"Yeah." The request had sparked his interest. "Why?"

"Because we might need it, and your favourite rifle."

"Hoofing!" The man from the Shankill looked happy, while Joe passed the message to London.

Chapter 26

Mac and Katya had nested together all night, sharing the same space, body heat and exhaustion. Almost conjoined and cocooned in their granite refuge in a spooned position and clinging together for mutual support. Mac was beginning to feel differently about her. She was no longer an SIS file number or code name. She was now a comrade in arms that had saved his life. The woman that he had made love to in London was fast becoming the woman that he loved. As he drifted in and out of sleep, he cuddled closer into her warmth and felt it almost melt his soul.

They both woke with a start when they heard the door of the small stone building creak open. The first rays of the sun were just beginning to change rocks into discernible shapes as they stole the night from the mountain's rugged slopes. Katya grabbed her weapon and sighted it toward the building. She held her breath as several armed men began to search along the path, with others now inside the goatherd's hut. Mac whispered, "They've found the bodies." "Yeah." Katya scoped the searchers and whispered back. "But they're not like the last lot." She clicked up the ACOG. "These men are locals."

She knew how people from the valley dressed and moved. The grey/brown pakol hats were worn differently in the valley, in the Tajik manner, Massoud style, and the Tajik tribal blankets or patoos were tightly rolled up and tied over a shoulder so as not to interfere with weapon handling. Mac sighted his weapon and came to the same conclusion. "Weapons tight," he smiled. "It might be the cavalry." He could see from the look on Katya's face that she had taken the comment literally and was looking for horses. "No, I think it's the NRA." She continued to scan with the sight. The two operators did not break cover but waited in the dark recess of the rocks until Mac's comms device vibrated. He glanced down.

FLASH MESSAGE
FRIENDLY FORCES ARE AWARE OF YOUR LOCATION.
WILL TAKE YOU TO CALLSIGN INDIA.
STANDARD REVCON PROCEDURE.
ERNIE

And then a shout in English.
"MAC?"

Mac touched Katya's shoulder tenderly. "We'll be OK." She gently stroked his hand.

He unzipped his rucksack, removed a torch, and fitted a red filter. He then flashed it three times toward the track and received five flashes back. Before he closed the comms, he quickly messaged London.

07.15
WITH FRIENDLY FORCES.
MOVING NOW.
MAC

★★★★

Ghazi's plan, like all good plans, was a simple one. But it was simple because it needed to be. He had planned complex operations as a captain in 333 Commando, but things had been very different then. The limitless logistics, air and artillery support, and the all-encompassing security blanket of the American mission called

Operation Enduring Freedom, had gone. He could no longer conjure up airframes to move his men or order up close air support when he needed it, because:

The hunters had become the hunted!

His only option now was to revert to classic guerilla tactics, the same butcher-and-bolt strategy that had worked so well against the Russians and the previous Taliban government and their Arab allies. The Insurgency hoped that such raids would eventually wear down Kabul's resolve to keep their best fighters in Panjshir. Ghazi thought it was a good plan because it was simple, and complicated never worked in Afghanistan. And it was always better to attack an enemy when and where they did not expect it. He had chosen his target carefully. The plan was based on information gathered by a network of informants across Panjshir. It was real-time intelligence with constant updates on the enemy's strength and intentions. Keen Tajik eyes keyed text messages that reported on everything that moved in the valley.

The first target would be the main Taliban vehicle checkpoint at the entrance to the valley, which would be a diversionary attack by the British and his cousin Farzin. The secondary objective would be the Badri fighters occupying the small mining village of Khosdeh-Rutya near the town of Khosden, once a stronghold of Ahmad Shah Massoud and a symbol of Tajik resistance. The village was defended by the Taliban's best fighters for a good reason. It contained a functioning and very profitable emerald mine under Chinese ownership and was part of a black economy that supplied the Taliban with over fifty million dollars' worth of fine Panjshiri gemstones every year.

Ghazi intended to split his troops into two separate assault groups to attack the Taliban in the village. The British team would deal with the main checkpoint and then extract to continue with their mission. He hoped that they survived the battle and that the two guests that they were so concerned about survived to meet them. The weather was worsening now, with a light dusting of snow making the going slippery. The line of fighters in front seemed to be endless in the tight confines of the mountain defile that led ever upward, but there were only fifty NRA men. Local intelligence sources placed the enemy's strength at thirty. Conventional modern tactics always tried to deploy a three-to-one advantage to assault an enemy position. He did not have that luxury.

But his men weren't conventional and were fighting for their homes.

He strode purposefully up the sharp incline with his beloved M4 rifle cradled in his arms. There was now a long file of fighters painfully trudging up the mountain path. Traversing a mountain brings its frustrations. An uphill climb is a stop-start affair, and if a man at the front slips, the time it takes for him to regain his feet is amplified as it works its way down the column. Being at the very back of a single file, while clambering up a slippery mountain on a load carry, is the worst place to be. But these were his mountains, and he knew every twist and turn, and could read the ground. Ghazi looked at the summit of the next mountain. Soon they would hit an old Mujahadeen resupply trail that would lead them straight into the village – and into battle.

★★★★

Joe checked his GPS. Ricky was covering the rear, squatting with his Colt Commando C8 tight into his shoulder. He turned and flashed a broad smile. The young Londoner looked in his element. The Increment team leader remembered when he had felt the same, but the carnage of Iraq and Afghanistan had somewhat worn away the adventurous side of the older man.

That's why old soldiers last longer on the battlefield than younger ones. The caution comes with age.

Joe looked at his watch. Time to move!

They had six hours before they had to be in position above the checkpoint. The plan was to be in overwatch of the target as Ghazi was ready to attack. He held the radio that the NRA leader had given him to coordinate the attacks. It was a Harris HH-7700 handheld, supplied to the Afghan commandos by the Americans but also used by the Badri 313 Brigade. It was meant to be a multiple-channel hopper for covert communications, but it could also be used to listen to the Taliban if the NRA techs hit the channels they were using. There was to be strict radio silence until the assault.

All the vehicles had now been checked and all the equipment apart from the weapons had been loaded. The only new addition to each vehicle was the white Taliban *Shahada* flags that Farzin and his commandos had affixed, hanging limp in the winter sun. The whole team was now prepping the kit, as each man was lost in his thoughts. Two of the Triples had taken out their prayer mats and were preparing themselves for battle in a more spiritual way. Farzin and the other sat opposite, smoking and telling jokes; it was their way of preparing for action. Joe was not surprised by this. The Tajiks were generally less judgmental than the Pashtuns he had known. The religious and the secular could coexist when one side gave the other space.

Shiner lovingly cleaned his Sharpshooter while hoping that the zero was still perfect. He would not have a chance for a check shoot before he engaged live targets. Ricky and Tam busied themselves with their weapons. The NRA had gifted them two very old-looking RPD machine guns for fire support. Both men stripped and examined every worn piece of the Soviet-era kit and then lightly oiled the working parts.

"These are still in pretty good nick," Ricky said. "Yeah," Tam replied, checked the cocking mechanism on his. "They built these fuckers to last." Ricky was gradually getting used to his Glasgow burr, almost delivered at machine-gun pace, but just nodded because he didn't quite catch the last bit. "Not so sure about this, though; what do you think?" Ricky was holding a belt of dodgy-looking ammunition that had seen better days. He started looking at each individual bullet in the long line of link. He pulled out the loose-looking rounds and replaced them. Tam looked across. "If we can salvage 400 rounds from this lot, that should be enough." Carl moved to the back of his vehicle and removed the green plastic case that contained the NLAW. He unclipped the latches and looked inside with a grin. "Beautiful."

"Beauty is in the eye of the beholder," Ricky quipped, as he handled the black Hornet Nano drone. "And this is my masterpiece." He checked the battery level. No doubt his favourite toy would be needed soon. Shiner removed the missile launcher from its protective case and picked it up. He felt the weight and smiled again. "So, what's the big deal with this bit of kit?" Tam asked. "It's a game changer, mucker." Carl placed the 2.5 optic sight against his right eye and then reeled off the weapon's specifications as if he were giving a lesson.

"The NLAW is a fire-and-forget missile system that will take out any known tank."

The Belfast man pointed towards the large green polystyrene cone on the front.

"Because in there is a 150 mm HEAT (High Explosive Anti-Tank) shaped charge designed to cut through just about anything." He hefted it in both hands. "It only weighs 15k, and here's the kicker. It can be used directly at a target or on what they call OTA, or Overfly Top Attack, where it explodes about one metre above the target and bangs that big HEAT round through the weakest part of the armour. And the best thing is, mate, it was put together in my wee country and in my own wee town." The Ulsterman picked up the NLAW, made sure the carrying strap was secure, nestled it into the rear of the Toyota, and covered it with a blanket. To Tam, it looked like a doting dad putting his baby to sleep.

"Impressive stats, but will it work?"

"We do great engineering in Belfast, mucker. Yeah, and let me tell youse again, I was an anti-tanker in 45 Commando and this fucker is a game changer."

The conversation finished abruptly as Joe said, "OK guys, final briefing before we start." There was a sense of urgency in his voice. Even in the relaxed rank structure of the India team, there was a place for orders. He was speaking without any of the usual slang terms, because each time Joe spoke Farzin translated it into Dari. He concluded by saying, "This is not going to be an easy mission and it's not one that any of us signed our contracts for. It will be a direct attack on a Taliban position." He looked at the men gathered around him. All the men had a similar background and training as him. "Does everybody understand that?" The sea of smiles reflected from the gathered warriors answered his question.

"OK lads, let's go." As they climbed into the cars, Joe once again checked that the tracker on his watch was working, and then tapped in the GPS coordinates of the FUP (Form Up Position) for the checkpoint attack. His plan, too, was kept simple. Ricky would do an overflight of the target with the drone and then he, Carl, and Tam would provide fire support as the Afghan Commandos readied the vehicles and then led off to breach the checkpoint. They had an hour to drive to the target.

The Triples pulled out onto the road first and the Increment's cars followed. Joe's heart was beating faster now, and he had the dry feeling in his throat that he had always had when leaving the safety of a FOB (Forward Operating Base) in Helmand or jumping out of a helicopter in Iraq with Task Force Black.

Nerves or adrenaline?

Chapter 27

Mac and Katya continued climbing uphill with the NRA rescue party, occasionally helping each other. Katya now wore a black hijab to allow for any cultural sensibilities, though she did not think the Afghans leading them minded either way. But she was a spy, and it was always good tradecraft to blend with the environment, both physically and culturally. The men in front were used to the mountains and moved quickly and quietly, but suddenly they came to a standstill and then froze completely. The leader of the rescue party, and the only one who spoke any English, turned towards Mac, pointed towards the side of the path and whispered, "mines."

Mac knew what he was looking at: a Soviet-era PFM-1 Butterfly Mine, also known by its nickname of *Green Parrot*. A distinctive bright green plastic wing of the device was clearly visible and wedged between two rocks. These mines had a wing on either side to allow them to autogyrate when scattered from a helicopter. They looked anything but dangerous - and had in the past been mistaken for toys by a generation of Afghan children that had lost legs, hands, and eyes.

The PFM-1 was meant to injure rather than kill, but they still did kill kids quite often. Over a million of these anti-personnel mines had been deployed by the Russians during the Soviet occupation. They were used to impede the movement of the Mujahadeen in the mountain passes, and they seemed to be doing the same job now. The group's lead man started to clear the path ahead, using his pakol hat to carefully remove the light dusting of snow in front of him.

This will slow things down, thought Mac.

He did not really know where they would finally meet the extraction team. He knew that they must start moving south eventually. He also knew that they were near what the old-time Mujahadeen crudely called *Kir Khar* or The Donkey Dick. It was one of the main transit routes used to resupply the former insurgency against the Soviets, and he had travelled it many times before. He looked back at where Katya was crouching and still covering the rear with her MX.

She's probably ambushed it! Mac's respect for her increased by the day. Her professionalism was impressive. He checked his watch to see if his tracker was still working.

★★★★

Collette observed the tracker on her desktop as things were starting to happen. The Increment's tracking triangle was moving quickly towards the entrance of the Panjshir Valley, and Mac's was moving slowly into the mountains. Both groups seemed safe for now, but they were still miles apart. She felt uneasy. She had no idea how or even when the India team would assist the NRA insurgents, but she did not want to know the details. She knew that, once you let the dogs of war slip, you could not call them to heel, and death and repercussions always followed.

Mac's report had raised eyebrows at the Ministry of Defence, who still did not think that Putin would invade. The Russian formations that Katya had named indicated a massive deployment of armour, amounting to a forty-kilometre tank column striking directly into the heart of Ukraine to surround Kyiv. The MoD's brass hats did not think it was a realistic game plan, but they had still authorised the immediate dispatch of another one thousand NLAWs. But Collette still needed to get more supportive intelligence to convince them of the time frame. She had to get Babushka back to London for a proper debriefing, so she needed a helicopter extraction as soon as Mac and the Russian were secured by the Increment. She reached for the phone to dial Danny Mac's number.

★★★★

The MI6 woman was under pressure to deliver the follow-up CX from Babushka. No intelligence agency likes to rely on single-source information. Every piece of the information puzzle they call military intelligence must ideally be corroborated. All the data produced by the Spellcraft team strongly indicated that a Russian attack on Ukraine was imminent. The technical intercepts harvested in a thousand ultra-modern ways also said that a full-scale invasion could be on its way. But this data also came with a health warning from the 'techies' at the building called *The Doughnut* at GCHQ Cheltenham:

The Russian military, and especially the GRU, has mastered cyber disinformation.

Collette knew that that was much easier to produce than sound intelligence. Even in the twenty-first century, the only real way to know what an enemy intended was to have an agent inside his organisation. The CHIS, or Covert Human Intelligence Source, was still the crown jewel of spying; in the end, HUMINT usually trumped all.

I need to get Mac and Katya back here and debriefed.

Her thoughts were disturbed by the chirp of her desk phone. She looked at the number, if it was yet another call from the MoD, she would not answer it. But it was Damian Brown. She picked it up at the fourth ring.

"Hi, Collette."

"Hi." She could not help smiling when she heard his voice. "What can I do for you?" There was a pause as Damian phrased his answer. "Work or pleasure?"

"Work," Collette snapped.

"Yeah," he laughed, "I thought so. Just wanted to know whether you have had any contact with Mac. I'm getting RFIs (Requests for Information) hourly and wanted to know the timeframe for Babushka's product. Is that possible?"

"No, Damian." Collette looked across at her computer screen and checked Mac's tracker. He was still a long way from the Increment; they were static at the entrance to the valley, and Mac and the Russian were at least thirty clicks from them, to the south and halfway up a mountain. She was now beginning to regret allowing the cooperation with the NRA.

"The only thing I can confirm at present is that Mac and, I presume, Katya are not far from the GPS coordinates that your asset provided. But I've not got a good feeling about it." She had quickly determined that if they were not with the Increment, they were with the NRA insurgents who were about to attack the Taliban. "No, I'm not happy about this, love." The word slipped out of her mouth before she realised she had said it.

"I'm on my way up," her ex-husband said.

Collette slumped forward, leaned her elbows on her desk and held her head in her hands. She had not slept properly for days. Leadership can be lonely. She was looking forward to seeing her ex - at least he understood. She thought of Mac and just knew that he was in danger.

★★★★

The killer recognised the village as soon as they approached it. Very little had changed in the last thirty years. The only real difference was that this unofficial Mujahadeen emerald mine had now become an unofficial Chinese Government-owned one. China had been buying up mineral rights while the USA and NATO had been bogged down in an insurgency and were too busy to notice. It was the same hillside village he had been watching from the other side of the valley. The old stone dwellings were now deserted and stacked up the mountainside like tombstones, one seemingly draped over the other. The great grey granite rock that looked like a skull was also instantly recognizable.

He could also see the entrance to the old workings where they had hidden the evidence of the ambush. It was a long, rough-hewn tunnel that Panjshiri miners had carved into the very heart of the mountain. The locals had used it as shelter from the Soviet bomb runs in the old days, and as a place to store food and weapons. But the locals had gone, and only the residue of betrayal and some skeletal Russians remained in the mine's dark recesses.

They had arrived in a convoy of American Humvees. It amused him; it was the ultimate irony. The High Mobility Multipurpose Wheeled Vehicle was the signature piece of American equipment that screamed 'US Army'. The Pakistani ISI had received them from US Aid for help with the almost yearly flood problem and had then gifted them to the Haqqani Network.

He had needed to use his influence with the Badri Brigade to get his men assigned to this part of the valley. Over a lifetime of killing, he had developed a unique homing instinct that always led him to his prey. He knew that the Russian woman would be drawn to this dark place. He touched the outline of his knife, resting in its leather sheath on the inside of his forearm. He felt a familiar thrill.

And I will be ready!

Chapter 28

The small group of NRA insurgents they had joined was now part of a much bigger one. And as soon as Katya and Mac had hit the old Taliban MSR (Main Supply Route), or what the locals called the Kir Khar, she knew where she was, and she knew by their direction of advance and what they were carrying that they were on the attack. It seemed a bizarre situation: the Russian spy was now under the protection of the people she had been ordered to destroy all those years ago.

The mad, bad memories of her Spetsnaz days flooded back in. The cold nights, with tracer rounds stitching the dark. The crack and thump of the high-velocity round that you only heard if it missed you. She stopped and looked around. She felt like the granite walls of the mountain path were closing in, and the cold eyes of the dead were watching her. She suddenly felt cold to her core.

"You OK?" Mac said. Katya snapped out of the trance. "Yes," she whispered. "But I know this place, and it hasn't good memories for me."

"Or me," Mac said. "Cold winters, poor clothing, and the imminent fear of death."

Mac checked his GPS and then moved closer to the Russian spy. "The GPS location we were looking for is not far from here, on the valley floor."

"How far?"

"Maybe ten clicks." Mac used military slang for a kilometre.

"That's where I need to get to," Katya whispered.

"The only thing we need to do now is get back to London." Mac seemed adamant.

Katya turned towards him, her Panjshiri eyes blazing in defiance.

"I have come here for a reason." She checked her weapon. "And I'm going, whether London likes it or not." And then she said softly, "But I need your help."

★★★★

The big man with a black beard was waiting as they moved along the track. He was standing by a small mule that had an old Soviet 82mm mortar tube on one side of its skinny frame and its base plate on the other. The small animal seemed to be trembling with the cold. The man was stroking its mane and gently whispering into its ear. He smiled as Mac approached him on the increasingly narrow mountain path.

"As-salamu alaykum," the big man growled, as he gave the traditional Arabic greeting used in all Islamic countries.

"Wa' alaykumus-salam," Mac replied.

"Is the mule OK?" Mac said in Dari.

The man replied in perfect English. "Like all Allah's creatures, she sometimes needs encouragement. She feels like our organization in its fight against the Taliban. It's a small horse with a heavy load, and she is tired, and no one is helping her." He turned from tending the mule and beamed a smile. "Christian McCann?"

"And you must be Ghazi?" They shook hands. "As you Brits say, fucking roger that." Both men laughed.

The Russian SVR woman pulled her hijab more tightly around her face. It was always better to adopt a low profile in the valley.

Muslim men are always more comfortable talking to other men, and not so much with women. It was a cultural norm rather than misogyny, but more deeply ingrained in rural societies. But she need not have worried about that with the NRA man.

"And this must be our other guest." Ghazi grinned. "I see you like wearing a hijab."

"It keeps the wind out of my face," Katya said.

"Sometimes these things are useful, but not as useful in the valley as that." Ghazi pointed towards the MX Rattler the Russian spy was holding. "But it is our job to keep you safe now. I hope you do not need it. We want your time with us to be successful and not too stressful."

"What's the plan?" Mac said.

"The plan is to reunite you with your British colleagues as soon as possible. But we have some work to do first."

"What work?" Mac said.

"We are going to attack and destroy a Taliban unit."

Mac looked across at Katya as she rolled her eyes. "When?" The big Afghan checked his watch. "In about two hours." He was still smiling.

Not too fucking stressful. Mac smiled as well.

★★★★

The insurgents moved into their attack positions almost soundlessly. Men born on a mountain are more attuned to its all-pervading silence and move more carefully by nature. There was only the slight scuff of feet and the occasional dull clunk of metal as the NRA prepared the mortar line. The barrels were moved as soundlessly as possible onto their baseplates and clamped into place. Each insurgent took out the two mortar rounds he carried slung in his patoo blanket as carefully as possible and placed them onto the ever-growing pile of 82 mm ammo as he filed past. The men were well drilled, as if they had practised for such an event their entire lives, and maybe they had.

Katya looked up towards the high ground on her right. The last of the winter sun was being replaced by a red sunset, a scarlet blood-red that she had only ever seen in Panjshir. She spotted the ominous outline of a 'Dushka' 12.7 mm heavy machine gun, just breaking the outline of the darkening sky. All around them, warriors crept into position.

Mac could see what was happening; he could almost read the plan of attack. It was straight from the old Ahmad Shah Massoud playlist, the Tajik version of shock and awe. A mortar attack coordinated with two Dushka heavy machine guns, with intersecting fields of fire, and then a mad infantry charge. Mac pulled his small binoculars from his rucksack and looked down at the old stone village below. It was supposed to be occupied by the Taliban but looked totally deserted. Then he saw something. The last of the sunset shimmered over a line of fighters trudging wearily up the hill from the valley floor. They were not moving tactically, which was a good sign. He focused his standard British Army Avimo binoculars with another few clicks. He looked at their kit and equipment, mostly American: M4s, M4s with M203 underslung grenade launchers and lightweight Protec Kevlar helmets with night vision fitted.

It looks like the Badri Brigade. Not a good sign!

★★★★

The team's vehicles stopped to prepare for the checkpoint attack short of the target. It was quiet in this part of the valley; its population having fled the Taliban occupation. Joe looked up. A golden eagle soared in graceful loops above them, seemingly the only party interested in their forward deployment for the attack.

He's hunting as well!

The team busied themselves unloading the weapons from the cars, as the Triples took up fire positions to secure the perimeter. They would be the first to mount the vehicles and break through the checkpoint once things went noisy. Joe looked across at Carl as he hefted the NLAW onto his back and checked his Sharpshooter. Tam also checked for brass inside his M4 and his Glock 19 pistol. Looking for brass, or 'check chamber' was the term soldiers used when they partially opened the chamber of a weapon with the cocking handle and checked for the reassuring dull glint of the brass cartridge inside that indicated that it was loaded correctly and 'good to go'. The team finished their preparations and then mounted the vehicles for the attack. Joe had studied the ground and selected a blind spot to the checkpoint where he thought the fire support team could leave the cars and deploy. The three vehicles pulled up four hundred metres from the checkpoint, hoping for a soundless insertion.

They opened the car doors as quietly as possible and gathered the weapons they needed. Tam and Ricky hefted the heavy RPD machine guns across their shoulders while they advanced uphill with their C8 carbines. Shiner's Sharpshooter was cradled across his left arm while he powered up the hill with his precious NLAW on his back. They moved as quietly as possible up the rough track that Joe had identified, with frequent stops to listen for the enemy, until they reached an ideal position with a direct overwatch and line of fire above the Taliban checkpoint. Tam and Shiner selected firing positions as Ricky set up his RPD facing the target. He then busied himself with the Black Hornet aerial surveillance platform.

Time spent in reconnaissance is never wasted!

He had heard that a thousand times during his secondment to the Special Reconnaissance Regiment. The Londoner removed one of the Hornet nano drones from its pouch and carefully checked the cameras and battery life. The little drone had three forward-mounted cameras that provided fantastic clarity.

Good to go!

He opened the small tablet that would provide a live camera feed from above and gently released the Hornet from his hand. The little helicopter drone lifted with a flutter into the thin air of the valley as the team gathered around the tablet to look at their objective. The drone was almost soundless now at three hundred feet, and gave a literal bird's eye view. The valley would be a tourist's dream at any other time. The snow-covered Hindu Kush soared on either side as the blue-green ribbon of the river bisected its raw beauty. The last of the winter sun glistened off a thousand rocks along the river, which looked like a long opal necklace set with diamonds that stretched into the distance.

Ricky used the small joystick on the control panel to hold the drone at the hover as he scanned towards the checkpoint. It was a fortified building that had not changed since Massoud controlled the Valley of the Five Lions. The only thing the Taliban had altered was to rip down the posters of the Lion of Panjshir, which had adorned the walls on either side. The checkpoint stretched across the road and up onto the hillside, where a Taliban strongpoint protected it.

An American-manufactured MRAP was parked almost directly in front of the building. It appeared to be manned and mounted with a US Browning .50 calibre heavy machine gun that scanned ominously in their direction. Ricky assessed the enemy's strength. As he watched, a bored guard, who looked like a local policeman, left the main building and stretched. He was unarmed. Ricky could see him hide behind a wall, take a cigarette from his trouser pocket, and light up.

The Taliban had banned smoking in the valley since they arrived but could not stop people from wanting to smoke. The door of a nearby red freight container opened, and the man ducked back behind the wall. A black-clothed Taliban, armed with an AK47 looped loosely over his shoulder, looked up at the sky as if to check the weather and then shouted back inside the container. Three other Taliban guards appeared, adjusting their clothing and equipment.

A guard changeover, Ricky guessed.

Shipping containers were used all over Afghanistan for storage and accommodation, shops, and as makeshift prisons and torture chambers. It seemed strange to see them in a landlocked country, in the middle of a half-deserted valley. Billions of dollars of US aid had arrived in these ubiquitous bits of abandoned Americana. The rusted red container was serving as a place for the Taliban guard force to rest had 'TX Logistics, Texas' stencilled on the side.

Ricky then made a complete circuit of the valley with the Black Hornet to check for hidden surprises before he pressed the recall button. The little drone landed in his outstretched hand five minutes later.

"What do you think?" Joe asked the team.

"What are we going for?" Tam pitched in.

"Meaning what?"

"Maximum or minimum damage."

"According to London, minimum." Joe could almost feel the doubt that crept from his collection of special forces operators. They all knew that half-hearted assaults generally fail.

"Any suggestions?" Joe knew it was a wise leader who always sought counsel.

"That's gonna be difficult, Joe." Carl 'Shiner' Wright was scanning the checkpoint through the sight of his Sharpshooter and gestured toward the NLAW, which was prepped and ready to go and next to him. "Because when this fucker blows that MRAP away, it will incinerate everybody inside it."

"OK." Joe sighted his own weapon. "We just do what we need to do." Joe had outstanding issues with the Taliban anyway. He had lost good friends in Helmand.

"Fuck it, let's just do it!" Joe had made his decision. He ran through the plan one more time with the team. The Increment went into cover, looking down at their target, Carl with the NLAW and with the two others manning the RPDs. Joe then opened the radio to listen out for Ghazi's radio check that would inform him when the NRA was in position for the main attack.

Carl observed the MRAP through the scope of the NLAW and checked the red square-shaped safety switch. He had selected OTA or Overfly Top Attack. He knew it would blow his location as soon as he fired the missile. Although the back blast from an NLAW was significantly less than any other anti-tank weapon, it would still throw dust and snow into the air and betray the team's position. They had very little time to disable the armoured vehicle, engage the checkpoint with the two RPD machine guns and extract to the vehicles manned by the Triples on the road two hundred feet below. There was quiet now as each man concentrated on his immediate task. Joe had the channel to Ghazi open and heard only the gentle hum of static.

The team members were still listening to the hissing sound of the Harris radio that Ghazi had given them. They would engage the checkpoint as soon as the first shot was heard. Time seemed to stretch for ever. Sometimes, waiting is the worst part of warfare. It had always been the same, since a man long ago had chosen his first weapon and worked out how to use it to kill another man.

To Ricky, it was just like waiting for the bell to ring at the start of a fight. The stress slowly built up, only to be released in a flurry of controlled violence at soon as you heard the first *ding*. Not that Ricky feared violence - after all, it was one of the things he was good at. He nestled the butt of the RPD machine gun into his shoulder and watched over the sight. The Taliban guard force were now completing their changeover. He watched as three of them entered the rear ramp of the MRAP. *Poor fuckers,* he thought. *Not a good place to be.* He had hoped the MRAP would be empty before Carl used the NLAW.

Tam was manning the other RPD. He had carefully placed the belt of machine gun bullets clear of the surrounding rocks, so it would not snag, and had acquired his target. He would pour fire towards the rear door of the guard house as soon as the NLAW took out the MRAP. Joe had asked him to fire high to minimize casualties. But Tam was an ex-Para. If they stayed in the guardhouse, they would live. But they would be caught in a cone of fire overlapped by both guns if they deployed.

Big boys' rules.

Shiner again checked the safety on the NLAW. His Sharpshooter was resting next to him on the ground. As soon as he had destroyed the MRAP, he would ditch the tube of the missile launcher and pick up his favourite rifle. Joe sat with his back against his rucksack, facing toward where he could clearly see his Triples. They had adopted fire positions protecting the vehicles. A wintry sun glinted on the windscreens. The white Shahada flags flapped in the slight mountain breeze. The Harris HH-7700 radio was still buzzing in the background. It was like white noise for his thoughts. The longer they waited now, the greater was the risk of discovery, and every minute stretched a nerve.

Could I have done this a different way? Probably, but too late now. It's shit or bust!

Chapter 29

In Afghanistan, and especially in the Panjshir Valley, warfare is tribal and generational. It is bound together by brotherhood, blood, bloodshed, and revenge and is, therefore, very much a family affair. Ghazi stood between the two mortar teams as he watched the Taliban fighters of the Badri Brigade trudge up the ancient, cobbled street of the village. The man on his right was his uncle and the oldest man in his unit, whom they called Firuz Rocket. The mortarman on his left was Ghazi's cousin and the old man's son, still called 'Little Rocket' even though he towered over his father. Firuz Rocket had been a famous Mujahadeen when the Soviets had been in Panjshir, and he had taught his son everything he knew about how to fire a mortar. A good team with lots of practice can fire over twenty rounds a minute. Ghazi knew that he had the best two men for the job.

He watched the Talibs' slow progress up the hill. A mortar strike always works better in an open space but within a confined area, and the narrow main street of the deserted village provided both. It is especially effective when, as here, there are stone walls to contain and reflect the blast: the sharp steel fragments of a mortar bomb could then bounce off the walls into the human flesh that was unwittingly making its way into the killing zone. Ghazi was happy. He turned on the Harris radio selected Joe's channel and sent.

"Hello India One, this is Golf One." He spoke loudly even though he did not really need to.

"STAND BY, STAND BY."

****

Ghazi's voice breaking through the white noise of Joe's handset was a welcome relief. The waiting, the worst part, was over. The team needed no further instructions and snapped into action. As Joe replied, "India One, roger that," he thought he could hear the faint thump of mortars further down the valley.

Tam and Ricky got comfortable and adjusted their fire positions behind the RPDs, as Shiner pressed the NLAW into his shoulder and looked through the cross-sight until the inverted arrow of the graticule rested slightly over the top of the MRAP. The Taliban below were about to be attacked by a blend of weaponry that spanned fifty years and two Tajik insurgencies. The old-school Soviet RPDs were combined with one of the most advanced anti-tank weapons ever devised. Technological innovations and microchips from six countries combined to make the NLAW a tank killer that would swoop down on the MRAP at over 400 miles an hour. Carl had selected OTA, or Over Top Attack. He clicked off the safety and thought he could feel the internal computer whirring as it automatically assessed both the target and the distance, and then armed the 155mm HEAT round. When the magnetic and optical sensors finally triggered the shaped copper charge flying one metre above the target, there would be no survivors.

Shiner depressed the trigger. There was a whirring as the weapon acquired the target. He counted down the three seconds required to lock it on. The Ulsterman counted in the old-fashioned parachutist way:

One thousand, two thousand, three thousand.

The missile pinged a lock-on, and there was a whoosh and a blinding light as the missile left the launcher, climbed briefly, and then dipped sharply towards the target. The impact below was accompanied by the twin chatter of the RPDs stitching across the checkpoint. Shiner quickly threw the empty tube down, snatched up the Sharpshooter beside him, and sighted it. "Fuck me!" The damage had surprised even Shiner. "That's fucking carnage."

Two burning bodies of what had once been Talib fighters were clearly visible, having been blown out the back of the MRAP's open ramp. The ultra-expensive, state-of-the-art APC (Armoured Personnel Carrier) was ablaze, its exterior shell warped by the pressures of the explosion inside its walls. Joe shouted "STOP!" and the two RPDs complied. "WATCH and SHOOT." This was a command familiar to any British Army soldier: it meant you ceased fire and waited for enemy movement.

As Carl (Shiner) Wright scanned the area with the sight of his rifle, he spotted a couple of Taliban fighters that had been sheltering behind the checkpoint's low sandbagged wall. Unfortunately for them, they were on the wrong side of it. He acquired the first target as he was frantically sighting his own weapon and placed a heavy 7.62 round into his back. The other Talib was just standing and turning towards him as he caught him with two rounds in the chest. The force of the bullets pushed him over the sandbags, and then there was only the crackle of the burning MRAP and the sound of floodwater rushing over the boulders in the Panjshir River.

"Let's go!" Joe checked his watch as he led the mad scramble back towards the cars. Shiner slung the empty NLAW across his back and moved with his Sharpshooter. Ricky and Tam grabbed the RPDs and ran with their rifles slung over their shoulders. The quickest route down was over a scree run that toppled with them as they half ran, half slid towards where the Triples had prepped the doors of the cars for a quick getaway.

The Afghan Commandos covered them as they mounted up and then took the lead as they sped towards the checkpoint. The subterfuge of the Taliban flags was no longer required as they carefully negotiated the carnage of their former target. There was no one left alive. The lead vehicle stopped, Farzin debussed and opened the barrier, and then they were finally in the Panjshir Valley. A series of loud explosions sped them on their way as the ammunition still stored inside the MRAP's hull started to cook off. The team was now speeding towards the sounds in front of it, where the crump of mortars and the staccato crack of gunfire rebounded off the valley's walls.

Tam was driving the second Increment vehicle, with the Belfast man riding shotgun on the passenger side. "I know you were anti-tanks, Shiner, but we didn't have that kit when we were in. How did you learn to use it?" The Ulsterman smiled and gave the answer "YouTube, mate!"

★★★★

The mortar strike had been particularly effective with its first salvo. Two bombs had exploded simultaneously within the tight confines of the village street, and half the Badri 313 men were down. The killer they called White Death was one of them. An 82mm mortar bomb had landed next to him, and a large razor-sharp shard of it had taken the head off the man in front. The blast had lifted the assassin bodily, as with a swat of a giant hand, and smashed him into a granite wall.

He did not know how long he had been out as his eyes twitched open. He tasted a bitter mixture of dust and blood in his mouth as his head cleared. He knew he had been wounded, although he felt no pain; a piece of Russian shrapnel thirty years before had prevented that. He touched his face lightly with his fingertips. A tiny sliver of the bomb had punctured his cheek, and he felt blood oozing from it. He pulled it free and held it in the half-light to examine it. He was soaked in blood, its clammy wetness and its odd metallic smell pervading his senses. Then he realised why. He felt the heavy wet weight of the headless Badri fighter pressing down on his chest. Their blood had been mixed, and they were now blood brothers in suffering and death. He pushed the corpse away from him and tried to stand, but his legs would not bear his weight. He banged his head again on the wall as he fell. Where there was once strength, he found only weakness. The last thing he heard before losing consciousness was the heavy crack of AK47s and M4s in the distance as the NRA started their advance through the village.

★★★★

Vauxhall, London

Damian looked concerned as he entered Collette's office. He knew that she was under pressure. The further up the intelligence food chain a person progressed, the more Her Majesty's Government expected. And, at his former wife's rank, an IR or an Intelligence Request was more akin to a peremptory demand. Faceless bureaucrats who never really ventured far from the corridors of power became instant experts wanting quick answers when they were squeezed from above. Collette and Damian both remembered how the so-called 'Dodgy Dossier' had been compiled before the second Gulf War. The Blob in Whitehall had just moulded some fiction with a little fact and a lot of supposition until it met their needs, and then developed a game plan around it. But, of course, there had been no Weapons of Mass Destruction found though lots of people had died. Collette and Damian had been junior officers in Six in 2003, but they had vowed that something like that should never happen again. Damian could tell that his ex-wife was not in a good place. Her face looked pale, and her eyes tired.

"When did you last sleep properly?" he said, with genuine concern in his voice. "I don't really remember." Collette smiled wearily. "Not since the guys have been on the ground, anyway." She busied herself by straightening her pink notebook in its usual position on her desk and placing her pen precisely beside it.

"You need to start looking after yourself, Collette."

"There was a time when I thought I had somebody to look after me," the betrayed wife, rather than the MI6 woman, answered sharply. A brief awkward silence ensued before the secure phone rang. Collette was not going to answer it.

"If this is those bastards at Defence and Foreign Policy again, I shall scream."

"No, it's probably Langley." Damian used the VX term or metonym for the CIA headquarters in Virginia, USA. "I wanted to get your feedback before I talked to them." She looked at the number and recognised it. It was a man whom she had worked with, a good man. Alex McMahon was her opposite number at Langley; they had worked together to foil a terrorist bomb plot on the Queen Mary 2, four years earlier.

"Alex, how can I help you?" Collette said sweetly.

"A little bird tells me," Alex said, "that you have people in my old stamping ground."

"A little bird?"

"Yeah, well, not strictly true, more like a very complex satellite surveillance system backed up by TECHINT in the Panjshir Valley and HUMINT within the NRA, but you get my drift."

"What do you want?" Collette said.

"Anything you have on Ukraine. I'm getting the same shit from above that you probably are."

"Yes, but I need something from you. Do you want to play ball?"

"Pitch away," Alex said.

"We will need a Reaper on standby to help extract our people." Collette was referring to the MQ-9 Reaper long-endurance, multi-role UAV used extensively by the CIA. It was armed with four AGM-114 Hellfire missiles and two laser-guided bombs.

"You've got it." The CIA man had had no hesitation.

"And we might need a US resettlement package for a very interesting Russian."

"I'm pretty confident that you'd get that, too.

When do I get the green light for the information?" Damian was standing by her desk, listening on speaker. He lifted his thumb. "You've got it." Collette had selected Alex's secure email, quickly attached the latest report, and sent it. "As always, it's a pleasure doing business with you," said McMahon. And he rang off.

CHAPTER 30

The killer once again opened his eyes in the pitch blackness. He listened as he tried to clear his head. A thousand strange thoughts sought to cloud it. His damaged brain had conjured up the same vivid dream. He was a child, back in his home village in Nuristan and in his mother's arms. They were wrapped around him tightly in a death embrace. They were cold, and he had to use all a four-year-old's strength to release himself. His first view of death was of the woman who had loved him most. They had battered her head in with an axe while she protected him. Her blood had made them think that he, too, was dead. History had repeated itself; the headless man's blood had camouflaged his survival, and the NRA had gone.

His mind refocused on his mission. The only weapon that the Tajik insurgents had left behind was his own. The mortar strike had turned it into a useless horseshoe shape and it was obviously beyond repair. But he still had some advantages. He still had his NVGs (Night Vision Goggles). He removed his Kevlar helmet and felt carefully for other injuries.

None serious.

He knelt on one knee as he looked through the NVGs. The village had become green and ghostly but visible. He was surrounded by death, but he liked it. He focused the goggles and realised that he was the only person left alive. Some of the Badri men had been dispatched with a gunshot between the eyes - *there was no mercy in the Valley* – while others had been mutilated by the mortar strike. The sight did not distract him. Death was his friend. He slowly got to his feet, steadied himself, and felt for his precious knife in its leather holster on the inside of his left forearm. It was still there. He smiled.

He then pulled the NVGs forward over his face and smiled. The killer, whom they called Igor Dumo Kalash, or the White Death, now half walked and half stumbled down the hillside, his direction dictated only by the slope that the deserted stone settlement was clinging onto. His brain seemed to be on autopilot, his body devoid of both pain and emotion. His only concern was his mission. He knew where he had to go. Somewhere cold and dark - and just like his soul. The dark had always been his friend, and now he had his NVGs to give him an edge. He balanced his knife in his right hand; its fine carbon steel felt light and well-balanced. As he stalked towards the old mine, the black polymer hilt felt good in his grip.

★★★★

The team was speeding through the valley now. The Triples led the way, with the white Shahada flag still fluttering from the front of each vehicle. The place was more deserted than usual. However distant, the crump of mortars and the crackle of small arms usually had that effect. Driving into danger rather than away from it was something counter-intuitive for the Increment, but necessity always drives action. Joe was at the wheel of the Toyota, while Ricky was studying the Firm's iPad. It clearly showed the small blue triangle of Mac's current position, just further down the valley, from where they could hear the din of combat. Sound travels further in the Panjshir Valley. It resonates from its mountainsides and reverberates along the river, doubling in intensity in a natural echo chamber.

"How far have we got to go?" Joe was concentrating on keeping pace with the Triples up front, while maintaining a decent distance so that he could help them if they ran into trouble, and he knew that the 333 Commandos were hoping for some.

"About 15 clicks." Ricky flicked the screen and checked the topography. "But they are a decent climb uphill. They must be in amongst that shit up front." He looked worried.

"Ghazi is supposed to deliver them to us."

"Do you trust him?" Ricky asked.

"Yeah." Joe turned the wheel sharply to avoid a boulder on the road. "He needs us as much as we need him."

"Why?" Ricky checked the rearview mirror for Tam and Shiner's car.

"They need US and UK help, and that will only come covertly through Six and Langley."

"Do you think they'll get it?" Ricky rechecked the screen.

"Fucked if I know, buddy. It's not our bosses making the decisions, it's the spineless bastards in Whitehall and the Beltway, but I hope so. The Panjshir people deserve our help. They are the lads fighting for their country when every other fucker has run away."

The conversation was interrupted by the radio. "Hi, Joe, this is Tam." Tam was looking at the live feed coming from the satellite. The picture was in green and ghostly grey.

"Send," Joe answered.

"We have what looks like a VCP (Vehicle Checkpoint) up front, five clicks."

"Roger that. Type?" Tam zoomed in on the screen. He could pick out the detail easily.

"It looks like a snap VCP, four armed men and a vehicle."

"Hello Farzin, you roger that?"

The senior 333 Commando travelling in the front car answered with his usual pseudo-cowboy accent. "Howdy Joe, let us clip their horns."

Joe decoded the 'cowboy'. "If they need clipping?" the Increment boss said, as the Afghan Commando changed lingo into Royal Marine slang.

"Hoofing!"

★★★★

Katya had always thought that the saddest sight you could see after a battle was the dead. Poets and patriots have always talked about *the Glorious Dead,* but there was nothing glorious about how you looked when your life had been violently ejected from your body. The sight brought profound sadness to any soldier involved in combat, and she was no exception. The NRA was now searching the bodies for 'items of intelligence', which is usually military code for looting. And why not? The Badri men had better equipment than they had.

Searching a dead body has its own technique, refined and taught by people who have seen it go wrong before. First, a visual check of the whole area of the corpse for trip wires and boobytraps. Then you grasped the fallen with both hands on the side furthest away from you and pulled, so you could immediately let the body fall back into position if there was a grenade. After that, it was a straightforward search. The Russian woman noticed that the older insurgents got this right, and the younger ones copied their example. It occurred to her that the oldest of them might have searched the bodies of her former Russian comrades in the same way. She tried not to think about it.

Mac was sitting with his back to a low stone wall and appeared deep in thought. He was turning the large coin Massoud had once given him in his right hand as if in a trance. Katya now knew that this was his method of problem solving. The movement of the silver Thaler suddenly stopped; the coin was flipped into the air, rotated multiple times, caught, and placed back into his pocket. She knew this was a sign that he had come up with a solution.

"What's the plan?" The Russian spy had her own plans but wanted to know whether Mac's intermeshed with them.

"We stay here until morning. Find somewhere to rest up, eat, wash and sleep."

Katya smiled; she was now beginning to detect the sour odour of the unwashed on her own body, subtly mixed with the slight tang of goat shit. It was not the scent she was used to wearing. *It is pungent and strong, but I don't see it catching on,* she thought.

"That sounds like a great idea. Where?"

"Somewhere away from here, behind the lines, maybe at the top of the village. I will ask Ghazi."

"But we will be further from the road and the mine."

"But we will be safer until morning. If there's a counterattack, we will get a warning. Remember - the Badri guys have NVGs and the good guys haven't."

"That sounds like a plan." Both operators wearily got to their feet and went to talk to the NRA commander.

★★★★

Farzin put his foot down as the Toyota sped towards danger, just as mortal danger sped towards the Taliban. The Triples had earlier stopped momentarily, discussed their plan, checked that the car doors opened easily, loaded the RPDs, and checked brass on all the weapons. It was going to be a standard car drill, something they had practised a thousand times with their British Special Forces mentors in Kabul. A four-man team splits into two groups. The two operators in the front seats step out of the vehicle - in this case, with the two old Russian machine guns - and engage the enemy from behind the open armoured doors of the car. The other pair exit on either side, fan out while they have covering fire, and then engage the enemy VCP from the flanks. Both pairs then use fire and movement to fight through the enemy position. It only needed SAS, or *Speed, Aggression, and Surprise*, to work, because action is always faster than reaction.

★★★★

Mac checked the door of the small stone-built house for booby traps before he pushed it open with his shoulder. It was one of the few houses left that still had a roof. It had been a family home before the Taliban had arrived in the Panjshir Valley, and it looked like they had left in a hurry. Mac shone his small pen-light torch over what they had left behind. A smashed framed photograph of Shah Ahmad Massoud lay on the uneven stone floor. Some scattered cooking utensils cluttered the area near the open granite hearth, along with a large, blackened cauldron.

Katya picked up a small stuffed animal, a child's toy, by the door. It was made in the traditional rural way, hand sewn, usually by the mother, from any material that could be recycled. This small figure looked like a horse and had been made from the hemp of a seed bag and dressed in pieces of bright clothing. It was a sad sight, maybe dropped from a baby's grasp as the family struggled to escape. There had been widespread reports of massacre since the fall of Panjshir. She held the small toy and thought,

I hope they made it.

Mac spoke. "It's not the Lanesborough at Hyde Park Corner." He was referring to Katya's usual London hangout.

"Please don't worry, Mac; it's better than the hole in the rocks we shared on the mountain, and I was born in a house just like this."

"Where?"

"Further up the valley, near Bagram, a small village on the side of a mountain near Charikar. It was the only part of the valley held by the Soviets then." Katya's memories made her look misty-eyed. "It was slightly larger but had the same layout. I will get a fire going." Katya moved to a small cupboard to the side of the main hearth and opened it. There was enough kindling to start a decent blaze. "This is the same as where my mother kept her firewood." And she started to clear the hearth.

Mac picked up the cauldron. "I will collect water."

He had lived in such surroundings for more months than he cared to remember. Your perception of comfort changes according to circumstance. This small house would have been the height of luxury when it had been a choice between living inside four walls or shivering on a mountainside. That was a lifetime ago when he was helping Massoud against the Soviets. A thought occurred to him as he checked the action on his MX Rattler and closed the door behind him.

I'm an insurgent against the people who, a year ago, were the insurgency. Afghanistan is some fucked up country!

When Mac had left, Katya busied herself tidying the small cooking space. She momentarily felt snatched back to a simpler, happier time. She started to prepare a meal from the ingredients that Ghazi had provided. She would make a traditional Panjshiri dish called Korma. It was a thick stew with a base of fried onion and garlic. The meat was of unknown origin, although she suspected it might be from one of the mules that hadn't made it through the battle. Ghazi also provided some vegetables, chickpeas and spices. She worked quickly with the knife from the Badri man she had killed. By the time Mac returned the fire was burning, and the small room was warming. The smoky aroma of wood pervaded the small space and made it seem more welcoming.

Mac knocked on the door rapidly four times and creaked it open. The Russian had gone instantly from domestic to defensive and was aiming her MX at his shape as he walked through the low stone doorway. Mac beamed a smile. "Hardly a nice welcome back."

"It's still Panjshir, Mac," she responded.

"Yes, and you are right to take no chances."

"So, what's the plan?" Katya placed the weapon down.

"I think we eat, and then we wash, and then we sleep, and then tomorrow morning, we meet up with the extraction team and get the fuck out of here."

Katya's eyes seemed to twinkle.

"Anything else?"

"After we wash?" Mac could smell his own pungent odour.

"Yes, after we wash and before we sleep." She turned, took the cauldron from him and placed it on the fire. He sat down with Katya and placed his arm around her. The flames of the fire danced and highlighted shadows across the whitewashed walls.

There was a moment of silence, and then he said, "The eat, wash, and sleep routine. Does it necessarily have to be in that order?"

Katya turned towards him. Her emerald eyes widened and twinkled as they reflected the flickering flames of the fire.

"No, any way you want," she said, as they kissed.

Chapter 31

The fighter at the Taliban VCP had just arrived in the Valley of the Five Lions. He was from Kandahar and felt the cold as soon as his bones started to chill in the Hindu Kush. He had been flown into Kabul airport in a Pakistani Air Force C-130E Hercules transport aircraft. He had been given an intelligence brief on Panjshir by the ISI officers that had arrived at the same time and rushed by truck with his other comrades to join the offensive to crush the Tajik apostates in Panjshir. It was not the first time he had seen action. Zalmai had already fought ISISK (Islamic State Khorasan) in both Kunar and Nangahar and was used to killing. The Taliban soldiers that fought against ISISK were now Kabul's answer to any internal unrest, whether it was women protesting in Kabul or the Tajik dogs they were now attacking in the mountains.

He looked through night vision binoculars that had once belonged to an ISISK commander. The road in front was clearly visible as a light green strip against a darker green background. It straddled the river as far as the eye could see. The first moving thing he saw was a set of headlights breaking over the edge of the horizon. A single car travelling fast. He immediately cocked his AK47 and shouted at his comrades to get ready. It was a curfew and a free-fire zone, so they could kill anybody still on the road.

Farzin slowed down and stopped two hundred metres from the checkpoint. He then looked through his own NVGs and made an assessment. He scanned the road beyond the VCP, where he could see a Ford Ranger pickup truck. This vehicle had been the backbone of the Afghan National Army and was now the Taliban's favourite ride. The Afghan commando was checking that the checkpoint did not have what the military textbooks called *defence in depth*. It appeared that it did not. Farzin pulled out a torch and flashed it six times at the vehicle; this was what informers in the Valley had said was the Talib recognition signal. The Triple smiled as he got three flashes back. "OK," he muttered quietly to himself. "Let's round them up." And he gave his orders to his team in Dari.

★★★★

Zalmai did not quite know why he felt so uneasy, but he knew something was not right. He focused his NVGs and saw what looked like a Shahada banner. The white flag was never usually flown at night, for obvious reasons. "Be careful, brothers," he shouted as the white Toyota with the flag rolled towards them and stopped. They were the last words he would ever say, as a line of 7.62 machine gun bullets stitched a pattern across his chest.

"GO!" was the only word the team leader had to shout, and the well-drilled team went to work. Farzin and his comrade opened the front doors and engaged their primary targets with the RPDs, and two Talibs were down. The two commandos at the rear were already out of the car and engaging two other Talibs that had overcome the shock of combat and had managed to return fire. Farzin felt two rounds smash into the armoured door of the Land Cruiser with resounding clangs. Aimed double taps from the Afghan commando's M4, followed by sustained bursts from the RPDs, silenced them. The team then stormed through the enemy position, stopping only to put a single shot through each Talib's head.

There was no mercy in the Valley.

Farzin checked the petrol gauge in the Ranger; it was three-quarters full. They would steal the fuel. He picked up the Motorola handset and sent his contact report.

"Hello India One, this is Farzin."

"Farzin send," came the immediate reply.

"Checkpoint clear, four X-rays down. Yankees, no casualties. Ammo good."

"Well done, cowboy," said Joe.

"Hoofing!" said Farzin.

Within fifteen minutes, all three vehicles were driving down the valley towards the pick-up area. The small blue triangle showed Joe where Mac and Katya were sleeping, but an approach uphill at night through what might be a battlefield was not a wise move. They would have to wait until morning, and the two agents would have to come to them. He sent London a flash message. They would need the helicopter extraction. He then sent a message to Mac.

FLASH FIELD URGENT

From India One.

Going firm in the general area of

GPS Latitude. 35.29559° or 35° 17' 44" North.

Longitude. 69.50077° or 69° 30' 3" East.

Will await your arrival.

Joe

★★★★

You know you are tired when you can sleep through scattered bursts of gunfire. The last flames still glimmered in the hearth as Mac woke with a start. It sounded like the sharp crump of an RPG grenade from further down the village. He guessed the NRA was clearing the last of the houses by the road. They had slept interlocked in warmth and love amongst the family's former bed covers and clothes. A goat skin rug that Katya had found hidden under the sleeping platform had insulated them and provided comfort. She woke just after him, and they both prepared themselves. Nothing was said as they worked together to leave. No words were needed. The two lovers who, moments before, were sharing their body heat were now working like intelligence operators on a joint mission. The first equipment check is always the most important. The first thing the MI6 man did was check his comms. He smiled as he read Joe's message and prepared for the day.

The Russian SVR woman codenamed Babushka nodded to Mac as she disassembled her own MX Rattler while Mac checked his MX for brass. Only one of them would clean their rifle at a time. She then assembled hers before Mac started to clean his. They then removed every piece of kit from the rucksacks and checked it for serviceability. Katya took the combat knife she had used for preparing the food the night before and placed it in her waistband.

And then the final check. They worked together, one operator checking the other for loose equipment or rattles. They then scoured the small house for anything they might have left behind. Mac then checked the Firm's handheld. He could see the Increment's tracker down in the valley, not far from the GPS location they had been given. He looked at the time. It was just before sunrise. He then opened the heavy wooden door that had protected them in the night and walked out into the cold breeze of a Panjshir winter. A light flurry of snow invaded the warmth of the small house as Katya slung her rucksack onto her back, placed her weapon in her shoulder, and followed him. The two spies were now on their own, as the NRA was too busy with the Taliban to provide an escort. It was at least five clicks to the RV (rendezvous point) over what, at that moment, was the most dangerous part of Afghanistan.

Chapter 32

Collette's office, VX

After Damian left the office, Collette did not know whether she was relieved or disappointed. The visit had been all business and solely focused on what the Americans wanted in trade for helping them in Panjshir. Their previous very enjoyable post-marital tryst was left unmentioned. Her former husband never usually had a problem mixing work with pleasure. *Maybe he was a reformed character?* She dismissed the thought as she dialled Danny's number.

The former intelligence officer was having the closest he ever got to a religious experience in the twenty-first century. He had just had his first sip of a very expensive Laphroaig old-strength cask whisky when his personal mobile sounded with the opening bars of Rule Britannia. His grimace turned to a grin when he checked who the caller was.

"Collette, how are you?"

"Fine, Danny, and you?"

"Tip top." He took another sip. "What can I do for you?"

"The reverse of before." The MI6 woman veiled her speech. "I will ring you on the other means to chat."

"Roger that." Danny stopped the call, took his encrypted phone from his desk drawer, and turned it on. It vibrated straight away, and Collette spoke.

"We need an urgent extraction from Panjshir."

"When?"

Collette cut to the chase, "With an airframe on standby to move ASP from tomorrow early morning, Kabul time."

"Can you give me precise timings?" Danny was aware of the difficulties of the request.

"No, unfortunately not. Things are somewhat fluid at the moment."

"How many pax?" Danny used the military abbreviation for passengers.

"Ten; is that possible?"

"Yeah, that's possible, but the airframe will have to wait on the Tajik side of the border to get the call, and then it will be within two hours of the LZ (Landing Zone) in the Panjshir."

"Yes." Collette looked at the trackers on her desktop computer. "That would work."

"OK, I will talk to our friends in Dushanbe, but I might have to negotiate with the NRA leadership."

"When will you know if it's a go?"

"Give me two hours, and I'll ring back." Danny looked at the glass in front of him and placed it to one side. He now had work to do, and the Laphroaig would have to wait.

"But like the whisky I'm sipping, it's going to be expensive. Whose budget?"

"Mine."

"OK, I will make the calls."

"Thanks, Danny."

"Always a pleasure, Collette." As Danny rang off, she hit the internal speed dial for her ex-husband.

Damian and the Spellcraft team can pay for this one.

★★★★

Mac and Katya were descending the long steep village path that would take them through what had just been a battlefield and down into the valley. The weapons were hidden from view but readily accessible under the traditional Tajik patoo blankets they wore around their shoulders. The MI6 officer knew that the extraction phase was usually the most dangerous part of any military operation or spying mission. As it was in this case, as the element of surprise had gone, the enemy was everywhere, and the people who had been protecting them were now busy just protecting themselves. Mac went through a mental checklist to assess the risks as they both negotiated the slippery cobbled path. He called them the what-ifs.

What if they had been betrayed? After all, the Taliban ran agents as well.
What if they ran into a Badri patrol?
What if the NRA had been defeated?

There were always more questions than answers involved in such an internal brainstorming session, and that could lead to a thousand dark thoughts. He tried not to think of them. In the end, if you could not mitigate the risk, you just had to accept it.

You made your decision and took your chances. And it was what it was; spying is a dangerous game!

As they moved through the village, the evidence of the recent attack was everywhere. The distinctive smell of gun smoke hung in the air. The soundtrack for their exfiltration was provided by a distant, odd, angry exchange of gunshots, with the fearsome crump of a mortar or the crash of an incoming RPG.

The two operators also had to sometimes negotiate a passage through and around the dead. In the killing area of a mortar strike, six Taliban bodies had been tipped haphazardly into the confined space, one man's limb interconnecting with the next until the whole path was covered in a gory jigsaw of death. They had been stripped of their boots, weapons, clothing and dignity. It was a sad sight. Mac noticed that some had received a single shot to the head, while the last man in the row did not even have a head. Mac and Katya had seen such sights before, in previous insurgencies.

There was no mercy in the Panjshir Valley.

Mac stopped in his tracks and just looked up, his face reflecting his appreciation. A Panjshir dawn is like no other. The burgeoning sun was just beginning to break the skyline, its deep red glow picking out the snow-topped mountains opposite like sparkling jewels. It made the contrast between life and death starker, as the life-giving sunlight shimmered over the dead. It was like life and death instantaneously combined in the same moment, the light and darkness of existence illuminated by nature. He looked around at Katya, who was also looking up. They both seemed connected at that moment, in the presence of those who had ceased to be, both looking over the edge of life and into the future. He felt a connection with her that he had never felt with anyone else. He snapped out of his thoughts and checked his GPS. The silence of the morning was broken by the distant wail of the call to prayer. Death and warfare stopped for Islamic devotion in this part of the world.

"How far?" Katya pulled the blanket around her shoulders; the sight of the dead made her shiver.

"Four clicks, but a dangerous four clicks." Mac took a knee and looked through the scope of the MX. "We might have to go into hard cover for a while." 'Hard cover' was SF talk which meant taking immediate shelter to prevent a firefight or compromise.

"OK." Katya pulled down the hijab covering her face, "But let's try to get as close as we can. I need some time on target."

"What target?" There was an edge of concern in Mac's voice.

"I will tell you when we stop," she half whispered. "But it's something that I need to do before I leave Panjshir."

"OK, I will help you if I can." From the tone of Mac's voice, she knew he meant it.

★★★★

Katya and Mac had taken shelter behind a stone wall, the last vestige of what used to be a mosque. The sun was rising over the other side of the valley and warmed their faces. Mac used his binoculars to scan the valley floor. He focused on the grid reference where the Increment should be waiting and immediately understood why they were not there. The position was bare-arsed, without a scrap of cover, and Mac guessed that the India team leader was waiting somewhere safe until the flight was inbound. He took the Firm's handheld from his rucksack and checked their latest position. The blue triangle indicated that the team was tucked in by the mountain. Mac pulled out and checked the old Russian map; the position was marked as an old mine-working.

"OK, they are near the old mine; we will go to them," the MI6 man said.

"That's where I need to be," Katya answered.

"What do you mean by that?" Mac was still scanning the valley.

"It is what I wanted to tell you, Mac. It is my secret, and I need your help."

"Secret?" Mac said, "Our lives are full of secrets, Katya, so I think we can share another."

There was a pause as Katya considered her reply. "When I was in this valley before, I was in love with a young man who died. I believe that he is still in the place his murderers put him. I want to recover his body."

"You can't be serious." Mac looked across at Katya, and as their eyes met, he knew she was. "We will work something out, but the living take preference." He looked into Katya's eyes again. "And only if it doesn't endanger the lives of the guys that have been sent to help us."

"Agreed." The Russian woman smiled.

"OK." Mac slung his rucksack on his back and moved towards what once was the doorway of the ruined mosque.

"Let's go."

★★★★

They had parked the vehicles off the road in what appeared to be an old mining area. A high berm made up of the detritus of a hundred years of emerald production shielded the team. This served two purposes: it both hid the vehicles and made an ideal defensive position. The Triples had set up the two machine guns facing towards the area of potential threat. The remainder of the unit busied themselves servicing the kit. Ricky checked the battery levels on the Black Hornet base station while Shiner checked the action on his Sharpshooter. Tam was still checking the cars. In the British Army, it's called a 'First Parade Service', normally carried out at the start of the working day, but in the Increment it also happened any time you needed the cars for the next phase of an operation. The sequence was always the same. You checked the tyres, the oil, the water levels, and the brakes, but:

Fuel was the most urgent problem.

Joe and the team were now within five clicks of the suggested LZ, but that was a non-starter tactically. The GPS coordinates they had been given placed the landing zone in a wide-open area, overlooked by both sides of the valley and within heavy machine gun range of any Taliban vehicle that might be driving along the only tarmacked road. A drastic rethink was needed. A perfect night-time/dark hours agent extraction was no longer likely. Joe's time spent on Special Forces operations in Iraq and Afghanistan with the SBS had taught him that, when a hot extraction was needed, giving a precise geographical point as an LZ just did not work. Hot LZs had to be flexible to be feasible, and a safe point of departure could only be chosen by the person on the ground. One of the maxims of Six training was 'the four Ps: *Proper preparation produces perfection.*

So, he needed to change the LZ. He pulled out the sat phone, activated the cypher mode, and waited. The phone beeped as it acquired the uplink, and then he tapped in the number. Ernie answered immediately. "Joe, how's it going?" The Increment boss seemed relieved to hear from him. "It's been interesting, Joe said.

He looked down at the SITREP he had tapped into text message format ready to cypher and send to London. A SITREP was the British Army's term for a situation report. It was a standard formula for quickly covering what Ernie needed to know and the actions that needed to be completed. "I'm passing the SITREP now," Joe said, and pressed Send.

06.15 KT (Kabul time)
Lat. 35.29559° or 35° 17' 44" North.
Long. 69.50077° or 69° 30' 3" East.
Arrived in the general area of pick-up.
We are awaiting the clients.
Helicopter extraction is needed as high levels of enemy activity prevent vehicle extraction to the border.
Team OK, Task OK.
At RV and waiting out.

There was a pause as Ernie scrolled through the text.
"What else do you need?"
"A helicopter, some luck, and a cold beer when I get back."
"I will try with the first, hope for the second, and definitely supply the third when you get to the Smoke."

"Sounds good; when will we know about the airframe?"

"Within one hour; I will text you back." Ernie was already speed-dialling Collette's secure line. "OK, roger that, and well done, Royal."

"Roger that, Boss," Joe said, as he finished the call.

Joe turned to the rest of the team. In the world of special operations, decisions are made by consultation rather than by command, and ideas are generated by group discussion rather than diktat. It was a way of harvesting the team's experience for the greater good. And anyone who shared the same risk had the same interest in getting it right. "OK, boys, what's the crack? Open to a bun fight, guys. What do we do now?" A bun fight in the Oxford Dictionary is defined as *a heated argument or exchange,* but in the Special Forces it is more like exchanging ideas to enhance operations.

Tam was the first to speak. He had been with Mobility Troop in B Squadron 22 SAS and knew everything to do with getting from A to B by car with a minimum of complications. "Hey, we've got problems with fuel, and there's a shit load of road to cover to Tajikistan." He shrugged. "I suggest we arrange a mobile RV with a heli extraction, just like we did in Iraq when a job was compromised."

"When will the air be on standby?" Shiner pitched in.

"I need that confirmed, but Tajikistan is two hours' flying time, so, inshallah, about two hours after we ask for it," Joe said.

"Well, let's get the pick-up done and then drive like fuck until we can call the chopper into a safe LZ." Ricky seemed to have found the obvious solution.

"OK," said Joe. "We meet the agents, get them into the cars, and call in the aircraft while we get the fuck out of Dodge. Does everyone agree?"

The statement was met with a nodding of heads. *Democracy rules,* Joe thought.

"Right." Joe looked towards the entrance of the old mineworkings and directed his question to Ricky. "Would I be right in thinking that your flying toys can help find our two guests?"

"Yes." Ricky pulled one of the small drones from its resting place by its control panel. "We have a superb lens on this." He was pointing to the tiny forward-mounted camera on the drone.

"OK." Joe pointed towards the side of the mountain. "If I give you a GPS fix, can you do an overflight to find them?"

"Yeah." Ricky flashed up the Black Hornet control station. He picked up the small bird-sized camera drone, held it in the palm of his hand and whispered to it. "We have work to do, little girl." And he let the drone power itself upward and then fly off towards the slopes above.

★★★★

London. MI6

Collette answered the phone immediately. The call display just said Hedges and Fisher, Danny McMaster's London-based security company.

"Hi, Danny."

"Hi, Collette, I have your helicopter."

"Excellent. When?"

"It can be ready to go in two hours. It will wait on the Tajik/Afghan border until it gets an approximate LZ."

"How many pax?"

"It's a Tajik M17 and has space for at least your ten."

"Thanks, Danny."

266

"Thank Amrullah Salah." Danny mentioned the former Afghan Vice President, who was organising the NRA offensive from Tajikistan. "It was done as a special favour for MI6, and he will need payback eventually."

"I will bear that in mind!" Collette was aware that political favours are never free.

"Can I give them the green light to move from Dushanbe?"

"Yes please, and thanks, Danny."

Chapter 33

The small piece of shrapnel that had made its permanent home inside the killer's brain had rendered him oblivious to pain and fear, the two things most important for human survival. He knew that he had been wounded in some way but was unaware of exactly where and had not had the time or inclination to find out. But he knew he was getting weaker, and that his end was near. He had used his NVGs all the way into the mine until the ambient light failed, and then he switched to infrared. He felt his way carefully along the long burrow of the horizontal mine shaft. He moved slowly, aware of his frail condition and the numerous boobytraps they had used to seal the mine all those years ago. He knew the way; his memory was still as sharp as the knife he carried. The infrared torch made the damp limestone glisten and illuminated ancient pickaxe marks on the bare rock. The only sound was the dripping of water, and the occasional flurry of leathery wings as a bat brushed past his face.

And then he arrived at the chamber. It had been used as a Mujahadeen store and hospital during the Soviet occupation. But thirty years before, it had been turned into a torture chamber. The area was illuminated by the glow of the torch, which made everything blood-red. The infra-red lit up the eyes of small, silky-skinned bats as they hung upside down from the cavern's roof like hundreds of shiny rubies. The young Russian man was still as he had left him, with his skeletal remains bound by ropes and attached to a makeshift cross in the centre of the space. This was where his best work had been done: removing a man's skin when he is still alive is a rare skill. At his feet lay the dummy nuclear device the Russian officer had tried to convince them was real. It was partly hidden by the bodies of the other Russians that formed a random heap of bones and skulls scattered around it. It reminded the killer of those pictures of the dying Christian God, Jesus, that Soviet soldiers had shown him as a boy.

The pilot's body hung together with its remaining tendons, perhaps preserved by the still-dry air. The young man's skull hung to one side, its jaw still attached by the last of the desiccated skin. The black cavern of the mouth gaped open and looked like it was still screaming. The killer remembered the living screams and felt cold. The tableau of torture made him think of the evil he had enjoyed, but also of his own death. He found a natural seat in the cave's wall and slumped his form into its recess.

Maybe this was the way it should end.

He had never been a believer. The Nuristani people had been forced by conquest to convert to Islam and had fought hard against it. The area had once been referred to as Kafiristan, or the land of the unbelievers. The ancient religion of his homeland was known as Kalash, and it was also his family name. It was an old faith that had existed before Islam, Christianity and even Buddhism. A dualist creed like that of Zoroaster, it espoused the idea of the twinned existence of good and evil locked in an eternal struggle, like two sides of the same spinning coin, which, on landing, for either good or ill, decided the destiny of men. As he thought about religion, he thought of his mother, who had protected him with her last breath.

He remembered her tight, cold embrace, her caved-in head, and her blood. He was now soaked in the Badri man's blood as he waited to kill Babushka. His mother had believed in both God and the undead. She had told him stories of avenging *Jinns, Divs,* or demons. He remembered the nights by the small house's open fire as she told him ancient folk stories. He remembered her lilting tones.

"They are the spirits of the undead, dispossessed but not extinguished. A Jinn cannot be killed by combat. One must find an object to store its soul in, so that you can command it."

The killer sat in the alcove in the wall and thought he felt the knife begin to warm against his skin and pulse rhythmically. It started to throb against the inside of his arm. He felt stronger, and he felt the power begin to flow again.

★★★★

It had only taken an hour for the two spies to find their extraction team. Mac had chosen the most secure route, traversing the side of the valley by a goat track and then dropping down a slippery scree run onto the mine-workings on the valley floor. They had stopped to identify themselves, but a flashing torch with the identification signal told them that the team had been following Mac's tracking device, and the slight buzz of the Black Hornet drone in the still air above confirmed it. The little drone swooped low over them, circled twice, and headed down onto the valley floor. They had been rescued. It was the first time they had both felt truly safe, or at least safer, since they had entered Panjshir. But there was no time for celebration. Ricky briefed Mac and Katya on the extraction plan as Joe flashed up the comms to call in the airframe. They had two hours before any pick-up, and they needed to be clear of the valley to achieve a safe extraction.

Ricky's last comment made sense. "If I were you guys, I would get some rest before we are out of here."

"Yeah, thanks, mate. How long have we got to wait?"

"Not long. We will move as soon as the airframe is in the area, but we need to be clear of the valley before calling in an LZ - maybe an hour, maybe two."

"Roger that," said Mac. The two spies talked as they found a place to rest.

"I don't think we will have time to look for Mikhail." There was a genuine tone of regret in his voice.

"No, I didn't think there was going to be." Katya sounded sad.

★★★★

Collette was at her desk and looking at a large TV monitor on the wall where the four essential working parts of the rescue mission were displayed. The team's tracker was now joined with Mac's in the same blue triangle in one corner of the screen, with the live feed from the American Reaper drone in the one opposite. The bottom of the screen showed a map and the estimated progress of the M17 from the Tajik border. The final space was filled with live satellite images from the Panjshir Valley. Everything seemed to be going to plan. Mac and the Russian had the protection of the Increment, and the helicopter had entered Afghan airspace and was on its countdown to pick-up. The armed Reaper surveillance drone was also inbound and should be on target to cover the exfiltration, as the team appeared to be ready to move away in their vehicles. She hoped to have the whole team back in Dushanbe by late afternoon and back in London the following day. It had been agreed with the FCO that the Triples would be evacuated and join the ARP (Afghan Resettlement Programme), as suggested by Ernie and Joe.

What could go wrong?

But she had previous experience of falling foul of the AFUF (Afghan Fuck-Up Factor), and *if something could go wrong, it would.*

★★★★

Mac and Katya felt safe. After a week where nerves had been stretched to breaking point, the sense of relief was palpable. They were both mentally and physically exhausted but greatly relieved. They were now clinging together and seated to the rear of the vehicles with their backs to a small stone wall. The sun had now fully risen over the valley and had vanquished the cold. Katya had rested her head on his shoulder. The body language said it all. The pretence that their relationship was purely professional had gone as they relaxed in the warmth of a Panjshir sunrise. He felt her hair against his cheek and closed his eyes as the gentle heat of the winter sunshine bathed his face. He turned and kissed her lightly on the cheek, and she kissed him back. It seemed like the stress of the last week had now lifted. They were going to be safe. He next heard the gentle purr of Katya sleeping as the feeling of safety, coupled with weariness, overcame them, and he closed his eyes.

As Mac dozed, the Increment team was busily preparing for the move. It seemed that every pair of hands was readying something. Two of the Triples were trying to sort out the last bandoliers of ammo for the RPDs, while the other two occupied the sentry position. Ricky was prepping and recharging the Black Hornet drone as Tam refilled the Land Cruiser with the remaining fuel from a jerry can. The big Ulsterman checked the frequencies they would need to call in the helicopter on the Harris radio. Joe was putting together the plan. He felt the weight of responsibility for everything as he studied the Firm's handheld and looked at the mapping and topography for the drive out. He needed to assess where, if he were the enemy, he would try to block them, and then think of a way around it.

He concluded that in that valley there was only one way in and one way out, and you could be observed from just about anywhere. The vehicles were channelled by the high ground in either direction, so they were probably better off driving towards Tajikistan, although this was the most obvious direction. At least this would give the airframe more fuel and, therefore, more time on target for the exfiltration. It was important, though, that they left as soon as possible while Terry Taliban was still getting a kicking from the NRA. He knew that, as soon as Kabul found their offensive was being outflanked, they would send more troops.

Chapter 34

Mac woke with a start. He was alone. He checked around him. Katya had taken her rucksack and weapon, *Fuck*. He knew exactly where she had gone. He felt the ground next to him; it was still faintly warm. He looked for tracks and saw a series of small size boot prints leading off towards the mountain. Mac made a quick decision as he briefly followed Katya's spoor, her small footprints hurrying quickly through the wet soil. He confirmed her direction. She was heading for where the Russian spy had unfinished business with the Soviet past. He needed to let the Increment know.

Mac's heart raced as he ran towards the team and found Joe still looking at the satellite coverage. It was the first time that Joe had seen any concern in the usually calm and controlled MI6 man's face.

"She's gone!" Mac barked.

"What do you mean, she's gone?"

"Precisely that."

"For fuck's sake," Joe muttered. His plans had dissolved in front of his eyes or, more precisely, when he had not been looking. "Any idea where?"

"She talked about needing to get to the old mine."

"What the fuck for?" He had lost one of his clients just as the plan was coming together.

"It's a long story, and I've no time, but I need to go after her."

"I can't let you do that," Joe snapped. "We have an extraction inbound and strict instructions from London for you to be on it."

"You haven't a choice, pal. I'm just letting you know. London doesn't make my decisions in the field." Mac turned on his heel and returned to track his fellow spy.

"Fuck!" was all that Joe could think of saying as he looked across at Tam and Shiner. He did not really have any choice but to follow. But the responsibility of leadership made sure that he did not rush thoughtlessly into danger. The what-ifs ran through his mind.

What if the Russian girl is doing the double?
What if it's a trap?
What if the Taliban get to them before us?

He then made his discision, "OK, lads, let's get after him; we'll give him some space but watch his back." "Roger that," the guys said in unison as they grabbed their weapons.

★★★★

It did not take long to pick up the two sets of tracks. Joe knelt to examine the spoor. They were both in the same direction, but Mac was moving quickly. He checked the Firm's handheld and picked up his tracker. He then unfolded an old Soviet map from his tactical vest and compared it with the screen.

"Mac's right: she's heading towards the old mine working," he said to Carl.

"What the flying fuck for?" Carl grunted in perfect Shankill Road.

"I'm a team leader, not a mind reader, Shiner! But my guess is it's something to do with her past."

"How long have we got to find them?" Tam and Ricky had joined the two other operators.

"An hour - tops!" He looked at Mac's tracker again. "And unless we find them, we're going on the longest E and E (Escape and

Evasion) exercise ever devised." He had an hour at most to recover the people he had been sent to extract from Afghanistan, or they were all in the shit.

★★★★

Katya held the MX Rattler in the 'ready' position lightly in her shoulder. She also had a red filtered penlight torch in the left hand cupped under the weapon's forestock. She was moving carefully now, placing each foot tentatively on the ground, weight on the heel first and then rolling it onto her toes, almost like a ghost walk. She knew that the Soviet Army had widely used anti-personnel devices like the PFM 1 butterfly mine in the Mujahedeen's tunnel network, and now was not a good time to lose a leg. The faint red light had picked up another set of footprints in the darkness. They were a man's boot prints, a tall man, a large man. It was too dark to know precisely how old they were, but they were recent, *and no footprints were going the other way.* She paused for a moment and scanned her front, with the sight on the MX set to infrared. The tunnel stretched into the darkness along with the boot prints. The right footprint was dragged along in the dust, as if the man were injured.

As she stood, a flutter of leather brushed her face. "BLAY'D" (*Russian for FUCK*). She shouted more loudly than she had wanted to. A small bat was entangled in her hair. She swiped her hand across her head and grabbed it free, and it fluttered off into the blackness. Her heart was beating harder now. The Russian spy took a deep breath to compose herself and then moved, following the trail into the darkest part of the tunnel.

★★★★

Igor Dumo Kalash, the killer from Nuristan, had sensed the presence of his prey before he heard her. Noise resonates in a cave, and Katya's swear word bounced in a sound wave that echoed along its limestone walls. The knife seemed to know she was there before he did. It was now warm in his hand and pulsing. He felt its edge. He imagined it thirsting for blood. The cold carbon steel needed nourishment. It needed her warm red blood. His hand held the knife tightly. He felt the polymer handle fit snugly in his palm as if it wanted to be there. And then he had a thought:

Was the knife his tool, or did he belong to the knife?

He pushed himself further back into the recess in the rock as she brushed past him. She screamed; her face contorted into an involuntary mask of grief as she was assaulted by the full horror of the scene. There was the boy she had loved a lifetime ago, skeletal and crucified and illuminated in red. The strength left her legs, she fell to a kneeling position, and then he was on her. Katya was dragged backward by an unseen hand with demonic strength. She left the dusty floor of the cave as if she had been jerked by giant strings, and then a growling red mask of hate was inches from her face. It was the face of the Devil.

The killer drew back his arm and felt the power of the knife flow into every part of his body. He felt omnipotent and strong. But Katya recovered her wits. She had landed hard on the cave floor and could hardly breathe. She reached into her waistband, and her knife was in her hand as she watched the killer draw his back for the fatal blow. And then he stopped, and his face turned from killing rage to one of puzzlement.

She was there. Reflected in the face of the woman he was about to kill. He saw his mother as he tried to plunge the knife into the Russian woman's neck. Her gentle face floated before him, superimposed over Katya's. He tried to pull back the knife, but the blade resisted. He pulled harder, but the knife pushed stronger, and then he *knew*. He remembered his mother's words:

"One must find an object to store its soul in, so that you can command it."

But he had always let the Devil's Jinn command *him*. He thought again of his mother, felt her loving arms encircle him once more, and smiled. In that fatal second of hesitation, Katya lunged upwards and plunged her knife up to its hilt into his neck while she stared into the killer's smiling face. Just as the blade sank home, the killer's head exploded outwards as a silenced double tap from Mac's MX Rattler thudded into it from just ten feet away.

★★★★

Joe came on aim with his C8 Carbine as two figures staggered out of the tunnel's darkness. He immediately recognised Katya and Mac, who was holding the Russian woman up with his arm around her waist. They were both blinking and trying to adjust to the light. Katya was drenched in the killer's blood, along with fragments of skull and brain. As Ricky and Tam went into fire positions to cover the flanks, the team leader and Shiner rushed to help. "Where's she been hit?" Joe swung his rucksack from his shoulder and reached for his medical kit. "She's just in shock. She will be OK," Mac replied, as he gently supported Katya as she slumped onto the ground.

The Russian spy was ashen-faced and sobbing silently. Joe was the team's combat medic. He placed his hand on her neck and felt her cool, clammy skin. Her breathing was far too rapid. He checked her pulse; it was racing. Her eyes were enlarged and saucer-like. He gave his diagnosis. He had recognised all the classic symptoms of traumatic shock.

"She just needs time to rest," Mac said. "How much time have we got?"

"The extraction is about forty-five minutes out." Joe checked his watch. "And we have no time!"

As he said that, the SVR officer looked up. "I will be OK." It was as if the frail woman who had just emerged into the sunlight had reverted to the former Spetsnaz girl. She lifted the MX Rattler from where it hung by her side and checked the weapon. "I'm still OK to fight." Mac was already moving as he said, "OK, let's get to the cars and get the fuck out of it."

From further up the slope, a man had been watching. The NRA were not the only people with spies in the valley. In hard times, a little money buys a lot of information. The hungry farmer had been supplied with a local Roshan mobile phone and ten US dollars by the Taliban. As the British team and the Afghan commandos sped away, he tapped in a number.

★★★★

It was a race against time now. The Triples in the lead car were driving fast, and the two Increment vehicles kept up. The telephone poles that lined the road flashed by faster as Ricky put his foot down. The original plan called for the helicopter extraction to be at an LZ of the team's choosing, but, like all the best-laid schemes, especially in Afghanistan, it had gone astray. Ricky was following the distant white dot of the Afghan commandos' Land Cruiser. He glanced at the fuel gauge, which seemed to be emptying fast. Next to him, Joe flashed up the Firm's tablet. It had the same display Collette had on her desktop, showing all the variables that ensured they could get home, but it all could change instantly.

One part of the screen showed the current satellite coverage of the Panjshir Valley. In another, a small red triangle showed the inbound helicopter against a geo-positioning map of Afghanistan. The bottom of the display alternated between the live feed from the Reaper surveillance drone and a small yellow arrow that represented its position. It had just crossed into Afghanistan's airspace. Now he needed to find a decent LZ before the fuel ran out.

Collette was looking at the same set of images. She checked her elegant Cartier watch and reached for the phone. It was time to get the techs to patch her through to the Command-and-Control facility at Creech Air Force base in Clark County, Nevada. Collette had worked with UAVs (Unmanned Ariel Vehicles) before in Baghdad while, according to the USAF's mission statement, they were engaged in *anti-terrorist operations using remotely piloted aircraft systems that fly missions across the globe.* The Reaper MQ-9 had recently replaced the Predator that Collette had used, operating out of Balad Air Force base in Iraq. It could carry a heavier weapon load, including eight Hellfire missiles and two laser-guided 230kg GBU-12 bombs. It had an operational altitude of 50,000 feet and a range of 1,850 km. Collette knew that, sitting in their control centre at Creech, there would be the drone's pilot, the sensor operator, and the mission intelligence coordinator. The aircraft would be flown remotely from the nearest Reaper hub to Afghanistan. The hub's location would never be confirmed by the CIA, but the MI6 woman guessed Qatar, or even Tajikistan. Her secure line rang, and she pushed the speaker button. "We are patching you through to Nevada," the tech said in echoing tones, and then three short rings and a voice answered. It sounded like a young woman receptionist.

"Hello, caller. Can you give me your access code?" Collette tapped in the random series of numbers that Alex McMahon, the

CIA man, had supplied, and she was through to the Command Center at Creech. The Reaper team was in position. The pilot was sitting to the left of an array of TV monitors in a high-backed swivel chair, and the sensor operator was to his right. The module looked like a giant computer gaming system, with the two screens angled outwards in a diamond shape that allowed them to view the drone's live feed simultaneously. A series of other screens told them everything they needed to operate the sky-borne killing machine. The intelligence officer was at the end of the room, hooked into the communications system. Each team member wore a gaming-type headset with the team's encrypted channel.

Collette knew how things at Creech worked. The Reaper team would have been fully briefed on the AO or Area of Operation, the mission, and what the Americans called *'the Intel profile'*. The Intelligence Coordinator was the first to speak.

"Hi, I'm the Intelligence guy; how can I help you?"

"Have you all the mission details you need?" Collette asked.

"Yeah, we're all ready to roll." The voice had a Texan accent.

"Time to target?" Collette said, as the man coordinator checked his display.

"We have overwatch in ten minutes. Will you need ordnance?"

"What's available?" The MI6 woman knew that a platform might have already been involved in another mission.

"We have a full load if you need it." That meant the Reaper had all its munitions on board: eight Hellfires and two laser-guided bombs.

"Hopefully not, but maybe!" Collette answered. "It could be a hot extraction."

"Roger that!" said the Texan.

Chapter 35

The Panjshir Valley looked beautiful, spread out below from forty thousand feet. It was divided between the stark shadow of the mountains of the Hindu Kush on one side and bright glimmering snow on the towering heights of the other. A long bending ribbon of green/blue water bisected the lowland between them. It was a colour that caught the light and reflected it with amazing clarity.

The most beautiful parts of the world are sometimes the most dangerous, the pilot thought, as he touched the small joystick on his control panel in Nevada and the Reaper turned to swoop, hawk-like, from altitude into a valley in Afghanistan. He tapped the Brit team's last coordinates into his keyboard and tilted the stick slightly to vector the Reaper towards them, and then he spotted the three-car package on the road below.

Collette was now listening to everything the Reaper team was saying. It was frustrating as it was the CIA's show now, and she was just a listener thousands of miles away from both the US Command Center and her team on the ground. The CIA officer controlling the drone had a clipped Bostonian accent that oozed confidence.

Pilot: "I have located Yankee One. Please confirm." They had designated the Increment cars as Y1." The Intelligence Coordinator came back within a minute.

"This is Intel. Confirmed."

Sensor operator: "Sensor. Roger that, confirmed." The sensor operator was a twenty-two-year-old CIA woman who had only just qualified from what they called *The Farm,* the vast CIA training facility of Camp Peary, near Williamsburg in Virginia. Her voice was light, Californian, but equally confident.

The pilot was the first to see the Taliban vehicles. As a matter of routine, he scanned down the only main road in the valley and then focused the Reaper's nose camera onto what had once been an Afghan Army Ford Ranger pick-up. The Ford appeared to be the lead vehicle of a five-car convoy.

Pilot: "Our friends have company - confirm."

Intelligence made the assessment. "Confirmed - five vehicles: one Ranger, one MRAP, and three trucks."

Sensor: "Confirmed - five vehicles: one Ranger, one MRAP, and three trucks."

★★★★

Joe was peering through the slightly misty windscreen of the Land Cruiser, looking for an LZ, when the Harris radio squawked into life. It was an American voice.

"Hello, India One, this is Tango One, over." Tango One was the helicopter's callsign. "Hello, Tango One. Send."

"Hi, Tajik Airlines here. We are ten minutes out and happy to welcome you aboard." The voice was American.

"Hello Tango One, I will send a possible LZ in two."

"Tango One, Roger that." Joe looked at the Firm's handheld, looked at the car's speedo, noted the speed, time, and distance, and got an approximate grid reference.

"Hello, Tango One. Pick up at MGRS..." He quickly reeled out the grid reference from the handheld while scrawling it on the back of his hand with a biro. Then "Hello, all stations India, this is Joe. Extraction inbound in ten minutes."

"Roger that." All the India callsigns were answered in numerical order.

Joe sighed with relief. It looked like the plan would work. The Tajiks would block the road to the front. The two remaining cars would block from the rear, and the helicopter would land as near to the road as possible. Simple plans always worked best in Afghanistan, *but what about the Afghan Fuck Up Factor?*

The AFUF was about to kick in. Joe's handheld computer tinged a warning. They had company. He examined the live feed and spotted a small convoy of vehicles closing fast. The only time you usually got a convoy of cars travelling fast in this part of the world was when it was either part of a tribal wedding celebration or a rapid troop movement.

Afghan tribal weddings might be a bit more dangerous than British ones, but they still didn't need an MRAP as a wedding car.

Joe then immediately picked up the radio handset to warn the incoming airframe.

"Hello Tango One, this is India One, over."

"Send, India One." The pilot answered immediately.

"Prepare for a hot extraction."

Radio procedure was forgotten for a moment on the airborne end. "How hot?"

"India One, we will not call you in until we have a secure LZ."

"Tango One, Roger, that would be greatly appreciated," the American pilot said. "We will hold over your position."

Joe said, "Thanks."

Katya had spotted the Taliban vehicles. She had been intently examining the rear-view mirror and spotted a small blip on the road closing fast. "Mac, we have company," she said calmly, her voice sounding a bit more Russian than usual. Just as she had identified the possible threat, Mac's satellite phone tinged from inside his rucksack. It was a text message from Collette: "*I will ring*". Mac opened the Iridium 9575 phone. As soon as he snapped open the ariel, Collette's voice was on the other end. "Mac, I have an emergency SITREP. Stand by."

"I'm standing by. Send." This was standard procedure when a lot of information needed to be passed quickly.

"You have five Taliban vehicles, including an MRAP with a .50 cal and three trucks. A Ford Ranger fronting and six up. The trucks have Badri Brigade markings and are closing fast. Reaper is on station and will help with extraction. Any questions?"

"No," Mac said, as he picked up the India team Motorola radio. "Hello Joe, this is Mac."

"Joe: that's Lima Charlie (loud and clear) to me."

Mac quickly passed on the enemy threat and finished the call.

"OK, Joe. You call it!"

★★★★

Joe, as the Increment team leader, had operational control. A successful helicopter exfiltration would have to pull together three different elements. Firstly, they would have to arrive at the approximate LZ and secure it soon. Then, they would have to wait until the Reaper was on call, and, finally, they would have to engage the Taliban vehicles to make time and space for the very vulnerable airframe. Joe rechecked the handheld. The Taliban were closing, with the faster Ford Ranger in front by at least half a click (500 metres). Joe picked up the team Motorola radio.

"Hello, all stations. This is Joe."

"Farzin, send."

"Mac, send."

"Tam, send."

"All stations India - STAND BY." Joe used one of the Special Force's most significant terms, the same words the SF use when they breach a building with an explosive entry. A countdown usually comes next.

In the rear Land Cruiser, Carl prepped the door of his vehicle and checked for brass in the Sharpshooter. In the driving seat, Tam grunted "game on!" in Glaswegian. He grabbed his C8 from the footwell and secured it under his seat belt and over his knees, so that he could help Shiner engage the threat to the rear when the car screamed to a halt. They would use the armoured car as hard cover as they took care of the Talib Ford Ranger.

Chapter 36

The Reaper pilot tracked the Taliban convoy. He held the drone stable and locked the live feed onto the lead vehicle. He could clearly see the individual features of the occupants, shouting at each other in the back of the pick-up. A CIA man in Nevada was looking at a group of men in a Ford Ranger in Afghanistan whom he was about to vaporize.

The voice of the Intelligence coordinator sounded in his headset. "You are clear to engage the convoy at your discretion."

Pilot: "Roger that."

Sensor Operator: "Roger that."

Pilot: "Launch checklist."

The girl's voice: "Checklist."

Pilot: "Power." There was only a brief pause as the sensor operator checked one of the screens. "On."

The pilot then went into a well-rehearsed checklist. "88-bit."

The young woman answered almost immediately. "In progress."

The pilot continued the checks. "Weapon power."

The CIA girl said, "On."

The pilot: "Code weapons."

Sensor operator: "Coded."

Pilot: "Weapon status."

Sensor: "Weapons ready."

Pilot "MTS auto track."

Sensor: "Ready."

Pilot: "Laser."

Sensor: "Laser selecting. Laser armed."

Pilot: "Lasing arm is hot,"

Sensor: "Lasing and writing range."

All the weapons were now armed and ranged. The pilot selected a Hellfire missile for the Ranger. He again studied the faces below and switched off the safety on the trigger.

★★★★

In the Increment's rear vehicle, both operators listened for the countdown to action. Joe's voice was clear and steady and almost emotionless.

"3-2-1. GO, GO, GO!"

Tam slammed on the brakes and pulled the handbrake as the Land Cruiser slithered to a halt with a scattering of gravel and a juddering of brakes. The vehicle now had its side to the approaching Badri Brigade convoy. At lightning speed, both operators clambered across the vehicle, through the doors furthest away from the threat, and split in opposite directions, Shiner to the front and Tam to the rear, as they came up on aim. There are two places on an armoured vehicle that are even safer to use as a fire position. Shiner was instantly looking through the Trijicon ACOG scope of his L129A1 Sharpshooter rifle. He was leaning over the front of the car, where the engine block would give him extra cover from fire. Tam took the position at the rear, with his C8 carbine over the rear axle, which afforded him similar protection. Any incoming Talib round would also have to penetrate both armoured skins of the car. It was the perfect place to take them on, with car drills that had been perfected in training on a hundred different windy range days in Wales. The Talib convoy was still six hundred metres away as Shiner picked out the driver through the front windscreen of the Ranger. He held the rifle steady and concentrated on controlling his breathing, placed the bearded face in the centre of the graticules of the scope, and took up first pressure on the trigger.

In Nevada, the pilot pressed the trigger and said, "3,2,1, rifle." The first Hellfire streaked towards the target. At the same time, Shiner pulled the trigger on his Sharpshooter.

The pilot watched the screen as he counted.

"3,2,1, impact." The front Taliban vehicle disappeared in an orange flash 40,000 feet below.

Shiner was silent for a second while trying to process what he had just seen.

"Fuck me, Tam. Did you see that?" The Belfast man grinned.

Tam laughed. "Yes, ya mad fucker, what round was that?"

"A fucking Hellfire, old mate; it's my favourite. We have friends above looking after us, but they're not fucking angels."

In Nevada, the pilot smiled and selected the next target. He snapped down a toggle on his firing control to switch to bombs. He could now see that the remainder of the Taliban convoy had stopped, and the Badri Brigade fighters were trying to deploy from the troop trucks. *Schoolboy mistake,* he thought. The fighters had left the green canvas covers over the rear of the trucks. Although it made the vehicles warmer in the Panjshir winter, it also made them more difficult to deploy or even escape from.

Shiner and Tam were now taking on the Taliban fighters while they attempted to rally. As soon as Shiner identified a target, he engaged it. A Talib leader was talking into a radio while kneeling. Shiner's scope settled on his upper torso, and he pulled the trigger. An armour-piercing bullet slammed into him, and the radio dropped to the ground. Tam was hammering away with the C8.

He stopped and snapped open the M203 grenade launcher below the rifle, placed in a 60-mil grenade, and popped it off towards the mess that had once been a convoy. There was a sharp explosion as it landed amongst fighters trying to skirmish towards them, using the gulley at the side of the road.

The pilot again made an assessment.

Pilot: "Weapons status."

Sensor: "Weapons ready."

Pilot: "MTS auto track."

Sensor: "Ready."

Pilot: "Laser." The bombs were ready to go.

Sensor: "Laser selecting. Laser armed."

Pilot: "Lasing arm is hot."

Sensor: "Lasing and writing range."

Pilot: "3,2,1, rifle."

Pilot: "3,2,1, impact."

The remaining Increment vehicles had stopped after the countdown, just in time to hear the explosion that had destroyed the front Taliban car. Then the two 230kg bombs exploded with a deafening roar that seemed to echo up and down the valley. Pieces of twisted metal were still hitting the surrounding area as Joe made his assessment and picked up the radio.

"Hello Tango One, over."

A calm American voice answered.

"Hello, India One, send."

"India One, ready for pick-up." Joe hoped they could get away while the enemy was still in shock.

"Tango One; is the Lima Zulu secure?"

"India One, it's hot but under control." Joe hoped it was.

"Roger that, two minutes." Just as the helicopter pilot said that the team heard the distant drone of the M17 closing fast.

The Taliban that managed to escape the carnage were fighting back now, and incoming bullets were kicking up the tarmac just before the team's refuge. And then there was a resounding crash as the first .50 cal bullets from the MRAP smashed into the Land Cruiser. The pilot in Nevada could read the situation on the ground. He switched the ordnance back to Hellfire and went through the checks.

Pilot: "Laser." The missile was now ready to go.

Sensor: "Laser selecting. Laser armed."

Pilot: "Lasing arm is hot."

Sensor: "Lasing and writing range."

Pilot: "3,2,1, rifle."

Pilot: "3,2,1, impact."

There was a deafening explosion, and the MRAP had ceased to exist. The armoured turret spiralled upwards, seemed to tumble mid-air, and crashed onto the road. There was a brief silence and then another sound, an ever-louder drone of the approaching helicopter. Joe used the team's Motorola radio.

"Hello all stations, this is Joe. Stand by for extraction." As the noise of the incoming M17 got louder, Tam came up on the radio net.

"Hello Joe, this is India Two. We are held." The remaining Badri Brigade men had now gone to cover, and Tam and Carl knew that without their continued covering fire a safe helicopter extraction was impossible. "We will hold here while you extract." The two operators thought that this was the only option.

Then another voice broke the airwaves. "Hello all stations, this is Farzin." The 333 Commando leader panted as he ran towards where Shiner and Tam were defending the rear of the LZ. "We will cover you while you get out."

Joe was just processing the new plan when the four Afghan commandos ran past him towards the firefight and danger. Joe shouted into the handset, "You're coming with us." Farzin was still running as he shouted back into the radio. "No amigo, our country, our fight. We are staying." The four Triples were now at the rear Land Cruiser and using their extra firepower to subdue the remaining Taliban. The incoming rounds were now only sporadic – Shiner's Sharpshooter punished any Talib who broke cover. Joe identified the lull as an opportune time to call the M17 in.

"Hello Tango One, this is India One." A spent round landed at his feet as he shouted "NOW, NOW, NOW!" over the noise of the old Russian war machine, as it swooped down to rescue them.

Farzin was now arguing with Tam.

"You must go!"

"No, you guys go."

"We never intended to leave. We are staying. This is our fight, not yours."

Joe led the way onto the helicopter that had landed on the road within fifty metres of his vehicle. He stood by the door to count the passengers onboard. A helicopter extraction under fire is a strange experience. The downdraught from the aircraft almost pinned the Increment's team leader to the ground, while the heavy smell of aviation fuel reminded him of the imminent danger. The downdraught had also formed a light swirl of snow that obscured his vision. And then the first of the passengers arrived, wraith-like figures from the cold.

Mac quickly clambered on, followed by Katya and then Ricky. The last two aboard were Tam and Carl. They moved back with what the British Army calls fire and movement, with one man moving as the other was in a fire position covering his back. And then, in an almost telepathic response honed by training, they both turned and made a zigzagging run for the door. Carl 'Shiner' Wright was the last person on and still held his beloved Sharpshooter rifle by the pistol grip. He tapped Joe on the arm as he launched himself into the cabin and shouted, "LAST MAN." The old ex-Soviet aircraft lifted, turned, its engines struggling with the altitude, and powered itself out of the Panjshir Valley and towards safety.

Epilogue

Your past affects your present and will permanently shape your future. And sometimes the darkness trapped in the past comes home. The Ukraine War was now a year old. It had dropped off the front pages of the mainstream media in London, and the only places it made headlines now were in Russia and Ukraine. Both populations now called it The Long War. As in Soviet times, the Black Tulip was flying with its usual cargo of carnage. 'Black Tulip' was what Russian families had called one of the largest aircraft in the USSR, the Antonov An-12, when it was delivering 'Cargo 200', or the war dead from the Soviet/Afghan war. The aircraft's design had changed a little, but its function was the same. The transport plane designed to carry paratroopers was once again carrying coffins from a war much closer to home.

Some local officials had told them that the war dead were coming home, so, just as in Soviet times, the families were there to meet them. The mother of Mikhail Andrei Petrov had never expected to be able to bury her son. She was in her eightieth year and had been mourning his loss for over thirty. She had thought he would always be lost. But he had been found, she was told, by some tribesmen in the Panjshir Valley, where his helicopter had crashed. They called themselves the National Resistance Front of Afghanistan and had contacted the Russian Embassy in Tajikistan. She was grateful. All the zinc caskets looked the same when they arrived in the village, but only her son was returning from a previous Soviet occupation. The others were from the present one. At the rear of the crowd, a younger woman pulled up the hood of her traditional fur shuba coat and shivered with the cold.

Living in America has softened me, she thought.

A tear rolled down her cheek as she watched the priest bless the coffin. The mother leaned over, placed the medals on its black zinc lid, and kissed them.

The Cross of St George.
The Order of Military Merit.
The Order of Military Merit to the Fatherland.
The Order of Zhukov.

They had been given to Mikhail's mother by a veteran, an Afghansy comrade of her beloved son. She did not know where they came from, but it was enough that they now honoured her dead boy. The younger woman, after watching this, turned, and left.

She had kept her promise.

★★★★

An agent debrief has no time constraints when you are an ex-SVR spy chief working for MI6 and the CIA. They had thirty years of espionage to sort through. Mac was allowed to stay with Katya throughout the debriefing process. It started in a pleasant, detached house in Surrey and then moved to the CIA headquarters at Langley. The intelligence officers conducting the information review were always polite and respectful. Katya knew that debriefing was a painstaking and deliberate process. Each interview is recorded and cross-checked. Each event or date is also recorded, verified, and then collated. The interviews start early and end late until the last scrap of information is squeezed out of the turned asset, and then you are free.

Katya's pre-emptive intelligence about the Russian invasion had undoubtedly saved the lives of Ukrainians and prevented Kyiv from being overrun within the Kremlin's original timeline of ten days. Colonel Katya Sokolov's initial assessment had been accurate: modern Western anti-tank weapons had made tank warfare less predictable. And she especially liked her new MI6 friend, Collette, who, when she finally left for America, had wished her well and meant it.

★★★★

The National Resistance Front of Afghanistan is still at war. The nucleus of the organisation is still the Afghan commandos or Triples. After the firefight, Farzin and his men had melted away into the Panjshir Valley like a fresh snowfall in the sun. Farzin, the great Ghazi, and the rest of what was the Northern Alliance are still fighting in the Valley for the land that they love, despite being abandoned by the West.

★★★★

The killer they called 'White Death' is still entombed in the blackness of the mine. The Tajiks are religious and deeply superstitious, so his body still lies where it fell. The decaying corpse was covered in feasting bats when it was discovered. The killer had instilled as much fear in death as he had when he stalked through the darkness of his resting place. The Tajiks believe in the old ways. So, the skeletal hand of Igor Dumo Kalash is still grasping the knife that he had lived by and died with. It would normally be an attractive item for a tribesman, a Spetsnaz-issue

6.5-inch Bopoh-3 fighting knife of deadly black tungsten steel with a rubber-reinforced polymer grip. But no one picked it up. They sensed the evil that emanated from it, maybe from the presence of a Jinn or even the Devil himself.

★★★★

Danny did win the contract for the Qatar World Cup and was looking forward to getting some sun. London in the winter is not good for older bones. After Qatar, he would kick back and do some decidedly sexagenarian things like cruises and long holidays in warmer climes. Maybe!

★★★★

Collette and Damian see a lot of each other now. In more ways than one. When you have known true love once, once is enough. Both are still busy. The security and intelligence services are always working flat out. The perpetual cycle that turns raw information into verifiable and accurate intelligence is always turning, and somebody must always feed it. The foot soldiers of the intelligence war are still working. Ahmad and Lou are still recruiting their sources, meeting them, and debriefing them, thereby providing the fuel that powers the Security Service machine.

The Increment goes on protecting deployed agents in the field. Ernie has retired now to his house near Poole and his local golf course. Joe now runs the Firm's India assets from the same office in Slough and will sometimes disturb Ernie's golf swing for some advice. No official report has ever been made about the Panjshir extraction, and it is only mentioned by the men who fought there.

Carl (Shiner) Wright and Tam are now team leaders deployed in Ukraine. Ricky is now an MI6 handler in London. They all intend to get together every year on the anniversary of the extraction and do what soldiers do best: drink beer and share war stories. Or, as the ex-Royal Marines say in Royal Navy slang, 'tell dits'.

★★★★

If you are ever in Naples, Florida, at about sunset, go to the beach and you may find them. A couple walk hand in hand and turn to smile at each other with a frequency only engendered by mutual love and respect. The man is wearing Bermuda shorts in paratrooper maroon. He is fit, straight-backed, and walks like a man who sometimes climbs mountains. The woman is beautiful, wearing a figure-hugging pair of knee-length white shorts and the man's old Army tee shirt. She looks like she, too, could climb a mountain. That is because they both went to the Valley and climbed the mountain together.

The Author

W, T. Delaney is the pen name of a former Royal Marine and security contractor who now writes books. During his time in the military, he served in 45,41 and 45 Royal Marine Commando Units. He qualified as a Royal Marines Physical training instructor in 1985 and was attached to the Special Boat Service. He also served four years as a covert special duties soldier at the end of his service. A second career on London's security 'Circuit' led him to various tasks ranging from body-guarding an Arab Royal Family to providing security advice and protection to both Fox News and NBC News as they covered events in Iraq and Afghanistan. After a ten-year contract as a US contractor teaching intelligence collection to the Iraqi security services and the Afghan National Army. He retired to write intelligence-based action and adventure books. His first book 'A Shadowing of Angels' was published in 2016 and was followed in 2019 by 'A Falling of Angels'. The final book 'An Evil Shadow Falls' completed the trilogy in 2021. All three of his previous books are available on Kindle, paperback, or as audiobooks at:

A Shadowing of Angels
A Falling of Angels
An Evil Shadow Falls
Authors Republic.
Chirp audio books

Authors Web Site wtdelaney.com

THANKS

Thank you for reading 'The Long Shadow of Panjshir' I hope you enjoyed it. If you have, please take the time to leave a review and let others know how much you liked it.

Thank you once again.

Bernie Plunkett MBE Msc Mlitt

(AKA W.T.Delaney)

ALSO BY W.T DELANEY

The Sam Holloway Trilogy

Book 1

A SHADOWING OF ANGELS

The first book of the Sam Holloway Trilogy is 'A Shadowing of Angels' which was released in 2016.

The story unfolds in the murky and dangerous world of covert intelligence collection and the 'Circuit; the name given by private military contractors to UK-based security companies. Set in 2016 this adrenaline-fueled spy-based adventure novel highlights the struggle against the evil of the Islamic State. Samantha Holloway is a highly trained intelligence operative and special forces officer working on the Circuit when an American hostage is snatched by ISIS in Iraq. Sam's team is contracted to launch a search and rescue mission. The search starts in London amongst radical Islamist organisations and reaches its climax in the very heart of darkness- the Iraqi town of Mosul, under the demonic control of Daesh. A Shadowing of Angels is the first book of the Sam Holloway Trilogy. All three interlinked novels are all based on a factual historical backdrop. The writer had drawn on his own experiences of working as an intelligence officer in both Iraq and Afghanistan to craft the story.

***** Brilliant, Delaney's background nails the authenticity once again...'
***** A cracking listen that had me hooked to the end...'
***** Realistic that races off the page.
***** Wow!! What a cracking book!!!

Ashadowingofangels

Author Website Wtdelaney.com

THE SAM HOLLOWAY TRILOGY
BOOK 1
A FALLING OF ANGELS

The next book 'A Falling of Angels' was released in January 2020. It is based in London in 2019, after the Islamic State has collapsed and a team of British jihadists is on its way home with mass murder in mind. A British spy operating within the Daesh reveals a complex attack aimed at the seat of Government, and Sam and her team of former special forces soldiers are contacted by the security services to help. As the story unfolds, the team race to prevent the attack against the backdrop of a secret CIA plan to locate and capture the terrorist mastermind organizing it. But when the truth emerges, Sam realises that London isn't the only target.

★★★★★ Five stars again for Delaney.
★★★★★ I listened to this in two sessions.
★★★★★ Brilliant, Delaney's background nails the authenticity once again.
★★★★★ This audiobook is as gripping as the first.
★★★★★ Delaney is a tour de force! I literally couldn't put this book down. He makes the complex murky world of counterintelligence infinitely entertaining. Loved it!

Afallingofangels

The Sam Holloway Trilogy

Book 3

AN EVIL SHADOW FALLS

An Evil Shadow Falls is the final part of the Sam Holloway trilogy, in which the former Special Forces officer and her team of warrior contractors face their most dangerous mission yet. In a wild adventure that starts in London and ends in armed intervention and death on the high seas. A nuclear warhead had gone missing, and a terrorist mastermind, inspired by the events of 9/11 and a fanatical vision of Armageddon, is planning a mass-casualty attack against the West that can only be measured in the metrics of madness. The Security and Intelligence agencies must make sense of a complicated jigsaw puzzle of clues, technical intercepts, source reports, and inputs from foreign intelligence services if they are to prevent Ground Zero 2. In a race against time, Sam's team, now including an unlikely ally, a refugee from London's postcode drug wars, and an MI5 agent within ISIS must find the deadly device before it detonates. The last book in the Samantha Holloway series starts in London, has its back story in the wild mountains of Afghanistan, and ends on a stormy night in the mid-Atlantic, with the Special Boat Service on standby and ready to deploy from a Royal Navy warship in support of the Spartan team. But even the best-laid plans rarely survive contact with the enemy. The team must draw on all their combined skills and courage if they are to thwart a murderous plot that carries with it a horrifying echo of an all-too-possible future reality.

***** Brilliant, been there, done that, Delaney nails the authenticity once again...'
***** An audible treat that had me hooked to the end...'
***** The action races off the page!
***** Wow!! What a cracking story!
***** This is essentially a 'rattling good yarn', a highly topical good vs evil adventure story, fast-paced and packed with incidents.

Anevilshadowfalls

Printed in Great Britain
by Amazon